SKI
WEEKEND

PRAISE FOR *SKI WEEKEND*

"This is a suspenseful book that had me thoroughly hooked from page one. . . . The emotional journey of *Ski Weekend* is relentless . . ."
—*READERS' FAVORITE*, five stars

"This book will send so many chills up your spine, you'll feel like you're alongside the snowbound characters. The only time I don't recommend reading this book is right before bed. You won't be able to sleep, and you won't want to."
—JEFF ZENTNER, award-winning author of *Rayne & Delilah's Midnight Matinee*

"[A]ll the intensity and thrills of *The Hunger Games* packed into one car over a snowy weekend. Secrets, lies, strong characters, and twists will keep readers turning pages. If you've ever wondered how far you would go to survive, you need to read this book."
—EILEEN COOK, author of *You Owe Me a Murder*

"Ross weaves a stirring tale where each of her characters wrestle with choices that could result in life or death—some survive, and some don't."
—PAUL GRECI, award-winning author of *Surviving Bear Island* and *The Wild Lands*

"Ripped from the headlines, *Ski Weekend* is so real you'll be shivering with the characters, fighting the elements, and asking yourself—what would you be willing to do to survive? Forget Netflix and chill. Binge this book."
—SORBONI BANERJEE, Emmy Award–winning journalist and author of *Hide With Me*

"This pulse-pounding story of survival mirrors all the highs and lows of the hit reality TV show *Survivor*. In my case, I knew I could quit any time, but these kids aren't so lucky. Buckle up—this is one wild ride!"

—CORINNE KAPLAN, two-time *Survivor* and *Amazing Race* player and reality TV star

"Captivating and shocking! I loved it!"

—ELISE LEE, owner at Away With Words Bookshop

✹ 2021 Firebird Award Winner in Young Adult Fiction

✹ Featured in *Cosmopolitan*'s "15 Compelling Fall 2021 Books to Add to Your Reading List"

SKI WEEKEND

A NOVEL

REKTOK ROSS

SPARKPRESS

Published by SparkPress, a BookSparks imprint,
A division of SparkPoint Studio, LLC
Phoenix, Arizona, USA, 85007
www.gosparkpress.com

Published 2021
Printed in the United States of America
Print ISBN: 978-1-68463-109-4
E-ISBN: 978-1-68463-110-0
Library of Congress Control Number: 2021905238

Interior design by Tabitha Lahr

For those who said yes when everyone else said no.

CHAPTER 1

December 20 · 8:45 p.m. · 6,005 feet
Northern California, 10 miles south of the Mount Sierra Pass

We're almost to the foothills when the trouble begins. Flashes of red and blue light up the stormy night sky as police cars hurry along the side of the snowy mountain highway. My heart does this flip-floppy, somersaulty thing in my chest as I watch them line up, blocking the path ahead. I just know this is something bad.

The surrounding cars slow, but my brother is too busy messing around with the stupid car radio again to notice. He's got the volume turned up so high it takes all five of us yelling over his throbbing techno music to get his attention. Finally, he looks up and then slams on the brakes so hard the SUV's tires buck and squeal beneath us. We skid clear across the left lane, heading straight for the massive semi-trailer truck in front of us.

I let out a scream, my overactive imagination going straight to that place where I like to envision worst-case scenarios. This time it's our car plummeting straight off Highway 90 and exploding into a fiery ball of teenager parts and ski gear.

1

Somehow tire tread miraculously connects with concrete, stopping us mere inches from the truck's bumper. For a moment, we just stare at each other in shock. My best friend, Lily, does this deep-breathing meditation exercise she learned in ACT boot camp, pinching her nose and blowing out air slowly, while Champion jumps up from the floor, attempting to scramble all ninety pounds of animal muscle and fur onto my lap. I wince as sharp claws dig into my jeans and his wet nose burrows against my chest, hiding there. Gavin's dog is on the verge of a full-scale panic attack, and he's not the only one.

"*Cāo, Stuey!*" Lily yells next to me, breaking the silence.

I roughly translate this into the f-bomb. Lily curses in Mandarin when she's upset, a habit she picked up hanging out with her dad in the kitchen of their family-owned Chinese restaurant. Some words I know by heart now.

"My bad." Stuart turns around in the driver's seat, giving his girlfriend an apologetic half smile. "Sorry, Lils. I didn't know anyone was braking."

"Jesus, Stu! You need to pay attention!" I say, finding my own voice. *"We could've died!"*

He groans loudly. "Alright, now you're just being dramatic, Sam. We're fine, aren't we?" Eyes the same shade as mine twinkle back with laughter. Sometimes I'm convinced our bluish-green seafoam-colored eyes and pale skin that never tans are the only things my little brother and I have in common.

"Barely," I mutter, my pulse still racing from our near miss. I pull out a few peanut butter treats from my pocket and coax the trembling dog back to the floor.

"Just be more careful, okay, babe?" Lily is already grinning at Stuart, letting him off the hook. They've only been dating a few months and are still in that yucky honeymoon phase.

"And *this* is why they don't let sophomores on Ski Weekend," Britney says in the middle row in front of me, making the sign of the cross like she's thanking God we're still alive. "Who invited you on this trip anyway, Stu Poo?"

"Watch it, Miller," I warn. Stuart got his horrible nickname after an unfortunate accident freshman year. It was after his back surgery and the doctors overprescribed his pain meds and . . . well . . . it wasn't pretty.

Most people don't have the nerve to call him that in front of me, but not Britney Miller—Seaside High's queen of everything. Most popular. Head cheerleader. She's even president of our school's prayer group, which is ironic because Britney and her friends are the biggest assholes in school.

"Oh, relax. He knows what I mean." She grins at me, tossing her golden blond hair over one shoulder. "Everyone knows Ski Weekend is seniors only."

Stuart throws the gear into park as car horns blare around us.

"What's going on? Why isn't anyone moving?" Lily asks, adjusting her eyeglasses and tucking a strand of long black hair behind one ear. She cranes her neck above the middle row's headrest, but we're too far back in the SUV to see much.

Gavin's brand-new GMC truck is an extended-cab affair with two seats up front followed by two full row benches and a cargo area in back that we filled to the brim with our luggage, ski gear, my dad's cooler, and a twenty-four-pack of bottled waters for the weekend. It would be considered spacious with plenty of room for six people under normal circumstances, but not when you're crammed in between a dog the size of a small pony, Lily, and every school supply she owns.

When we chose our seats earlier, Lily climbed into the last row of Gavin's SUV thinking it would be the quietest spot for reading. Naturally, I took the seat beside her. That left Gavin's football buddy Hunter in the front passenger seat playing navigator to Stuart's terrible driving and Britney and Gavin in the middle row so they could flirt with each other.

"It's probably chain control," Britney says, applying another coat of pink sparkly lip gloss. I cringe as she pushes her lips together with a loud smacking sound. I still don't understand why Gavin offered her a ride with us.

Oh, wait. Yes, I do. Britney Miller may be terrible, but she's also gorgeous.

"Chain control?" Stuart asks. "What's that?"

Britney snickers. "It's when they stop the dumbasses with crappy little cars that can't make it up the mountain."

For the millionth time today, I find myself wishing I was home snuggled in bed with a good book and my favorite TV show, *Pit Bulls and Parolees,* on repeat instead of stuck in this SUV. I only agreed to come along on this stupid trip to make sure Gavin doesn't convince my brother to do something crazy. The last time those two were alone without supervision, Stuart came home with his arm broken in three places.

Stuart is only a sophomore and technically shouldn't be coming along this weekend—that's one of the reasons we're staying at Gavin's family cabin instead of the ski lodge with the other seniors. The other reason is that Gavin doesn't go to our school anymore. His parents made him transfer last year to some snobby boarding school in Boston.

"Just tell me when we're there," Lily says, cracking open her AP psychology textbook and turning on her book light. As she rustles through the pages, Hunter flips around in the front passenger seat to gawk at her.

"You're studyin'?" he asks in a thick Texas drawl, scratching at his goatee and looking shocked.

I hide a smile. Supposedly, Hunter Jackson's parents are super wealthy cattle ranchers with farms all over the South, but I've always thought his accent—and that southern good ole boy routine—was purely for show. Hunter grew up in sunny California like the rest of us.

"Obviously," Lily says, not bothering to glance up.

"But why?" he asks.

"Because some of us want to graduate," she says, snickering at her own joke before sliding on her noise-canceling headphones. Hunter and half the senior football players are on academic probation after they got caught cheating on last week's math final.

"Ugh! We're going to be so late." Britney switches from lip gloss to mascara, fluffing at her lashes using short, angry strokes.

"I bet it's that blizzard they mentioned on the radio," Stuart says.

"That's not supposed to hit until Monday," I correct him, rather glum about the fact. I've been getting weather alerts on my phone all week, hoping for an excuse to call the trip off. A nasty winter storm is supposed to roll across the Pacific Northwest next week, but we'll be home long before that happens.

"Good," Stuart says. "'Cause this weekend is gonna be epic."

"I'm getting laid for sure." Hunter flashes the grin of someone who is super attractive and knows it. With his rich, blemish-free dark skin and gorgeous brown eyes, he looks like a young Will Smith—maybe better—and has no problem getting girls at school, even with his rodeo cowboy schtick.

"You're so gross, Hunt!" Britney wrinkles her nose prettily. "Our bodies are a gift from God. We're supposed to save sex for someone special."

He winks at her. "They're all special, trust me."

I turn to my brother, ignoring them. "Just take it easy on the slopes, Stu. Remember what Mom said."

"Yeah, yeah." He waves a dismissive hand at me, annoyance creeping into his voice.

Using the sleeve of my sweatshirt, I wipe away the condensation forming on the car window beside me to inspect what's going on outside. It was barely raining when we left home hours ago, but now thick snow coats the sides of the glass and piles up alongside the highway. I blink, dumbfounded, as a burly, bearded man in camo exits his eighteen-wheeler truck and walks along the shoulder, heading for the police barricade. *Holy crap.* It must be ten degrees out there. He's either brave or crazy. Probably both.

Soon others follow his lead. They look like little ants, scurrying beneath the snow-covered mountains that rise and tower above us like some predatory, prehistoric monster. A shudder skitters down my spine. The Sierra Nevada mountains are so much bigger than I thought they'd be.

"See anything interesting?" Gavin asks me, his voice low.

I turn, and my gaze locks with those cool blue eyes framed by impossibly long black lashes. It's been so long, I almost forgot how good-looking Gavin is. Model-high cheekbones. Thick, full lips. Even the inch-long scar above his eyebrow only makes him more attractive. It really is a shame he's such a jerk.

Besides a brief "hello" at my house earlier, this is his first real attempt at conversation with me since he left for boarding school last year. He never even bothered returning any of my texts or e-mails. It sucked at first, but I'm over it now.

At least that's what I tell myself.

"Nope." I shift in my seat and look away.

"Really? That's all you have to say?"

I sneak another little glance his way. He's still staring at me.

"What?" I snap.

"It's funny," he says, looking amused as his long, elegant fingers play with the strings of his dark hoodie. "I thought you always had something to say about *everything*."

I scowl. "And I see you're still as charming as ever."

"Wouldn't want to disappoint," he says with a low chuckle before turning to the right, gazing out his own window. "I don't think that's chain control."

"Oh, yeah? What is it then?" I ask.

"Not sure, but I'm gonna find out."

When he looks back again, a devilish glint lights his eyes. I can tell he's going to do something stupid even before he zips up his leather jacket and flings open the car door next to him. A gust of wind rips through the opening and blasts my face as he steps outside.

"Get back in the car, you moron!" I yell, but he's already gone, the door slamming shut behind him. I feel hot doggy breath on my neck as Champion gets on all fours to investigate the commotion. As soon as his gaze lands on Gavin's now-empty seat, he whines softly.

"Did he really just do that?" Stuart's mouth makes a little "O" shape as he stares after Gavin's retreating figure.

"I don't know why you sound surprised," I say, fighting against a rising swell of annoyance as we watch Gavin jog toward the police blockade. This is exactly the kind of reckless behavior I expect from him.

Stuart gives me a look. "You promised you'd be nice," he says with disapproval as he buttons his bright yellow puffer jacket over his favorite sweatshirt—the one that reads: *Gamers, Because Somebody Has to Save the Princess.* My mother has tried to donate it to Goodwill multiple times, but somehow it always finds its way back into his closet.

"Sorry. He just makes it so hard," I say.

Stuart places a hand on the driver's-side door. "I'm going after him."

"Don't you dare!" My body stiffens at the thought of my brother outside in that gnarly weather. Stuart has the worst luck. Knowing him, he'd probably catch pneumonia.

Hunter rolls down the front passenger-side window just a crack. "Hey, Gav! Get back here!" he shouts outside as the frigid air rushes in through the small opening.

Stuart joins in, yelling, and then the dog matches them with his own high-pitched string of yelps. The three of them blend together to create the most awful melody ever. *Dear Lord.*

Lily yanks off her headphones. "Keep that beast quiet, would you?" she asks, her voice accusing like this is somehow my fault.

"He's *your* boyfriend!" I say, laughing. "You tell him."

"Hilarious. You know I was talking about the mutt—not Stuey." She reaches over my knees to press a finger into the dog's long black snout. "Shut it, flea bag."

I shove her hand away. "Ignore her, boy," I say, scratching the dog behind his pointed, perked ears, exactly how he likes it. He settles back at my feet, his dark eyes looking up at me lovingly.

Champion is a rescue, so Gavin doesn't know for sure what breed he is, but it's pretty obvious he's mostly German shepherd. His glossy coat is all black with a few flecks of brown around his feet and ears. He's so cute, I almost don't care he's smothering me, depriving me of any spare legroom.

"Would you shut up already? You're giving me a head-ache!" Britney angles forward and slaps Hunter upside the head. He cries out in surprise and his cell phone falls out of his hand, clattering to the floor at his feet.

"Hey! That hurt!" he says, rubbing at the back of his neck. "What's your problem?"

"This is all your fault. I told you we should've taken the I-6. Now look at us," she says.

"And I told you to be ready on time, sweetheart," he says, bending down to pick up his phone.

She eyes his untucked flannel shirt and baggy Wrangler jeans with open disdain. "Not like you would know, but perfection takes time. I'm not showing up in front of the entire school looking like some slob," she says, straightening the fancy rhinestone collar of her cream cashmere sweater.

He smirks. "Too late."

Lily and I snicker into each other's sides as Britney's glowing bronze skin turns scarlet. Her arm lifts as if readying for another attack just as the car door swings open and Gavin slides back inside the SUV. We all stare at him in anticipation. Even Lily closes her textbook.

He swallows hard. "I've got bad news."

"We're not getting up the pass, are we?" I ask.

He shakes his head. "Storm's worse than they thought. They're closing the road and making everyone turn around."

"Are you serious?" Stuart asks, his face crestfallen.

Poor Stu. He was so excited for this trip.

And yet, I can't help the little thrill I feel. Even if it makes me a horrible sister, I'm stoked to go home. If we turn around right now, I bet I can even get in an extra shift this weekend at the animal shelter where I volunteer.

"But we can't miss Amber's party," Britney whines, grabbing on to Gavin's hand. I swear she sounds like Minnie Mouse. Worse. Minnie Mouse on helium. "Everyone's expecting us."

"It's just a stupid party. Who cares?" I ask.

"You wouldn't understand." She looks back at me, her eyes shining. *Wait—is she crying?* "Amber just broke up with Kyle, and he's a total douchebag. If I'm not there, she'll do something dumb, like take him back." She sniffs. "She needs me."

"Hold your horses. I got an idea," Hunter says, rolling up a plaid sleeve. He reaches for the state-of-the-art navigation system in the dashboard in front of him and pushes a few buttons, bringing up a digital map. His hands run along the screen for a few seconds until he finds something he seems to like. "There it is!" he exclaims, poking at the display with a beefy finger. "My grandpappy and I took this shortcut last summer."

"I think we should listen to the police." Even if he is wearing that über-confident smile all cool kids have perfected, I'm not convinced.

"I agree," Lily says, patting my hand. "Turning around is the smart thing to do."

In the driver's seat, I catch Stuart rubbing at his lower back in that absentminded way he sometimes does. I can tell he's hurting, even if he won't say it.

"And Stu needs a break," I add. "He's been driving for hours."

"I'm fine," he says a little too quickly, and I know I'm right. The twenty minutes we took at that last rest stop wasn't nearly long enough.

"You're not fine. You need to rest," I say.

"Lay off, Grandma." Gavin arches a mocking brow my way. "He said he's okay."

Prick.

I clench the strap of my backpack lying on the floor between me and Lily and contemplate hurtling it at his handsome face. Gavin is the only person besides my parents that knows the extent of my brother's scoliosis. Even Lily has only heard bits and pieces and thinks my brother is fine these days, but Gavin has seen it all. The surgeries. The hospital stays. The pain meds. You'd think he'd be the first one agreeing with me, backing me up, but he always acts like this—like nothing's wrong.

Take this morning. Stuart just got his license and Gavin knows my brother isn't supposed to drive long distances, yet he did nothing to help me when Stuart hopped into the driver's seat, begging to test out Gavin's new ride. And here he is again. Doing nothing. Who cares how good-looking Gavin is when he's totally useless?

"Don't give me that look," Gavin says, groaning at me. "It's only one more hour. I'll show you." He glances around the car, his hand outstretched. "Someone give me a phone. My signal's crapping out."

Hunter tosses his cell backward as if it's a football, and Gavin catches it one-handed like when they used to run their winning plays on the field. Gavin was our star quarterback. Hunter, his favorite receiver. They single-handedly took our team to the state championship last year.

"Dude," Gavin says, laughing at Hunter's phone screen. "I can't believe you text this crap to girls."

"You're supposed to be reading maps. Not spying on Daddy's game," Hunter says.

Britney makes a gagging noise. "Stop calling yourself Daddy. It's creepy."

Gavin is still laughing as he raises the phone in the air. "Here it is. Right where Hunter said it would be."

Hunter grins. "'Course it's there. Would Daddy lead you astray?"

"See, Sam?" Gavin spins the phone around. On the glowing screen is a dotted red line that shoots off from the highway, cutting straight across the mountains until it lands on a big circle labeled MOUNT SIERRA. "That's the shortcut," he says, pushing the phone into my palm.

A tiny shock of electricity runs up my arm at the contact. For so long, I wasn't sure if I'd ever see Gavin again. I'd almost convinced myself I didn't care. And now here he is, looking at me. Touching me—

"Told you," he says with a cocky grin.

If only he wasn't such an ass.

"Just because it's on a map doesn't mean it's safe," I say, pushing the phone away.

"C'mon, Sam. It's our last winter break together. Next year you'll all be in college, and I'll be here ... all alone. Sigh." Stuart gives me his best hound dog eyes. He looks so pitiful, I feel myself cave. "We can always turn back if it gets worse," he adds.

"It'll be fine, Sams. I promise," Gavin says.

I'm not sure if it's the old nickname he uses or the smile he gives me—a rare one, genuinely sweet and hopeful—but a rush of warmth runs through me, melting my last shred of resolve.

I nod my agreement and Stuart turns the SUV off the highway with a victory roar, steering us toward the exit ramp as the snow really starts coming down. We skip hard across the road, sharp bumps jarring my backside. Champion looks up in alarm and tries to get to his feet again, but I push him back down as the car lurches left and Lily's petite, pointy elbow collides with my rib cage. I grimace, but there's no time to recover as we plummet down the ramp at an alarming rate.

Gavin and Stuart whoop and holler like we're back home riding one of their favorite roller coasters. Even Britney is giggling as she squeezes in close to Gavin, locking her elbow with his. Meanwhile, I'm tightening my seat belt with wobbly fingers and yelling for Stuart to slow down. Then I'm at it again—envisioning broken bones and guts and mangled steel. My fingers clench at the back of Gavin's headrest, accidentally poking him in the neck.

He swivels around. "Calm down, you freak," he says, but then he surprises me by taking my hand, squeezing it once before Britney grabs it back for herself.

As soon as we're off the highway, I let out a huge sigh of relief. There are more police cars here, lining the side of the access road, making a new barricade at the three-way traffic signal. Orange traffic cones block the northbound entrance of the highway. With nowhere else to go, we fall in line behind a row of cars about twenty deep.

One by one, the cars crawl forward and turn left to drive under the overpass to get on the southbound entrance, heading back to Orangeville. Only a few outliers go right instead, opting for the busy gas station on the corner. Its parking lot overflows with cars spilling onto the street while people run around in full winter gear, filling up on fuel and coffee.

"Should we get more gas?" I ask, eyeing the crowded pumps.

Britney's lip curls. "No way. Do you see that line?"

"We're fine," Gavin says. "We've got plenty of gas."

I can't help but notice he and Britney are still holding hands. I wonder how serious things are between them, though I'd rather die than ask.

"How would you know?" I ask him. "You've never taken this route."

His lip twitches. "Do you have to argue about everything?"

"Only when you're involved," I say sweetly.

"Break it up, you two." Stuart turns around. He's smiling, but I can hear the undercurrent of annoyance. Stuart hates when Gavin and I fight.

"We've got over half a tank. That's hours' worth—stop worrying, Sam," Gavin says.

As much as it kills me, I go quiet and let him have the last word. If we keep at each other like this, it's going to be one very long weekend.

Finally, it's our turn at the intersection. Stuart twists the wheel right and we blow past the gas station, heading east. Before long, the gas station grows smaller behind us until it's only a distant haze of light reflected in the rearview mirror.

Deeper into the woods we go, farther and farther away from civilization. Hunter keeps swearing we're going the right way, but we no longer see signs for lodging or food.

The darkness of night surrounds us, our only guide the high beams of the SUV's headlights. We're in the heart of the Sierra Nevada mountains now, surrounded by hundreds of miles of national forest.

I chew on the inside of my lip, hypnotized by the view illuminated ahead. Giant trees as tall as any building back home rise along the sides of the empty two-lane road. There are no colors anymore. Only black and gray and white of trunk and branch and snow. It's all so desolate. So unlike the sunny California coast back home. We might as well be in Antarctica.

"Beautiful, ain't it?" Hunter asks to no one in particular.

It is beautiful. But it's creepy, too, being out here in the middle of all this nothing.

My brother turns around in the driver's seat to say something to Lily. He takes his eyes off the road for only a second, but the car jerks and swerves dangerously close to the edge. He tries to recover by over-correcting too much and my head slams backward against the seat, sending a jolting pain skittering up my spine. Spinning wheels shriek against ice like a thousand nails on a chalkboard. Someone screams high and brittle—*Is that me?*—as the car heads for the giant snow bed lining the road. I fling my arms up in front of my face, preparing for the crash I know is coming.

Please, God, let Stu be okay, I think.

It's my last thought before the world goes black.

CHAPTER 2

10:15 p.m. • 13,100 feet
Old Donner Road

I awake to a perfect, dark silence. Hard leather runs along my backside, telling me I'm now horizontal in the SUV. My head angles upward, propped against something stable—a backpack, maybe? There's no way to confirm this because my eyes refuse to open.

"You have . . ."

" . . . up!"

"Please, you need . . . *right now, Sam!*"

Voices break through the eerie quiet, but I can't make any sense of them. Everything is muffled, like when Stuart and I were little and used to lie at the bottom of the pool to see who could hold their breath the longest even though I always won.

From somewhere in the car, Champion barks at a frenzied pace. The voices get louder. More urgent. Someone shakes my shoulders.

No, not just someone.

Gavin.

He yells my name over and over as though he cares. I open my mouth to tell him I'm okay, except nothing comes out.

My heart races, skittering a million beats per second as panic grips me. What's wrong with me? Why can't I talk? Or hear? Or see? I'm not . . . *I'm not dead, am I?*

Right away, I dismiss the idea. I can't be dead. Dead people don't think.

I hold in a deep breath and force myself to count to ten. *Relax, Sam. Just relax.*

Slowly, the sounds untangle for me.

"She's opening her eyes!" cries a voice I recognize as Stu's.

My vision is blurry at first. I can only make out large shapes. Dark shadows. I stare in confusion as one shadow in particular gets closer and closer until it looms over me. Then I blink again, and Gavin's face comes into focus.

"Thank God you're okay," he says, his blue eyes filled with an emotion it takes me a moment to recognize because I've never seen it on him before—fear.

I brace myself and sit up, surprised when my hands connect with Gavin's hard knees. He's somehow moved from the middle seat and now sits in the back row in between Lily and me. I realize my head wasn't resting on a backpack at all but cradled in the center of his lap.

"Stuart?" I turn toward the driver's seat where Stuart should be sitting and find it empty instead. My breath quickens. "Stu, where are you?"

"I'm right here," my brother calls back.

"Where?"

"RIGHT HERE," he repeats, louder.

I spot him a moment later in the middle row, crowded in between Britney and Hunter.

"Are you okay?" I ask, scanning his face critically, looking for any signs of injury. Other than that messy hair of his, I see nothing out of place. Truth is, he probably looks a lot better than I'm guessing I do based on everyone's expressions and the panicked way Britney clutches at the little cross around her neck.

"*Me?*" He looks stunned. "You're the one who passed out."

"*Gàn!*" Lily reaches over Gavin and grabs me by the shoulders, her lower lip trembling. "I was so scared! You wouldn't wake up!"

"I'm fine," I say.

"She needs to lie back down," Gavin says, pulling me back into his lap and gently pushing Lily away with his other hand. "That's what she needs to do."

"Everyone relax. She said she's fine," Britney says sounding bored, but I notice she's still gripping at her cross.

Gavin pulls off his hooded sweatshirt and balls it up, dabbing at my face with the heavy cotton. I try not to stare at the smooth muscles underneath his thin white T-shirt as he goes to work at my face. Six-packs aren't important right now. What's important are the tiny red droplets dripping down the sleeves of his black sweatshirt and onto the ends of his long fingers.

Oh, my. That's a lot of blood. My blood.

My stomach rolls as I wonder how bad off I am. I run through a symptoms checklist on myself like I've been trained to do with new animals at the shelter intake clinic:

Broken bones? No.

Dizziness? No.

Light-headedness? No.

Nausea—real nausea and vomiting, not the kind of nausea caused by seeing too much of your own blood? No.

Besides a tender throbbing in my mouth, I don't feel seriously injured. I wiggle my tongue around to find my cheek and lips are cut open and raw like hamburger meat, and a metallic taste fills my mouth. First relief and then embarrassment flow through me as I realize what happened. I must've passed out from fright during the accident and somehow bit through my skin.

"It's just a busted lip. I'm okay," I say, my cheeks hot as I push Gavin's hand away. It hurts a little to talk, but it's not unbearable or anything.

"You're not okay. If you were okay, you wouldn't be bleeding all over my new sweatshirt," he says, and tries to go at me again like he's plunging a toilet. His caretaking, while surprisingly sweet, leaves something to be desired.

I wriggle away before he can do any more damage. "I got it," I say, grabbing the sweatshirt from him and pressing it against my mouth.

"So ungrateful. Not even a thank-you, huh?" He laughs while I apply firm pressure to my mouth the way the vets at the shelter taught me, tilting my head forward. That's the right way to drain a muzzle injury; otherwise blood can pool up in the back of the animal's throat and it can choke to death.

My eyes widen as I look around and take in the car's state. It's like a tornado hit us. The insides of our backpacks are everywhere. Chewing gum, headphones, lip balm, and phone chargers litter the bench seats. Lily's deluge of books and pens sprawl across the floor at our feet. We weren't going fast enough for the airbags to deploy, but judging by this mess, we must've been pretty damn close.

At the front of the car, Champion whines softly for attention. He lies curled up in Hunter's old spot in the passenger seat. Someone must've moved him from the back seat while I was unconscious in order to give me more room. Just past the dog, the SUV's bumper is buried in between enormous snow ditches. Rows of towering trees surround the front and sides of the car, their thick branches pushing against the windshield while tiny hairline fractures like spiderwebs scatter across the glass. A few more inches and the branches would've burst through, skewering one of us sitting inside.

"*Holy. Shit*," I say.

"The car spun out of control," Stuart says, his voice catching. He slumps down in between Hunter and Britney. "I couldn't stop it."

"It was black ice," Hunter explains kindly, patting at Stuart's shoulder. "Ain't nothing nobody could do about that."

"I'm so sorry, Sam," Stuart says.

I dab at my swollen lip with Gavin's sweatshirt. "It's alright. Is everyone else okay?"

Lily rubs at her temples. "Eh, I think I hit my head, but no biggie."

Champion whimpers again in the front passenger seat. I call his name and pat at my seat, giving him permission to return. His ears twitch with excitement as he hops through the gap between the driver's seat and the passenger seat before clearing the middle row in one great leap. He smacks Britney in the face with his bushy tail as he goes by and then settles back down at my feet.

"Can we get out of here now?" Britney asks, her voice laced with impatience.

"We gotta check for damage first," Hunter says, and the three boys slip outside while the rest of us watch through icy windows.

Gavin and Stuart start by examining the rear tires while Hunter gets on his knees and runs his hands over the sides of the car. He disappears underneath only to pop up at the front bumper seconds later. Gavin and Stuart join him there. They move some fallen branches aside and get the dented hood up and back down right away, which the rest of us take as a good sign, until Hunter jerks open the front passenger door.

"We got a problem," he says, his bushy brows furrowed. "We're stuck. Real deep—maybe two feet."

"Uh, can't we use our hands and dig our way out?" I ask.

"Not exactly." He grins like I've said something stupid. I probably have. I don't know much about driving in the snow. "But don't worry, I got a plan."

"Wonderful. Another plan of yours," Britney says, her voice thick with sarcasm.

Hunter's smile grows bigger. "This country boy never runs out of plans," he says. "Now everyone outside while we try to get loose."

"Are you crazy?" Britney asks, wrapping her arms around her body like a shield. "It's freezing out there!"

"Sorry, princess. That's physics. The less weight inside the car, the easier it'll move." He opens her door and offers his hand, but she pushes him away and steps outside on her own.

Lily and I follow, pulling down the lever below Gavin's seat to lower the bench so we can climb out. Champion comes next, taking off at full gallop and then quickly finding a spot nearby and lifting his leg, turning the snow yellow.

Shielding my eyes against the raging wind, I glance around and suck in a shaky breath. This place looks nothing like the cute little ski villages I'm used to from our family vacations in Colorado. The roads there are groomed daily and the trees have perfect little blue lights wrapped around meticulously pruned branches. Here, the disheveled piles of snow make strange shapes resembling creepy white ghosts and the trees are like skeletons, twisting and grasping in the air, casting shadows. Even the harmless hoot of an owl, a mix between a whooping sound and a small dog's growl, is enough to make my skin crawl.

And the cold. *My God*, the air is so cold I can barely breathe. The wind cuts through my down jacket with savage intensity, turning my skin to ice.

Hunter has us start by digging away snow from under the tires while he runs around after us, using a can of Britney's extra-hold hair spray to break up the remaining ice. Even with gloves on, my fingers turn numb after a few moments. Britney starts to complain, begging to go back inside the car, but the rest of us ignore her.

After we've cleared some snow, Hunter places floor mats in front of the tires for traction and gets behind the driver's seat. He straightens the wheels and presses on the accelerator. We all watch him, holding our breath, but the car doesn't budge.

Next, he tries letting air out of the tires so they can grab more traction and propel the car forward. When that doesn't work, he tries using a car jack to shake the car loose. Then he has us rock the car from side to side, but it's no use. Nothing we do makes any difference.

"Well . . . that didn't go as expected," Hunter says, wiping the sweat from his brow as we slog back to the car, defeated, and return to our original seats. He turns the heat up, but it doesn't stop my teeth from shaking so hard I worry they might shake right out of my head.

"We're so screwed," Britney says, glaring at Hunter up front.

"Don't get your knickers in a knot," he says, kicking his crazy-looking black cowboy boots onto the dashboard—they actually have red flames running up the sides. "We'll just call for help. Trust me, you'll be at the spa right on time for your morning massage."

He sounds so confident even I feel calmer until we pull our phones out and discover none of us have a signal. Either we're out of range or the storm is messing things up.

Tense silence envelopes the car.

"So . . . uh . . . anyone up for a romantic late night stroll?" Stuart jokes, flipping around in the driver's seat to give Lily a suggestive look.

Britney cocks her head to the side as if giving his ridiculous suggestion real thought. "Actually, that's not the worst idea ever. Maybe you should go see what's out here."

"Hell no." Hunter gives Britney a sharp glare. "Everyone knows you stay in the car until help arrives. That's Wilderness Survival 101."

"And I say let him go if he wants to," Britney says, her mouth pinching up. "My friends got stuck like this last year. They walked up the street and right into someone's house."

"It can't hurt to take a quick look," Gavin says. "I'll go with you, Stu."

Stuart straightens the hood of his jacket, and I can tell my brother is seconds away from barging outside to play superheroes with Gavin. Sometimes I think all those dumb video games he plays go straight to his head, and Gavin's idiotic encouragement doesn't help.

"No way. You're not going out there," I say. "It isn't safe."

Stuart groans. "We'll be fine."

"Naw, man. She's right," Hunter says. "Didn't you hear about that dude last winter?"

"What dude?" Stuart asks.

"The UC freshman that got butchered." Hunter's voice drops an octave.

"Oh, please." Britney sounds disgusted. "You're making this up."

Hunter raises a hand to silence her. "The way I heard it, this couple turned off the highway for a little sexy time, but then their car wouldn't start. Dude went searching for a gas station while his girl stayed put, locking the doors and shit. Then right as she's about to fall asleep, she hears a tapping on the roof." A wide grin stretches across his brawny face. "Tap. Tap. Tap."

I hide a smile, pretty sure I've heard this story before.

"'Course, she assumes it's a tree branch scraping against the car until the cops show up," he continues. "They tell her to get outta the car, but when she looks back, you'll never guess what she sees."

"What?" Britney is on the edge of her seat, biting at her French-manicured acrylic nails. "What'd she see?"

"I'm glad you asked, darlin'," he says, licking his lips with relish. "She saw her boyfriend hanging upside down from a tree. Throat all slit. Blood dripping everywhere!"

Britney looks like she's about to be sick. "No way . . ."

He pumps a fist in the air. "Hell, yeah!"

Stuart's shoulders shake up and down in his seat, and then he bursts out laughing. "Nice try, man. But that's from a movie."

"No, it ain't," Hunter protests.

"You got the ending wrong too," Stuart goes on. "There wasn't any tree. He decapitated the guy with an ax." He turns to face me, his eyes dancing. "Remember?"

Now I know why the story sounded so familiar. Stuart made me watch that stupid horror movie three times last summer. Lots of blood and gore, just how he likes it, and some bimbo with big boobs being chased by an ax murderer—running up the stairs when she should be running down them.

"You asshole," Britney says, smacking the back of Hunter's seat. "I can't believe I fell for that."

"It ain't no movie. That's how it happened," Hunter says, shaking his head adamantly.

"I heard the same story," Gavin says. "Except there wasn't a boyfriend. The girl was at a gas station, and the killer got in her back seat with an ax. People were flashing headlights and stuff to warn her."

Lily yawns loudly. "Those are silly urban legends."

"A what?" Gavin asks.

"They're stories passed down from generation to generation," Lily explains. "We learned about them in psych class. They're supposed to stop kids from doing dangerous stuff. You know, like fairy tales. Keep your butt home, or you'll get eaten by the Big Bad Wolf."

"It ain't no urban legend," Hunter says. "No one is leaving the car—got it?"

I catch his eye in the front passenger seat. I'm still unsure if he's telling the truth or not, but his story served its purpose. I mouth a thank-you and he nods back with a little smile.

"Great," he continues. "Now that that's settled, let's eat!"

"Is food all you ever think about? You're such a pig," Britney says.

"Oink oink, baby." He laughs as he zips up his orange puffer jacket and hops out the front passenger door to get to the cooler in the cargo area of the SUV. "Thanks a lot, by the way," he says to Britney, his hand on the car door as the cold air rushes in. "Now I gotta freeze off my tail feathers just to get some dang chips."

Normally, the cargo area is accessible from the back row, but we packed the space so full of luggage and gear, there's no way to reach anything unless it's by going outside and using the rear door. Hunter pleaded to put the cooler in the middle row so he could have some "roadie snacks" on the drive up, but Britney shot him down, saying there wasn't enough room.

"Like I knew we were going to get stuck," Britney scoffs. "Besides, it's not my fault you're such a fat ass."

"The ladies like Daddy to have some meat on his bones." Hunter pats at his belly and laughs. "Oh, well. I guess it gives me an excuse to check the tailpipe."

"What's wrong with the tailpipe?" I ask with a small flicker of worry.

"Nothing—I hope," he says. "But we gotta make sure snow ain't building up and blocking things. If carbon monoxide gets inside, we'll be dead long before anyone finds us," he explains and then closes the door, heading for the rear of the SUV.

His answer makes me wish I hadn't asked the question. This is just wonderful. As if being stranded in the mountains isn't bad enough, now I have another thing to worry about—asphyxiation.

Moments later Hunter returns, shaking the snow off his body like a wet dog before sliding back into the front seat. His arms are filled with food. Stuart and I may have gone a little overboard packing this morning. He insisted on buying a six-pack of full-size Hershey chocolate bars and enormous party-size bags of sour gummy worms *and* honey-roasted peanuts. I crammed in some healthy options like my favorite snack-size pita chips and some string cheeses.

As Hunter distributes snacks around the car, Britney refuses, saying she doesn't eat "junk food" even though the snacks I brought along are organic. I eye her warily. She got nothing to eat at the rest stop either. Not that I blame her for skipping on gross fast-food burgers, but even I got a grilled cheese. It makes me think of the talk around school. Gossip isn't something I usually pay attention to, but her behavior makes me wonder. There are rumors that Britney and her friends starve themselves a few days before football games to be as cute as possible in their cheer outfits.

A bag of pita chips lands in my lap, making me forget all about Britney's rumored eating disorder. My stomach rumbles loudly as I rip the bag open, gobbling down food. Champion, the little beggar, whines annoyingly at my feet. He eyeballs my chips with utmost concentration like he's hoping one will fall out of my mouth and straight into his.

I cock a brow in Gavin's direction. "Hey, Farrell. Get your dog some dinner," I order. I love Champion dearly, but I'm not sharing my food with anyone.

After Gavin returns with kibble for his dog, Hunter pulls out cans of beer from inside his jacket pockets and waves them around like they're prized trophies. "Time to get this party started!" he shouts.

Lily's eyes go wide. "We can't drink that! We're not twenty-one."

"Good one!" Hunter laughs at her like she's told a funny joke even though she's one hundred percent serious.

"Lily's right. Drinking is a bad idea," I say, wriggling around in my seat. I'm sure Hunter and the others will make fun of me for this, but we have to be safe. "Alcohol is dehydrating, and we don't know how long we'll be stuck here."

"You're kidding, right?" Hunter asks. "It's only beer." He pops the top on the first can, and foam spurts out and dribbles down the sides as he passes it to my brother. Stuart gulps the contents down greedily.

"Yes, I can see that," I say dryly.

"Oh, relax. One drink won't kill anybody." Britney leans into the front and takes a can from Hunter. She turns around to face me, raising the beer in my direction and saluting me with a mocking brow. "Cheers, Sammy!"

My face heats. "I thought all you Bible-beater types didn't drink?"

"The Campus Crusaders are *not* Bible beaters." She looks offended. "Just because we love Jesus doesn't mean we don't turn it up!"

She turns to Gavin and bats her eyelashes, trying to share her beer with him. I smirk when he waves her off and continues chewing his peanuts, brooding out his window. Gavin doesn't drink. Even though it seems exactly like the sort of rule-breaking thing he'd be into, I've never seen him with even a drop of liquor. It's a little odd, but I'm not complaining if it means I'll have one less drunk idiot to deal with tonight.

My brother lets out a loud burp in the driver's seat while Lily looks on from the seat next to me, disapproving. I can tell she's annoyed by the way she sighs and opens her textbook, tearing through the pages. They're an odd couple. She's so studious and serious, and he's—not. They have fun together, but I secretly wonder how long it'll last once she leaves for Stanford next year.

Soon Hunter, Britney, and my brother are laughing their asses off like they're the greatest friends in the world, and my irritation turns to envy. I have to admit it looks like fun—or at least way more fun than I'm having. Sometimes it sucks being the voice of reason.

I clear my throat. "Oh, what the hell. Gimme one."

Stuart hollers with glee and lobs a can in my direction, cheering me on as I scull the beer. It's nice to be on the same team for once. I wasn't always this uptight, overbearing older sister. The two of us used to get into all kinds of trouble growing up. I was the instigator, encouraging him to do all sorts of crazy things. Bike riding with no hands. Bodyboarding on my boogie board at high tide. Eating an entire bowl of raw chocolate chip cookie dough in one sitting, salmonella be damned. But that all changed after Stuart's back problems began.

"My head's killing me," Lily says next to me, closing her book with a thud and kneading at her temples.

I lean to the left and put a hand on her forehead. It's warm but nothing worrisome. "It's just a headache. Yooooou're fiiiiine."

Oops. I think I'm slurring my words.

"It's the altitude." Unlike me, Hunter sounds normal even though he's already on his third beer. I must be a lightweight. "People can die from it. Like on Mount Everest."

I wish he would shut up. This death talk is ruining my buzz.

"You're okay, Lil." I attempt to pat her knee and miss, patting the leather seat instead. *Errr . . . I hope no one saw that.* "Go to sleep. You'll feel better in the morning."

The boys head outside with Champion to go pee in the woods before bed. None of us girls are desperate enough to join them. When they return, they have extra jackets from the cargo area stuffed under their arms that we use as blankets. The layers make it tolerable enough to allow Hunter to shut off the heater to preserve gas for a bit.

Stuart climbs in next to me and embraces Lily for a good-night kiss. Sister ick factor aside, I have to admit they're pretty cute—but not cute enough to make me switch seats with him when he asks. The back row isn't comfortable by any standards, but I doubt a big fat steering wheel in the middle of my chest will improve my sleeping situation.

Champion jumps into my lap and burrows his head against my chest, snuggling so close we become one person. Part dog, part girl. I adjust the jacket-blanket I'm using so it covers him as well and prop my backpack against the right side of the car to use as a pillow so I can sort of sit-sleep. The bottom part of Champion crosses over into Lily's side of the bench, and I watch with amusement as she slides her feet underneath his furry backside. She makes a disgusted face like it's killing her to do it, but there's no denying the extra heat his fur coat gives off.

Up front, Stuart and Hunter recline their seats and share the dashboard, each using it as a footrest. I try not to pay much attention to what Gavin and Britney are doing together in the middle row.

Wait—is that her head on his chest?

I turn away, telling myself I don't care.

Eventually, the blizzard shifts into high gear and the pounding on the roof gets louder. Wind kicks up swirling waves of powder that wash down the windshield like breaking surf. The absolute fierceness of the storm is mind-blowing. I close my eyes and try to convince myself not to worry. We're safe for now. We have shelter. Things will be better tomorrow.

Somehow it works, and I fall asleep.

CHAPTER 3

Day 2 • December 21 • 7:00 a.m.

When I wake, light streams through the windows and I see hours have passed. My bladder spasms painfully.

Ah yes, the beer. Great idea that was.

"Lil?" I whisper, reaching over the sleeping dog lying between us to nudge at my friend's limp arm. Her legs are curled inward, her body in the fetal position and rolled to one side, motionless. When she doesn't respond, I push harder until muscle moves under my fingers. "Hey, get up," I say louder, but her eyes remain shut.

A chill creeps up my neck that has nothing to do with the freezing temperature.

I lean over Champion, getting close enough to put my ear up against Lily's mouth. No air comes out. Lily isn't breathing!

No . . . This can't be happening.

I stare at her listless body in shock. I must be missing something. Doing something wrong. There's no way Lily is *dead*.

My hands shake as I crouch down and put my ear to her mouth again. For the longest moment it feels like no air comes out, but just as my heart goes from jackhammer to full-on nuclear explosion, I feel it. It's the tiniest whiff against my skin, but it's there.

I sigh with relief. Lily is most definitely alive, though her breath is far too faint to be normal.

"Wake up!" I yell to the others. *"Everyone get up!"*

Britney is the first to respond. She pops over the row like a deranged groundhog exploding out of its hole. "Can't you see I'm sleeping?" she asks with a groan. The scent of her sugary perfume wafts toward me, mixing in with the staleness of Stuart's leftover rest stop burger bag from yesterday. "*Glamour* recommends at least eight hours of beauty sleep each night and—"

"Shut up and help me!" I clutch at Lily's arm, unsure what to do.

"Jesus, Sam. Stop shouting," my brother says in a groggy voice. He twists around in the driver's seat up front and wipes at his bloodshot eyes, frowning at me. "What's so important that it can't wait until—"

"It's Lily! Something's wrong!"

Suddenly, Stuart is wide-awake, hurling himself over the center console and diving into the middle row. He inadvertently kicks Hunter in the face and smashes Britney into the car door in his rush to get to his girlfriend. "Lil?" he asks, hanging over the back of the seat. He grabs her arm and jerks hard on it. "You gotta get up, Lils."

"Stop it, Stu," I say. "Don't move her."

He ignores me, stretching farther down until he can reach the tips of Lily's shoulders. He grabs them and tries to shake her awake.

"I said stop!" I smack his hands away. "You're making it worse!"

"What's wrong with her? Why isn't she moving?" Britney asks, gaping at Lily. Even with all the chaos going on around beside her, Lily remains motionless. "Holy Mother of God . . . *is she dead?*"

"Shut up!" Stuart turns to Britney, red splotches forming on his cheeks. "Don't say that!"

"Don't tell me to shut up." She jabs a finger into my brother's skinny chest. "You shut up!"

Their yelling sets Champion off on a barking tangent. He leaps up onto my lap with such force I know I'll bruise later, before shoving off my knees and hurdling over the back of the middle row—his tail thrashing me in the face. He plops down onto the floor between Britney and Stuart, nipping and howling at their feet like they're playing some fun new game and he wants in. All the racket makes it impossible for me to think.

"*Everyone shut up!*" Gavin yells, and they all go silent. Even the dog drops to the ground, his ears going flat.

"Thanks," I whisper to him before turning back to Lily.

I pinch the bridge of my nose and focus all my attention on her. I don't understand what's going on here. Lily's lips are bloodless and waxy and tiny beads of sweat dot the top of her forehead, right below her dark widow's peak. Beneath closed lids, her eyes move back and forth as if she's in a deep sleep. It's almost as if she's fallen into a coma, but that doesn't make any sense. She was fine when we all went to bed last night, wasn't she? Normal teenagers don't just go to bed and slip into unconsciousness.

"Why is she like this? What's happened to her?" Stuart asks, his voice hollowing out.

I rack my brain, trying to think of all the conditions that could account for what I'm seeing. It can't be carbon monoxide poisoning, or we'd all be dead. Lily has no preexisting medical issues either. None that I know of, anyway. No epilepsy. No diabetes. She didn't even drink last night like the rest of us.

I make a frustrated noise. How can I fix Lily when I can't even figure out what's wrong with her?

"Sam?" Gavin asks. I look up and his eyes lock with mine.

"I don't know what's going on," I say, wetness pressing against my lids.

"What do you mean you don't know? You work at that stupid clinic!" Stuart stares at me with an accusing glare like I'm the freaking chief of surgery at Seaside General Hospital and not some high school volunteer at the local animal shelter. I've never even been with a patient without a vet around, for crying out loud.

"Those are dogs and cats, Stu," I remind him. "Not human beings."

"But you're always there," he says, his voice tight. "You must know something!"

"*I said I don't!*" I yell back so loudly Champion whimpers from his spot in the middle row.

"It's okay to be scared," Gavin says. Understanding floods his blue eyes. "But if there's something you can think of—*anything*—it could help."

"I'm not scared!"

Of course, this is a lie.

I'm terrified.

I unzip my jacket and pull it off, sweat trickling down my temple. It may be freezing outside, but the inside of the car feels like it's a hundred degrees. "What if—" My throat tightens on the thought, and it gets stuck for a moment. I swallow and try again. "What if I do something and make things worse?"

"Really don't think that's gonna be a problem . . ." Britney mumbles under her breath.

Hunter silences her with a warning glance before turning to me. His look is warm and encouraging. "Try somethin'," he says to me. "Somethin' is better than nothin'."

Gavin nods along. "You can do it, Sams. I know you can."

My heart thuds in my chest. They're right. I can't dwell on how inadequate I feel or worry I don't know enough. We're in the wilderness. It's me or no one. What I have to do is relax. Clear my mind. I close my eyes and force myself to take deep breaths in and out.

After a few seconds, the energy builds inside my body, turning into a familiar buzz I'm used to. It's an electrifying feeling I get whenever I assist the vets at the animal clinic. A sense of being alive that sets every nerve on fire. And then, in a flash of inspiration, I remember.

I've never had a comatose person on an operating table, obviously, but I've helped plenty of animals coming out of anesthesia. At the clinic we sedate them for all kinds of reasons like when we spay or neuter or during complicated teeth cleanings. Sometimes the animals have trouble waking up on their own. That's when we have to help bring them back.

I hear my favorite vet, Dr. Jayson, in my head. His strong and confident voice is clear as day: *The first priority is stabilization following the basic ABCs: airway, breathing, and circulation.*

Lily's a person, not a dog or cat, but—so what?—they're all mammals. The basics must be the same . . . right?

I get on the floor and crouch down next to Lily, leaning over her body to place a gentle hand on the back of her neck and under her chin to check her airway. Immediately, my fingers find a large knot on the bottom of her scalp. I part her fine black hair and peer closer until a nasty-looking bump about the size of a small lemon comes into view. Shame roils in my gut.

"This is all my fault," I say as understanding dawns on me.

"Don't be crazy," Hunter says. "You didn't do nothin'."

"No, you don't get it," I say. I'm having difficulty breathing. "She said she hit her head during the accident, remember? She told us her head hurt! I thought she was being dramatic and told her to sleep it off." I shake my head, near tears. "Do you understand what I'm saying? *I told a person with a concussion to go to sleep!*"

"Sam—stop!" Gavin snaps. "This isn't your fault. None of us knew anything was wrong."

"But *I* should've!"

Anyone with even the most basic medical experience knows that's the absolute worst thing to do. If someone has a head injury and exhibits symptoms like a headache or nausea, you want to keep them awake for as long as possible. I'd been so busy drinking—like an idiot, trying to fit in and have fun— that I'd ignored all the warning signs. And now Lily might die. Because of me.

Oh, God.

"How could I have been so dumb?" I whisper.

"Get a grip, Sam," Stuart says. His hands are on my shoulders, shaking me, and I realize I'm practically hyperventilating. "None of that matters, okay? Just fix her."

I take in a big gulp of fresh air and snap back to reality. If something bad happens to Lily because of me, I'll have plenty of time later to beat myself up about it. Right now, I have to do whatever I can to save her. Now where was I again?

I glance down at my hand, still clenching the back of Lily's head.

Oh, right. Airway.

Using my left pointer and middle fingers, I lift her chin to open her airway and pry her lips apart. My fingers flex and sweep over her clammy tongue, making sure it's clear before moving further inside, past her tonsils. To my relief, I see nothing obstructing her windpipe. Okay, good. That takes care of the airway.

Next is B for breathing. I already confirmed earlier that was working. Not great, but passable.

With the first two down, circulation is all that's left. I grab her wrist in my palm and search for the radial artery. It's easy to find since it's the vein closest to the surface of the skin. Keeping my hands steady, I place my middle and index fingers on top and check her pulse.

For one awful second I think the beats will never come, that I'm doing this all wrong, but then a weak throbbing moves beneath my fingers. I count the movement for fifteen seconds and multiply that number by four like you're supposed to. I'm so nervous I do the math three times in my head to make sure I've got it right.

"It's too slow," I say, swallowing down the rising lump in my throat. "Way too slow."

Britney blinks. "What is?"

"Her pulse," I clarify. "It's almost half what it should be."

"What does that mean?" Stuart asks. When I don't answer right away, he repeats the question, a note of hysteria entering his voice.

"It ain't good, man," Hunter breathes, putting a hand on Stuart's shoulder.

"Let's stay positive," Gavin says. "She's alive and breathing. Focus on that."

I try my best to stay centered and not burst into tears. If I start crying, my brother will lose it. Instead, I flex my hands, cracking at the knuckles, and work to put her in a recovery position to ensure her airway stays clear and help with her breathing.

First, I smooth down her wrinkled pants, making sure there's nothing bulky in the pockets, and then I grab her by the right shoulder and roll her onto her side so she lies as if folded in half. Her cheek and the left half of her body press against the seat while the right side of her body points up and toward the ceiling.

"Here—use this," Britney says, unbuttoning her coat and handing it to me. I roll it into a ball and stuff it behind Lily's neck to use as a pillow and prop her head up.

"Get her a blanket," Hunter orders. "We gotta keep her warm."

Gavin frowns. "What blanket? We don't have a blanket."

"Everyone keeps a blanket in their car," Hunter says.

"Well, *I* don't!" Gavin yells back.

"We could splash her face with water," Britney suggests. "I saw that on TV."

"Good idea," Stuart says. "I'll get water from the cooler and—"

"STOP!" I yell, and everyone stares at me. "Leave her alone," I say, letting out a tired breath. "There's nothing else to do right now. She's stable."

It won't help to tell them all the other things I'm worried about. That Lily's brain could swell. She might never wake up. She could . . .

I shake my head, unable to finish my thought. I don't want to think about all the bad things that might happen if Lily doesn't get help soon.

"She needs a hospital," Stuart says, his voice hoarse.

"Thank you, Captain Obvious." Britney snorts, throwing her hands up. "You see any hospitals around here, Stu Poo?"

"Don't be a bitch, Brit," Hunter says, frowning at her. "He's worried about his girl."

"I'm just being honest," she says.

"Well, we can't wait around hoping someone shows up," Stuart says. "We have to do something."

"Like what? We all agreed to stay put last night, right?" Britney looks at Hunter in the front passenger seat for confirmation. When Hunter doesn't respond, an angry note enters her voice. "You said help would come, remember?"

The thought of sitting around here doing nothing while Lily gets worse and worse makes my stomach twist with nausea. It's my fault my best friend is lying here half dead. Maybe I can't turn back time, but I'm sure not sitting on my ass and watching her die.

"I'll go," I say.

"I'm coming with you," Gavin says.

His quick response catches me off guard. Lily is my friend—not his. I wasn't expecting this.

"I'll be fine," I say.

"I'm sure you will be, but I'm still coming."

"But Gavy, you can't." Britney reaches for his knee, placing her hand on top. "You can't leave me here alone."

"You'll be fine," he says, already zipping up his jacket. "We'll be back soon."

He stares over at me as if challenging me to stop him from coming along. I can't decide if this gesture of his is admirable or more of the same bad decision-making I'm used to from him. Most likely he sees this as just another adventure, taking unnecessary risks and braving the outdoors to play the hero, but if I'm being honest, I'm not sure I care. They say there's safety in numbers for a reason. I could do far worse than Gavin for a traveling companion. He may drive me crazy, but even I can admit he's capable. Strong and fast. Smart. Most of the time, anyway.

"Let's do this," Stuart says, pushing at Champion's rump to grab the straps of his backpack and pry them loose from underneath the dog. Once it's free, he lifts the bag into his arms and climbs over Gavin's legs, reaching for the door handle.

"No way, Stu. You're not coming," I say. This is *not* part of the deal.

Not only is my brother slow and out of shape—his idea of a marathon involves movies and popcorn—but he has the absolute worst luck of anyone I've ever met. Stuart is always getting injured. He's had more hospital visits in one year than I've had my entire life, and that doesn't even consider his chronic back problems. If anything happened to him, if he damaged his spine again, it would be a nightmare. It's taken years of hard work and painful medical procedures to get him to a decent place.

"And why the hell not?" His eyes flash in my direction.

"Because . . ." I scramble for a reason he might accept. "Lily needs you to watch over her."

It's a cheap shot, using his love for Lily as a bargaining tool, but I'll do whatever it takes to keep him in this SUV.

"Nice try." He jerks the door open and steps outside, not looking back as it slams closed behind him.

"Hey! Get back here!" I yell, yanking on the seat lever and scrambling into the middle row to go after him. In my rush to leave, I land right in Gavin's lap.

"Relax," he says, grabbing my arm to stop me. "Let him come along."

"Don't be an idiot!" I say, my blood boiling.

This is why Gavin and I have never gotten along. We aren't talking about going for a walk in the damn park. This is the deadly wilderness in the middle of winter. People get seriously injured out here—even killed. And after what went down last year? How dare Gavin say this to me after what happened in Mexico.

Whenever Gavin is involved, things always wind up going sideways. Like the time he convinced Stuart to join our karate class, and they both went home with stitches. Or the time he took Stuart to the bike park and Stuart broke his front tooth. The list is endless, and I'm always worried one day it won't be something minor like a pulled muscle or a chipped tooth.

"You know I'm right," he continues, mistaking my silence for concession.

"I don't have time to argue with you! Someone needs to go after him before he hurts himself," I say, throwing the door open and dropping into the snow, frigid air rushing in to greet me. Shivering, I pull the warm hood of my puffer jacket over my head and do my best to push my fury down. No one gets to me quite like Gavin does, but I've got to keep my eye on the big picture—like keeping my brother's dumb ass safe.

My eyes lift toward the road, searching for him. As I suspected, he hasn't gotten far. He walks along the left edge of the mountain road, only a few yards ahead of me. A tiny grin pulls against my lips. I can't help but admire his bravery even while I resent his complete idiocy. He's going on a dangerous wilderness trek in the middle of the Sierra Nevada mountains, and he didn't even think to pack food or water? An extra sweater, at least?

"Stu!" I cup my hands over my mouth and yell. "*Get back here, you moron!*"

"You really need to learn to chill," Gavin says, ambling up behind me with Hunter in tow. "He's already got a mom, you know. He doesn't need two."

"Back off, Gav," I say.

"Not that I wanna get involved with whatever you and Farrell got going on," Hunter begins, and, unlike Gavin, he has the good sense to look wary of me. "But I think—"

I explode. "I don't care what you think!"

He holds his palms up as a sign of peace. "I think," he repeats, "that we got plenty of daylight left. Ain't too cold anymore neither, now that the storm's slowed. And all you gotta do is get to those red firs over there." He points to a cluster of giant trees with deep reddish bark off in the distance. They sit on a snowy, crested slope above the road we stand on. "That's more than high enough to see what's around," he says, and grins. "Now I know you're worried about your lil' bro, but even my grandpappy could make that hike, and he's eighty-five."

"C'mon, Sam, you know we're right," Gavin says, and lifts a dark brow. "Besides, what's the alternative? You gonna hunt Stu down and lock him in the trunk?"

Despite myself, my lips twist upward into a tiny smile. "The thought crossed my mind."

"He'll be safe, okay? I swear it."

Gavin looks so earnest I feel myself yield. I sigh, knowing I've been beat. At least if I'm with Stuart he won't be running around in the woods alone or doing God knows what else.

"Double pinky promise?" I ask him, and hold out my little finger. It's this silly thing we've done ever since we were kids.

He stares at me for a long moment. "You have serious issues. You know that, right?" he asks before taking my pinky and shaking it with his own.

I roll my eyes. "Go get him," I say, pushing Gavin forward with a little shove. "We've already wasted too much time."

"Yeah, you better get going. This weather ain't gonna hold forever," Hunter warns, his brown eyes flicking upward. It isn't snowing yet, but the sky is hazy and dim and the sun remains hidden. Puffy white clouds hang low, whirling above our heads.

Gavin blinks. "Wait—you aren't coming?"

"Hell no! There's too much work to do back here. First, I gotta line the windows to keep the warmth in." He ticks tasks off his fingers. "Then I gotta set up emergency signals. And then I gotta—"

"I just thought you'd want to come along," Gavin says, cutting him off, "since you're the one always bragging about hunting and fishing and building fires with your bare hands and all that."

Hunter smirks. "It's a hike—not *The Hunger Games*."

I tune them out and stare down the red firs we'll be walking to. My eyes narrow as I size up the distance between the car and those tall, thick trunks. It looks far but not much worse than the canyon trails behind my house. Back in middle school, Gavin and I used to hike them all the time on the weekends when Stuart slept in.

I can do this. I know I can.

The question is, can Stuart?

CHAPTER 4

8:50 a.m.

After Gavin wrangles my brother back to the SUV, Hunter dresses us like we're going on an expedition deep into the North Pole. He starts by layering sweatshirts and our warmest coats to protect our core. That's the most important part of the body to keep warm. Then he moves on to buttons and zippers, checking to make sure everything works and is secure, and piles on scarves and ski hats and multiple pairs of gloves and socks so we don't lose body heat through our head and digits. Lastly, he secures dark ski goggles around each of our foreheads to prevent snow blindness if it gets too sunny. Apparently, dangerous UV rays can bounce off the snow and get into our eyes, doing serious damage without protection.

I can tell by the twitching of Gavin's mouth that I look ridiculous, but Stuart gets it the worst. He's skinny to begin with, so Hunter has to give him even more clothes to wear than me. The result leaves Stuart looking like a kid in a fat sumo wrestler outfit—tiny head, enormous body. Of the three of us, only Gavin looks good in all the ridiculous layers and goggles, but Gavin would look good in a burlap bag.

Once we're dressed, Hunter distributes supplies for our journey. He pours almost half of the peanuts from the party-size bag into the front pocket of my backpack and hands Gavin a few string cheeses plus six of the water bottles. It seems like overkill for a short hike, but we have to prepare for the worst. We'll be all alone in the woods with no way to get help if anything happens.

Gavin volunteers to carry most of the extra weight. He stuffs the cheese inside his giant black mesh backpack and tries to put the water in too, but before he can fit them all inside, Stuart grabs half of the bottles and shoves them into his own limited edition Marvel *Captain America* backpack. I shake my head, hiding a smile. I still can't believe he uses that silly bag. You'd think he was six—not sixteen.

"Don't forget to watch the sky," Hunter warns as he escorts us to the road. "You catch two layers of dark clouds moving in different directions, and you hightail it outta there, got it? That means it's gonna dump."

Gavin nods. "Got it."

"And make sure you don't get lost. You know wilderness navigation, right? Like how trees grow on the north side of the mountain?"

Stuart looks at Hunter like he's sprung two heads. "Huh?"

Hunter groans. "A'ight, we'll keep it simple. Remember to always mark your path so you can find your way back." He grabs extra scarves and socks from the cargo area and secures them to the elastic bungee cords on the front of Gavin's bulging backpack. "Tie these around the tree branches, okay?"

"Got it," Gavin says, rearranging his pack to center it on his body. He inches toward the road.

"Make 'em tight."

"Got it," Gavin says.

"And you gotta remember to—"

"I said I got it, okay?" Gavin pinches the bridge of his nose and blows out a slow breath. "I swear, Hunt. If you give me one more instruction, I'm gonna tie *you* to this backpack and make you come along."

Hunter lets out a low chuckle. "Fair enough."

Champion tugs at the leash in my hand, eager to get going on our hike. I wave goodbye to Britney, who promises to lead a prayer for our quick return, while Hunter gives Gavin and my brother pats on the back for good luck. "You keep 'em safe, Sam," he says to me with a wink before heading back inside the car to work on whatever chore list he was spouting off earlier.

I turn to my brother for one last reassurance. "Promise me you'll be careful," I beg him.

He groans. "Would you chill out already?"

"Stu—"

He cuts me off, wrapping his arms around me and pulling me into a giant hug. He crushes me against his thin chest so tightly I almost choke. Stuart hasn't hugged me like this since . . . well . . . I don't know when the last time was.

The impulsive gesture makes me think of the picture my mother has of us on her nightstand from when we were little kids in grade school. Until he turned ten, Stuart used to hate sleeping in his bed alone. He had night terrors and was scared of the dark, but our parents wanted him to grow out of it, so they made him sleep with only a little white night-light for company. After my mother would put Stuart to sleep in his own bed, he'd crawl into mine and fall asleep next to me. In the nightstand photo she keeps, we're smashed up so close together in my little twin bed that my father used to joke he couldn't figure out where I started and where Stuart began.

I still feel like that sometimes, like Stuart is a part of me. I've been taking care of my little brother and watching out for him for so long, I'm not sure who I'd be without him around. And not in that hokey way people sometimes say, but like if he ever ceased to exist, so would I.

"I promise," he says, letting go of me and stepping back. "Now quit nagging."

Stuart is the first to start down the road, but Gavin soon pulls in front, taking the lead. I roll my eyes at his back. Of course, he has to be first in everything. I bring up the rear, Champion bouncing at my heels. The dog is ecstatic to be out of the car.

We barely get a foot down the path before Champion breaks free of my grasp with a powerful yank on the leash and plunges headfirst into the snow beds. They're at least five feet high, rising alongside the road and dividing it from the desolate forest on either side. I whistle and he emerges seconds later, covered from head to tail in snow. He looks like a ghost, his tongue flopping and tail wagging in the wind.

"Bad dog," I tell him, but I'm laughing as he races back to me. I grab his leash again as he tries to lick his apology. "Behave or you're going back to the car," I say, pushing his slobbery muzzle away, but I can't stop smiling at him.

As we continue onward, I keep my eyes peeled for signs of people and civilization. There's not much so far. No buildings or streetlights. No tire tracks. There's not even any trash on the sides of the road. Nothing but trees and snow and the occasional fluttering of wings as birds fly by overhead. It's eerily quiet here, save for the sound of ice crunching beneath our boots like some strange ambient background music. It's downright spooky.

Before long, Stuart is whistling notes from a dance track by some new DJ he's obsessed with, keeping rhythm with the beat and singing off-key.

"Cool song. Who sings it?" Gavin asks, turning around, hiding a grin.

"Nice try," Stuart says. "I may be young, but I wasn't born yesterday."

"What?" Gavin asks, attempting to look innocent.

"Oh, come on." Stuart groans. "You want me to say the singer's name, and then you'll tell me to keep it that way. Not falling for it, dude."

I chuckle. "Good for you, Stu!"

"Oh, shut up, Sam," he says. "That's your dumb joke. He learned it from you."

Gavin's eyes dance with amusement as he meets my gaze. "Guess it worked better when we were thirteen, huh?"

I refuse to smile back. It'll take a lot more than some stupid shared jokes from middle school for me to warm up to Gavin. We're here for Lily, that's all. Not some trip down memory lane.

And yet, I can't stop my mind from wandering back to that very first day we met.

It was almost five years ago, the first day of my eighth-grade year and Stuart's sixth. I'd felt terrible for my brother that morning. He'd been so excited to start middle school with me, but the doctors were making him wear a hideous plastic brace to school because his scoliosis had worsened over the summer. If that didn't work, they said back surgery was next.

Stuart had stood in front of the iron gates at the entrance to our school, looking paralyzed while the bigger kids rushed in all around him. "You can see my brace, can't you?" he'd asked, blowing out a long breath, staring at the looming building ahead.

"No, you look great," I said, even though you could. The fact that he was tall and thin only emphasized the brace more.

Someone bumped into him and he lost his balance, flailing to the ground. I hurried forward, helping him back to his feet and holding him upright. He stared down at my hand like it was some kind of bug and shook himself free.

We walked past the gymnasium and then the cafeteria while he rolled his backpack along behind us. The bag was bright blue with an ugly yellow stripe running down the center, two clunky wheels, and a massive rubber handle. The doctors wouldn't let him carry a normal backpack like the other kids because it put too much strain on his back. We got all the way to the lockers before he stumbled over his untied shoelaces and crashed into someone twice his size.

"Hey! Watch where you're going," a boy with a hooked nose said. He had long, greasy hair pulled back into a ponytail.

"Yeah, watch it, loser," said another boy standing next to Ponytail. The two of them looked big enough to be in eighth grade with me, but I didn't recognize them.

"What's with the suitcase? You going on a trip?" Ponytail asked Stuart.

"It's a backpack," Stuart said, his voice cracking.

"It's lame," the other boy said. He smirked, and the extra pudge on his cheeks wrinkled up like a shar-pei dog while my brother's face turned red. Stuart rubbed at his nose—a telltale sign he was about to cry.

"Get out of our way," I said, stepping in front of Stuart.

Ponytail got so close I could smell his bad breath, some gross combination of tuna fish and ammonia. He gave me a slow, ugly smile and snatched the roller bag with one hand, shoving my brother with the other. The push sent Stuart hurtling across the linoleum floor.

Without thinking I jumped on the kid, making my fists hard and tucking my nails in, like my dad taught me. I got in a few good licks, too, before Ponytail's friend grabbed me by the wrists. His grip was so tight, pain flared up my arms.

"Leave them alone!" a male voice called out, and powerful hands grasped my waist, jerking me away from the bullies' clutches.

The warning bell rang then and Ponytail and his friend scuttled away, leaving my brother's bag on the ground. When I twisted around, standing before me was the most beautiful boy I'd ever seen. Where the bullies were grizzled and rough, he was clean-cut with smooth lines, an angular jaw, and hair gelled back with every strand perfectly in place. He was regal looking—almost pretty—except for his eyes. There was fire there like the hottest blue at the bottom of a Bunsen burner.

"You okay?" Blue Eyes asked me, rolling the bag back to my brother.

I nodded, unable to form words.

"Wow! That was so cool!" Stuart said. "Like in the movies when Superman faces off with General Zod." He was gushing so hard, he practically drooled. For a second I was annoyed because, *hello*, I was the one who almost got punched.

"No big deal," Blue Eyes said, shrugging, but something dark flashed across his face. "I hate bullies."

High-pitched howling cuts through the memory and stirs me from the past. To the right of me, bushes rustle from somewhere deep within the surrounding forest and cause the hair on the back of my neck to stand straight up.

"Are those *coyotes*?" Gavin asks. Those bright blue eyes from my memory are now trained on me as the three of us freeze in place.

"I thought coyotes only came out at night," Stuart whispers, his face ashen.

I pull Champion in close to my side and spin around to face the woods. "Coyotes are only nocturnal near people," I explain. "I bet they hunt around the clock here."

I close my eyes, concentrating on the sound. It's impossible to gauge an accurate number. It could be two animals or twenty. The odd thing is that it doesn't sound like coyotes. Coyotes yelp in between their barks and howls, but that's not what I'm hearing. If I didn't know better, I'd say these are dogs, except there's no way wild dogs are running around in the deserted mountains.

Champion bares his canines into the woods as the howls grow louder, echoing off the mountains, distorted. His tail bristles and his back legs flex, preparing for a charge.

"Champ! *No!*" I jerk his leash and he goes silent. The boys inch closer to either side of me until they have me blocked in like they're my personal bodyguards. My brother holds his hands up, making two small fists in the air.

"What are you doing?" I hiss at him.

"Protecting you!"

"Nothing out here is going after a human, silly," I say, and shove them both away. "It's Champ we have to worry about."

"Champ's fine," Gavin says, reaching for the dog's long chin and running a finger along the old scar there. It's a souvenir from the time he got mixed up with an aggressive Rottweiler in the bike park. "This old beast can take care of himself."

"Yeah, well, I'm not taking any chances." I push at Champion's hindquarters, herding him into the middle spot so he's stuck between the three of us. My muscles tense up as I prepare myself for a fight. Nothing bad is going to happen to Champion while I'm around.

Thankfully, after another minute, the barking fades until it's so far away we can hardly hear it anymore.

"Gee, that was fun," Stuart says with a derisive chuckle.

I continue staring into the woods, hoping I might catch a glimpse that will explain what we just heard. If it isn't coyotes and it can't be dogs . . . what in the world is out here with us?

"Do you think it'll come back?" Gavin asks me.

I shrug my shoulders. "I don't know," I say, still trying to figure out what "it" is.

"What if it's werewolves?" Stuart asks.

"Werewolves don't exist," I say, rolling my eyes.

"Sure they do, and they're awesome," he says. "I saw it on YouTube. There are eyewitness reports and everything."

I groan. "You know YouTube isn't the actual news, right?"

He grins and gives me a knowing look. "You're just a hater because you never made it past the second level of *Werewolf*."

Werewolf is this ridiculous video game Stuart used to make Gavin and me play with him. The main character is a man who turns into a wolf and gains supernatural abilities so he can save the world from evil creatures.

"Yes, I did." I start walking again. "I beat you, remember?"

"No way," Stuart says.

Gavin's laugh is rich and deep behind me. "She's right, bro. She did."

"That never happened!" Stuart shakes his head.

"It did," I insist. "Last Christmas. Even *he* remembers," I say, pointing a finger back at Gavin.

Those magnetic blue eyes spark in my direction, and the necklace I wear hidden beneath three layers of clothing burns at my neck. I'd never tell him, but I still wear the beautiful gold locket he gave me for Christmas last year. I always assumed he'd forgotten all about that night and the way we'd almost kissed, but the way he's looking at me now—I'm not so sure.

"Hey, you're supposed to be on my side," Stuart says, elbowing Gavin in the ribs.

"Always." Gavin breaks eye contact with me, his grin widening, and damn, there are those incredible dimples of his. "And if memory serves right, I believe it's the third level Sam never made it past," he says, fist-bumping my brother as they crack up.

I groan and jog away from them to get some space, annoyed at myself for letting my guard down. Even if only for a few seconds, I can't allow myself to reminisce about Gavin like that. Thinking about him that way . . . it never leads to anything good.

Champion runs after me, catching up and nuzzling into my side. At least there's one male around that's not completely obnoxious. I reach down and scratch his ears, thinking about the day we first found him cowering behind some ragweed bushes in the canyons behind my house, scared and alone.

The animal shelter told us the chances of a blind puppy being adopted were slim to none. That the best thing we could do was to euthanize him. It was Gavin who learned about cataract surgery and raised the money to pay for it. The first time I looked into Champion's big brown eyes and saw him looking back at me—really seeing me—it was like witnessing a miracle. That was the moment I knew I wanted to be a veterinarian.

"Time to rehydrate," Gavin says, making us stop to drink some water. Since we don't have a dog bowl, I chug my water and then give Champion the other half, tipping it back for him. Almost all of it makes it into his mouth, and I smile with pride. I taught him the trick years ago when we used to take him hiking in the canyons behind my house. Gavin was always forgetting to bring along a collapsible dog dish.

"How's Boston?" Stuart asks Gavin in between sips. "What are the chicks like there?"

"Gross." I make a face. "Sister around, remember?"

Gavin shrugs. "They're okay," he says, stopping to tie a sock around the closest tree branch, marking our trail like Hunter instructed earlier.

"Yeah, you probably don't care anyway," Stuart says, finishing his bottle as we start walking again. "You've been back in town less than forty-eight hours and already have the hottest girl in school chasing after you."

"Britney and I are just hanging out," Gavin says, snaking

the lead from me. "She needed a ride, and we had room. I'm not getting down on one knee or anything."

My face stays blank, showing no reaction. I wish I wasn't so happy to hear Gavin and Britney aren't anything serious—not to Gavin, at least—but I am. And I sort of hate myself for it.

"Seaside isn't the same without Gavin Farrell," Stuart says.

I smirk. "Some might say it's better."

"I miss you too, Sams," Gavin says, turning back to me. His lips twitch in my direction before focusing on my brother again. "How's school? Did you ever sign up for that writing class?"

Stuart makes a face. "Writing is for losers."

"How can you say that?" I halt in place. "What about Shakespeare? Dickens? Hemingway?"

He giggles. "Exactly."

"I'm not sure about those dead guys, but King and Patterson are basically billionaires. Stephenie Meyer too." Gavin grins. "Definitely not losers."

I hide the smile tugging at my lips. If Gavin is agreeing with me for once, maybe Stuart will actually listen.

Stuart used to love telling stories. When he was stuck in the hospital after his back surgery and we visited him, Stuart would share bedtime stories each night before the staff kicked us out. They were fantasies filled with dragons and demons and magic and heroes and happily-ever-afters. The nurses that took care of him would even bring other sick kids into the room to hear his stories. Stuart was a legend in the children's ward.

"*Twilight?*" Stuart's nose wrinkles with disgust. "Please! Those were the worst vampire books ever."

"What's wrong with *Twilight?*" Gavin asks.

"Are you serious? Sparkling vampires?" Stuart lifts an incredulous brow. "Totally unrealistic."

I choke on my laughter. "You know vampires don't exist either, right?" I ask, jabbing him in the side.

"Sure they do. Just like werewolves," he says, and sticks his tongue out at me. "And they don't sparkle."

Gavin suddenly stops so fast I almost walk right into him. "Hey, is that a gas station?" he asks, pointing to a tiny, one-story building that sits tucked in between soaring trees. It's yards away from the main road, almost entirely hidden by snow-covered branches. A big red sign on top of the brick roof screams, "GAS!"

"Holy shit!" Stuart lets out a whoop and then we half run, half jog up the road, yelling and jostling each other. People! Food! Heat! *We're saved!*

But when we get to the small parking lot moments later, my heart sinks. There's not a single car in sight except for a faded red truck on blocks that looks like it belongs to decades past. Old tires litter the side of the building, and black plastic bags cover the two nozzle pumps, making them unusable. The place looks like something straight out of a gory slasher movie, the kind Stuart loves where a wood-dwelling masked killer hacks up teens with chain saws and machetes. *Jason Voorhees would feel right at home here*, I think, and shiver.

"It looks closed," I say as we walk up to the front door and lean into the windows, wiping ice away with our sleeves and peering through the glass to get a closer look inside. All the lights are off.

Stuart lets out an angry grunt. "Yeah, since the 1900s."

"Must be the storm," Gavin says.

I cock my head at him. "But wouldn't the storm be more reason to stay open? More people needing gas, right?"

"What do we do now?" Stuart asks.

Gavin's eyes flash in my direction with that mischievous twinkle I know only leads to trouble. "I bet I can find the key around here somewhere," he says, bending down and digging through the snowy asphalt to grab the biggest rock he can find. He tosses it from hand to hand, eyeing the large window in front of us, and winds his arm up.

"Uh . . . what do you think you're doing?" I ask with alarm.

He smirks. "Getting us inside."

"But that's breaking and entering."

Stuart slides a hand to my shoulder. "This is an emergency. It's for Lil, okay?"

Under normal circumstances, this is the kind of crazy idea I'd be talking them out of, but out here, so far from civilization, things feel different. The black-and-white rules of polite society don't seem to apply to us anymore.

"Be careful," I warn, and close my eyes, turning away to hide my face behind my forearms.

There's a loud cracking sound as Gavin smashes the front window with his rock and Champion barks in a panicked series of yelps behind me. When I glance up again, Gavin already has his gloved hand through the empty windowpane and is unlocking the door. He steps inside, motioning for us to join him. Before following him, I tie Champion to the post of a handicap parking sign so he can't come after us and get hurt stepping on broken glass.

Once I'm inside the gas station, I make a beeline for an old rotary phone tucked behind the cash register. It's bizarre looking, like an ancient artifact belonging in a museum somewhere. I wipe away the thin layer of dust covering the mouthpiece with my jacket sleeve and hold the receiver up to my ear. There's no dial tone.

"Damn. It's dead," I say, shivering as I wrap my arms around my body to ward off the frigid air and snow blowing through the window Gavin broke. So much for heat. It's almost as cold inside the dark, empty gas station as it was outside.

"Must be the storm," Gavin repeats, but with far less conviction this time.

My skin tingles as I take a good look around. The gas station has a musty and mildewy stench as if it's been locked up all winter, and the floors are as filthy as the counter. I think the tiles are supposed to be some kind of off-white shade, but the dust and dirt layer has turned them gray. The rows of wooden shelves are barren and empty. There's nothing here we can use. No water. No medical supplies. Not even an old can of food. It's obvious the place hasn't been occupied in ages.

"This place isn't closed for the storm. It's closed—period," I say.

Gavin swears.

"What is it? What aren't you telling us?" I ask.

"I didn't want to say anything before and freak you out, but the roads are strange too."

"Strange how?" Stuart asks.

"It's not like the roads near my cabin," Gavin explains. "The ones here haven't been plowed at all. Not that I can tell, at least. It's like there's no one around."

Stuart's eyes widen. "What if it's zombies?"

"*Zombies?* What are you talking about now?" I ask. Sometimes I really don't understand what goes on in that crazy head of his.

"What if that's why no one's around?" he clarifies. "Maybe the zombies have taken over and eaten all the people here. This could be a real *Night of the Living Dead* situation. I once saw this movie where—"

"Knock it off," I snap, losing patience. "Zombies don't exist."

"You don't know that," he disagrees, his nostrils flaring. "I saw this documentary on Netflix about these brain parasites. They can take over animals and control them. So why not people? It could happen," he says. "And don't even get me started on military experiments. And brain viruses! This is real shit."

"No one is here because we took a bogus shortcut," I say between clenched teeth, and turn to glare at Gavin. "I told you we should've gone back."

"Hey, you agreed. Remember?" Gavin's eyes flicker with irritation. "Besides, this changes nothing. We just have to get high enough to get our phones working and call for help."

I tremble with anger. "*But I told you.*"

"Would you two stop arguing? I'm sick of you fighting," Stuart says, and stomps off angrily, heading around the corner.

Gavin's mouth tightens. "What's done is done, Sam! I can't change the past, now can I? We have to keep going, and when we get home you never have to talk to me again, okay?"

"Fine with me!"

The back of my neck flames with indignation, and I'm about to bolt for the front door just as I hear my brother's blood-curdling screams behind me.

CHAPTER 5

12:00 p.m.

Gavin's face drains of all color and then we're both running for my brother, my annoyance at Gavin replaced by sheer black fright. What if it's Stuart's back? What if his other discs have given out, like the doctors warned us could happen?

What if he never walks again?

I hear another high-pitched shriek followed by my name.

"Stu! I'm coming!" I shout, running through the aisles until I find him at the back of the gas station. He howls in pain, lying underneath an empty wooden shelf that must've fallen on him somehow. His bright red blood is spattered across the linoleum floor. Of all the disaster scenarios that run through my head, I never could have imagined this one.

"Stu?" I drop to the ground, pulling his head into my lap. His skin is pale. Much too pale. He has enough strength left to say my name one last time before his eyes roll into the back of his head and he goes limp. "*Stuart!*"

I swear out loud, unsure what to do. You're supposed to raise a fainting person's legs above heart level to help with circulation, but I worry with that shelf compressing his body. Movement might do him more harm than good. *If* I can even move him. The shelf is huge.

"Can you hear me?" I loosen his jacket collar and stroke his cheek, trying to wake him.

Slowly, his eyes flutter open. "Sam?"

"*Good God!*" I let loose a sigh of relief. "You scared the crap out of me."

"Sorry . . ."

"Are you okay?"

"I think so," he says, staring down at the shelf in disbelief. "I don't know what happened. The damn thing fell on me."

"Can you feel your legs?"

He grunts and his eyebrows pull together, his face tightening with concentration. "Yeah. I feel them."

"Try to move your toes," I order.

"We have to get the shelf off of him," Gavin says, moving next to me, his mouth in a tight line as he hovers over us.

I lean down, grabbing the sharp edge of the shelf. Gritting my teeth, I give it a big tug upward. The damn thing must weigh over two hundred pounds! It barely moves an inch before I lose control and it slams back down on Stuart's body.

"What the hell!" Stuart cries, tears cutting dirty trails down his face. "Shit—Sam. That hurt!"

"It's too heavy." Gavin shakes his head. "We have to work together."

Heat rises to my face as I whirl on him. "Oh, so now you want to work together, huh?" I laugh humorlessly. "What about when I needed your help *keeping my brother in the damn car?*"

"Like I was supposed to know a shelf was going to fall on him?" His handsome face fills with exasperation. "You're acting crazy."

"*Me?*" Red explodes in my vision. "*I'm* the crazy one?"

Stuart groans. "Will you both shut up already? Just get this thing off me!"

I glance away, feeling like a jerk. I can't believe I'm arguing with Gavin when my brother is lying on the floor, bleeding.

"I'll get the top," I say, wrapping my hands around the shelf. "You take the bottom." Gavin nods, the annoyance in his eyes dissolving as he kneels down to grab onto the lower end of the shelf. "You ready?" I ask, looking over at my brother.

"Uh-huh." He pants and squeezes his eyes closed, bracing himself. "Do it quick, okay?"

Together, Gavin and I jerk the shelf upward, trying to stand as we hold either end against our bodies. My muscles strain, arms spasming from all the weight. It's so heavy I almost drop the damn thing back down to the ground again.

"Pull harder!" Gavin yells in my ear.

I press my lips together and tug until sharp edges of wood dig through my gloves and jacket sleeves, pricking my skin. My eyes water, and my knees threaten to buckle under the stress. Seconds later the shelf falls to the side with a big thud, freeing my brother.

"Sweet baby Jesus!" Stuart rasps, wiping away tears with the back of his hand. "I thought you were going to kill me!"

I drop back down to the ground and scoot in closer. Now that the shelf is off, I want to inspect the damage. Both of Stuart's pant legs are slashed from the thighs down and caked with blood. I place a light hand on the largest rip on his right thigh to see if he still has feeling in his legs.

"That's just a scratch," he says, his teeth chattering. "It's the other foot that hurts."

The instant I touch his left ankle, he lets out an earsplitting scream. The sound slices right through me, and I know something is broken. I whirl on Gavin.

"This is all your fault!"

Something like panic flashes across his face. "C'mon, Sam! Not this again."

"But I warned you!"

Stuart coughs. "Hey, guys—"

"He's fine. It's just a sprain or something," Gavin says. "You're overreacting."

"My overreacting is *not* the problem. You are! You're a crappy friend with terrible judgment, and you're always hurting the people around you."

It's not only about my brother's ankle, either, or that he never listens to me about Stuart. It occurs to me I'm still furious with how Gavin left things between us when he left for Boston last year. Or rather, didn't leave things.

Maybe we weren't close like he and Stuart were, but still. You don't spend that much time with someone and then leave town and never talk to them again. You don't ignore all their calls and texts. If he thought it was okay to up and ghost people like that, he had another think coming.

"That's a really shitty thing to say to me," he says. His eyes flash as his expression flips between hurt and fury.

"Too bad." I cross my hands over my chest. "It's the truth."

Stuart coughs again, louder and more insistent this time. "Um, guys—"

"*What?!*" Gavin and I yell in unison.

"Just wondering when you'll both stop bickering long enough to help me up?"

"Oh—sorry." The little jab of guilt returns. What's wrong with me? Why am I so focused on Gavin when my brother needs my attention? "Here, hold on to me," I say, reaching down to help him up. He drapes his left arm around my shoulders and stands, tottering as he clutches on to my arm for support.

"You two should just do it already and get it over with," he whispers into my ear.

"I'd rather stick needles in my eye," I whisper back. Gavin is an ass. If I never talk to him again after this weekend, it will be too soon.

I half lead, half carry my brother out of the gas station until we get to the parking lot and he's able to put pressure on his ankle. Even then, I stay glued to his side in case he needs me. Gavin unties Champion, taking hold of his leash, and the three of us move like zombies back down the road. We trudge step after miserable step with only one goal in mind: *get to the car*.

After a while, the abandoned gas station disappears until there's nothing behind us but the empty stretch of mountain and forest. Gavin and my brother make small talk, catching up on girls and football, while I stare at the road ahead in silence. I'm so mad, I don't know how to calm myself down or speak without screaming at Gavin again. To be safe, I resort to giving him the silent treatment. Or for all I know, Gavin is the one giving it to me.

The longer we walk, the more time I have to rethink my words. Maybe I was a tad harsh. Despite what I said, Gavin isn't a bad person. He doesn't cause trouble on purpose. I think he even has good intentions—most of the time. A lot of this is bad luck, pure and simple.

And can I really be mad at him for forgetting about me once he moved to Boston? Even if he never called or texted me after he left, so what? It isn't like he owes me anything. When it comes down to it, he's Stuart's best friend—not mine. What did I expect?

The more I think about it, the more I realize Gavin isn't the only person I'm angry with. I know I screwed up too. I should've stood my ground the other day and made the group turn around and go home. But damn it, Gavin always has this way of getting me to agree to things I shouldn't be agreeing to. It's like that parasailing trip last year in Mexico.

Gavin warned me he was going. He even asked me to help him sneak Stuart out of the house without my parents noticing. I knew it was a terrible idea. I even told him so, but I didn't stop them from leaving when I could have. If I had, Stuart wouldn't have wound up in the hospital with a broken arm, and Gavin's parents wouldn't have shipped him off to boarding school as punishment.

So, yeah, Gavin isn't the only one to blame.

We briefly stop to refuel, eating the peanuts and cheese for strength and guzzling down more water. The skies above us darken, ominous-looking clouds gathering and temperature plunging. As the wind whips my hair against my cheeks so hard it stings my skin, I recall Hunter's advice earlier about heading back if weather threatens. By the look of things, we don't have a lot of time to make it to safety.

The air around us turns thinner and colder the longer we walk. The chilliest day on the highest mountain slope I've ever experienced in Colorado pales compared to this. The air freezes every baby hair on my face, even the little ones inside my nose. I pull my scarf tight around my face, but it's little comfort. I'd need a thousand scarves here to keep warm.

The mountains turn deathly quiet other than the sounds of wind and our footsteps. No more birds chirping. No insects buzzing. It's so sterile and strange, like a frozen alien planet. I knew we were screwed, but I didn't realize until right now just how badly. I can't help but feel an immediate sense of danger as a dreadful thought forms in my head: *We don't belong here.* This isn't a place for humans. At least not without the proper shelter and gear and training.

We finally reach the SUV as the moon begins its slow rise above the mountains. Hunter is the first to spot us. He sprints down the road, screaming our names, and then helps us carry Stuart the rest of the way back to the car.

I open the door to the middle row and glance toward the back where my best friend lies motionless. My heart squeezes at the sight. Her eyes are still closed, same as when we left her hours ago. No movement at all or any sign that she hears me.

"How's she doing?" I ask Britney.

"No change," she whispers.

My eyes prick with wetness, but there's no time to be sad about Lily. I have to help my brother.

"What happened to him?" Britney's mouth drops as she notices Stuart's injuries.

"Long story."

She moves to the driver's seat so Hunter and Gavin can help me lay my brother down in the middle row. My arms and legs ache from exhaustion as we get Stuart in a neutral, flat position, and then I kneel on the floor next to him while Hunter and Gavin move to the front. They each take up half of the passenger seat so that Hunter's right side smashes against the car window and Gavin's left side overflows onto the center console.

Champion tries to crawl into the row with Stuart and me, but Britney wraps her arms under his armpits and pulls him against her. She keeps him half in her lap and half spilling onto the floor and the gas pedals, giving me space to work on my brother. Everyone turns in their seats to watch me while I inch up Stuart's left pant leg, steeling myself for the worst. My eyes widen as I take in what's underneath. The wet blood and ripped jeans did nothing to prepare me for what I see.

Stuart's left ankle is red and has swollen up like a golf ball. Long vicious cuts run along the length of his leg, a few of them still oozing fresh blood. Something is definitely broken, or at least sprained very, very badly. Worst of all are the wicked-looking wood splinters from the broken shelf that jut out all over his poor skin. My brother looks like a human pincushion.

"Pretty gnarly, huh?" he asks, watching for my reaction.

I force a smile and hope he doesn't notice my trembling fingers. "Let's get you cleaned up, okay?"

"Whatever you say, doc."

While I stare at his wrecked leg, I try to recall everything I've learned at the clinic. I've seen plenty of crush injuries before, though they're usually from car accidents—never a wooden shelf. The first step is to stop the bleeding so the animal doesn't bleed out and die on the operating table. Luckily, most of Stuart's cuts have already stopped bleeding on their own. The one exception is a large gash near his ankle that needs serious medical attention.

"This may hurt a little," I warn, unwrapping my scarf and using it to apply direct pressure to the cut.

He lets out a terrible scream. "*A little?*" he yells, his look accusing.

"Sorry," I say, but I don't let up. I turn toward the passenger seat, looking at Gavin and Hunter. "I need supplies. Soap. Bandages. Tweezers ... uh ... " I trail off, overwhelmed. This isn't the animal clinic back home. Where am I going to find all that stuff out here?

"I'll check the back," Hunter offers.

"You know what to look for to clean wounds and make a splint?" I ask.

He chuckles. "Girl, I've been an Eagle Scout since I turned thirteen."

"Okay, but do you have any medical training?"

"Seriously?" he asks, lifting a brow. "Do you know what an Eagle Scout is?"

"You're wasting time. You should both go." Britney leans into the middle row, slapping my hand away. She grabs the scarf I'm holding over Stuart's ankle and presses down on his wound. I watch in surprise as blood dribbles out from the sides of the wool scarf, getting all over her expensive cream-colored sweater, yet she doesn't move away.

"You sure?" I ask, impressed at her ability to manage both the ninety-pound dog and my bleeding brother.

"Go! Before I change my mind."

She doesn't have to tell me twice.

Hunter and I meet at the SUV's rear, but when I get there, I can only stare at the shiny black bumper, paralyzed. My breath quickens as an awful memory bubbles up like acid reflux.

Last fall, we had an aging poodle at the clinic. She was hit by a car, and the owner treated her himself with a makeshift splint. With a crush injury you can generally set a few bones and call it a day, but you should always watch for complications. By the time the owner brought the poodle to us, she was already near dead from a raging infection. We worked all day and half the night, but the dog died a horrible death. All from a broken bone.

Hunter puts a hand on my shoulder. "You a'ight?"

I shake my head, pushing away the horrid images. "I'm fine."

He opens the door to the cargo area, and we plunder through its depth for suitcases and duffle bags, searching for anything we can use. There isn't much. A few T-shirts Hunter suggests we shred into bandages. Some rubber hair ties I can use to secure things together. Little manicure scissors to cut with. I find my cosmetics bag and dump out the contents so hard its insides go clattering to the ground. Toiletries fly everywhere. Face wash. Toothpaste. Shampoo.

"Where the hell are my tweezers?" I yell at the empty bag.

Soft footsteps approach behind me. "Anything I can do?" Gavin asks.

"Do you have tweezers?" I ask, not bothering to turn around.

"No."

"Then go away."

"Please." He swallows hard. "Let me help."

I think about the poodle again, worry gnawing at me. "You promised he'd be okay! Why couldn't you listen to me for once?"

"I get it. You're still upset about Mexico. I know I screwed that up," he says, a muscle twitching at his temple. "But this isn't anything like that. Stu's fine—I've seen worse on the football field."

I sigh. "You don't get it, do you? We're not on a football field, Gav. Out here a simple cut can get you killed."

"Killed?" He snorts. "Don't you think you're being a little dramatic?"

"No." I push him back toward the front of the car. "Now go away."

"Sam—"

"Just leave me alone. I need to concentrate," I say right as Britney sashays around the corner of the SUV, pushing me aside and reaching inside the cargo area. I throw my hands in the air. "Am I the only one taking things seriously? What are you doing?" I ask her. "If you're all out here, who's watching Stu?"

"Relax. He'll be fine for thirty seconds." She grabs her humongous pink suitcase from the back and unzips the front pocket, pulling out a pair of crystal-encrusted tweezers. "Here," she says, pressing them into the palm of my hand. "I heard you screaming about tweezers."

Oh.

"Sorry," I say, feeling like a jerk. "Thanks."

She shrugs. "Don't worry about it."

We gather up the rest of the supplies and pile back into the car. I squeeze into the middle row next to Stuart and take a few calming breaths. Now that I have what I need, the next step is getting the splinters out.

The tweezers shake in my trembling hand. I've watched vets take splinters and ticks and all sorts of things off of cats and dogs, but I've never done it myself. You have to be super careful not to twist or jerk the tweezers. If you do it wrong, pieces can break off and remain under the skin, which can lead to infection.

The trickiest part for me isn't getting the technical aspects correct—it's the emotional part. This is my little brother, not some animal. It's been my job to take care of Stuart for as long as I can remember. I can't fail him.

It's more pressure than anything I've ever had to do at the clinic. I need to center myself. Maybe if . . . I squint and try to imagine Stuart as a skinny greyhound dog. To my surprise, it works.

My breathing slows and my fingers steady. Gently, ever so gently, I grasp the first splinter with the edges of the tweezers and pull it out of Stuart's skin. It comes away intact, and I feel a jolt of pride.

It takes twenty minutes to get all the wood shards out of his legs. After I finish, I wipe away the beads of sweat from my forehead, admiring my handiwork. Not bad for a beginner. Even a real vet couldn't have done it better.

"Thanks again," I say, handing the tweezers to Britney.

She eyes them with disgust, pushing them back toward me. "Uh, you can keep them."

Chuckling, I put the tweezers in my pocket in case I need them later and grab hand sanitizer from the front pouch of my backpack to disinfect Stuart's wounds. Antibacterial lotion or even rubbing alcohol would be better, but this is all we have. He grinds his teeth together while I slather the liquid over the puncture wounds and any big cuts he has, but otherwise he takes it in stride.

"Does anyone have a magazine or something I can use to splint his ankle?" I ask. At the clinic we use casts made of fiberglass, but out here I'll have to wing it.

"How about those western white pines? We can break off a branch," Hunter says, pointing out the front passenger window to a bunch of trees with fissured purplish-brown bark and a checkered appearance.

I nod. "Good idea."

He returns minutes later with a perfect branch the exact size and circumference of Stuart's shin. After making sure it's centered above and below Stuart's ankle and fibula for the best support, I use one of Hunter's flannel shirts from the cargo to act as a cushion between the back of Stuart's leg and the branch.

"Here," Hunter says, holding his Western cowboy belt in between his hands. An enormous silver buckle with a gold longhorn bull on it dangles off one end.

"Huh?"

"For the cast," he clarifies, leaning in next to me. I watch in amazement as he sets an intricate set of loops with the leather, expertly tying it around the splint to keep the branch, flannel, and Stuart's ankle secure.

"Whoa. You're like some kind of wilderness knot-tying pro."

He grins back at me. "If you think that's impressive, you should see my—"

"Hunt," Gavin warns.

"What'd I say?" Hunter asks, looking the picture of innocence.

I grin, trying not to laugh as I double-check the knot around my brother's leg. "This feel okay?" I ask Stuart. "It's not too tight?"

He winces. "Feels awesome. Never better."

I squeeze his shoulder. I can tell he's trying hard to be brave.

"Let's get some ice on you. It'll reduce the swelling and help with the pain."

Hunter and Gavin head for the SUV's cargo area and return with three long black men's socks filled with snow, twisted at the top into knots. I place one ice pack on Stuart's ankle and the other two on his bruised thigh. Once I've got that covered, Hunter helps me elevate Stuart's foot above his heart to reduce blood pressure and slow the flow of blood around his swollen ankle.

"Now stay still," I order as we stuff sweaters underneath his backside to keep him in place.

"So what's the verdict, doc?" Stuart asks, sweat dripping down his temple. "Am I gonna live?"

"Don't be silly! Of course, you're going to live."

Even if I am worried, I'd never tell him that. It's a waiting game now. All we can do is hope things will be fine and watch for any signs of danger: fever, nausea, vomiting, muscle aches.

"Thanks, sis," he says, and takes my hand in his.

I stare down in surprise. We haven't held hands since we were little kids. This used to be our thing—handholding—but he hasn't done it in years. Not since he decided he was too cool to hold on to his big sister.

Sure enough, some of my anxiety slips away. I have a feeling this handholding thing is helping me a lot more than it's helping him. I wonder if he knows it too.

It's funny. I'm always so worried about taking care of Stuart, sometimes I forget how he takes care of me too. Like Valentine's Day last year. There was a fundraiser for student government, and everyone bought roses for their friends and whoever they had crushes on. I was sure I'd be the only girl at school with no flowers.

I'll never forget that feeling of dread when the junior class officers came into homeroom to hand the flowers out. A tiny pit of humiliation grew in my gut as I buried my head in my textbook, pretending not to notice. But then I felt a tap on my shoulder and when I looked up, the class secretary was holding out a dozen beautiful red-stemmed roses—for me. Even Britney, the most popular girl in class, only got eight roses. At first, I was sure it was some mistake, but attached to each perfect rose was a note with my name on it. The card was signed, *Love, Your Secret Admirer.*

Later that night, after Stuart went to sleep, I checked the empty little shoebox under his bed where he stashes his allowance money. He'd been saving up all month for new video game controllers, but the box was empty. It was even better than having a secret admirer. I had someone who would spend his entire savings on me just so I wouldn't feel like a loser on Valentine's Day. That was the day I realized I had the best brother in the entire world.

I will not lose him.

CHAPTER 6

4:30 p.m.

We settle in for the long evening ahead. As a peace offering, Gavin suggests taking my spot in the back of the SUV to watch over Lily so I can sit with my brother in the middle row. I don't know if I'm ready to make peace with him, but I agree to the seating arrangements. Champion curls inward at my feet, lying on the floor and cozying up against my shins, nuzzling his snout into my boots. Up front, Hunter and Britney take the remaining two seats and fight for the next ten minutes over precious dashboard and center console space for their feet and arms. Finally, they reach an accord. Hunter gets the dashboard, but he has to sleep with Britney's legs in his lap.

Now that things have somewhat calmed down, I'm able to take in all the work Hunter did to the SUV to weatherproof it while we were out looking for help. He's rearranged most of our bulkiest ski and boarding equipment and placed it in the small gap between the cargo area and the last row of the SUV, reducing the amount of cold space. The mats are also now missing from the floor and have been rigged up and secured to cover the entire length of the front windshield and the windows in the last row to trap more warmth inside.

"Great job on the car, Hunter," I say to him.

"What am I? Chopped liver?" Britney scowls, lifting her chin.

"What do you mean?"

"You didn't think he did it all himself, did you?"

"Actually, I di—"

"What my sister is trying to say," my brother gives me a wry glance, "is thanks. You both did great."

"Thanks, Stu Poo," she says, beaming. "It was kind of fun, actually."

"Really?" I lift a skeptical brow. I find it hard to believe Britney enjoys manual labor. Very hard.

"Sure." She shrugs. "Kind of reminds me of my mission trip last summer. We built these little homes in Cozumel after Hurricane Ellen. At first, I only went because Bobby Mason is in my church group and he's gorgeous and was totally flirting with me all summer—even Amber said so—but it wound up being way better than I thought. All the families had a new house by the time we left, and some of them were sleeping in tents before we got there! And it was so spiritual." A serene look comes over her face, her voice dropping with reverence. "We prayed with the families every night, even the ones who didn't know English. It's, like, even though we didn't speak the same language, it didn't matter. We just understood each other. God's word is universal, you know?"

"That's pretty cool," Stuart says.

"It really was." She nods along. "And I didn't even care that Bobby wound up hooking up with Rebecca Welsh instead—even though she has a bad perm and wears clothes from Target."

I stifle a laugh.

For dinner, we split two of the six chocolate bars and a few handfuls of sour gummy worms while Champion gobbles up the dog food Gavin packed for him. He snatches it out of my hands, leaving trails of drool for me to wipe away on my jeans. After we've both eaten, I share my bottled water with him and use what's left to wash down my own meager meal.

The second we've finished drinking, Champion makes anxious little whining noises in the back of his throat and places a massive paw on my right knee, his eyes begging.

"Potty time?" I ask.

He lets out a quick answering bark, and the corners of his black lips move into a grin. There's a lot of debate over whether dogs can smile out of happiness or if they smile to be submissive, but that's only because those people haven't met Champion. He definitely happy smiles.

"I'll take him." Gavin inches out of his seat.

My stomach contracts uncomfortably as I remember I haven't gone to the bathroom since the rest stop yesterday.

"I've got it," I blurt. I'm not excited about venturing out into the woods at night, especially after the animal barking we heard earlier, but if I have to go in the wilderness, I don't want company. Definitely not Gavin's.

"You shouldn't go alone. I'll come with you," he says, and I can swear there's a note of worry in his words.

Britney's eyes narrow at him all the way to the back row. "She said she's okay. Leave the girl alone."

"Yeah, I'm fine," I agree.

"All the same, it ain't safe to go alone. No matter how *fine* you are." Hunter gives me a big wink.

I cock my head at the front passenger seat, confused. Is Hunter flirting with me, or is that just how he talks to every girl? I don't think I'm his type. He dates popular girls. Cheerleaders like . . . well . . . like Britney. Maybe all his charm is a southern thing?

Britney lets out a groan. "Relax. I'll go with her."

"Okay—whatever," I say.

It's not that I want Britney coming along with me, but there's no way to get out of this without drawing even more attention to myself and the fact I need to use the bathroom as badly as the dog does.

I slide out from underneath Stuart's legs and reposition his ankle so it's elevated on top of his backpack before flipping open the center console between the driver and front passenger seats. There's a pile of napkins on top from the rest stop yesterday. I shove a few of them into the front pouch of my backpack and step outside. Champion darts around me, flying out the door and barreling down the road like a wild banshee.

"Wait for me!" Britney calls, walking around to my side of the car. Since she gave her coat to Lily, she's now wearing one of the extra blanket-jackets from the night before. I can't help but notice with a cringe she's also sporting a hideous cream hat, fur-trimmed to match her boots and gloves.

Yuck. She probably took out an entire family of sweet little rabbits for that outfit.

I try not to let my revulsion show too much as she surprises me, grabbing onto my arm for support. We head for the line of trees closest to the car, a few feet off the road, as another door flings open behind us. I glance back to see Hunter leaping out of the front passenger seat.

"Where do you think you're going?" I ask.

"Wherever you're going, sweetheart," he says, and tips an imaginary cowboy hat in my direction.

"We don't need a chaperone." Annoyance flickers at me. I guess it's nice that everyone is so concerned for my well-being, but damn, can't a girl relieve herself in private?

"Don't worry. I'll keep my distance," he says with a sly grin, and I have a horrible suspicion he knows exactly what I'm up to and why I don't want him around. "And you're going the wrong direction."

"What do you mean?" Britney clutches at my forearm to stop from sliding further into the snow.

"Better head to the lodgepole pines over there," Hunter says, gesturing to a row of giant trees with brownish-gray trunks that appear orange from this distance. They're on the other side of the road, about a football field away from where we stand.

Britney lifts an eyebrow. "Are you kidding? That's way too far."

"You gotta get at least a few hundred feet away to avoid contamination. Or unwanted animal attention."

"Animals?" she squeals. "What kind of animals?"

"You know. Raccoons. Bears. Coyotes." He smiles a toothy grin. "Big Foot."

She gives him a dirty look. "Big Foot doesn't exist."

"Sure he does." His grin widens. "And he loves pretty blond cheerleaders."

I laugh. I'm really starting to like this guy.

"You're an ass, Hunt," Britney says, and jerks on my arm. "Let's go, Sammy."

She pulls me across the road, past the soaring pines and firs, heading for the trees Hunter pointed to. The wind blows so furiously I have to hold on to my faux fleece ski beanie with both hands. Snow whips into our eyes, almost blinding us.

With each step we take, we sink deeper and deeper into the snow. It's like walking in a vat of ice cream. We have to lean against each other so we don't slip and fall. If anyone had told me before this weekend that Britney Miller and I would traipse around in the snow, holding hands, I would've called them crazy. And yet, here we are.

Hunter moans with impatience and sidles in between us, grabbing our elbows to steady us and move us along faster.

He's so sure-footed you'd think he walked through feet of snow daily. But the one who puts us all to shame is Champion. The dog runs circles around us, jumping in and out of the snowdrifts as agile as a porpoise maneuvering through waves in the ocean. It's as if he was born for this.

A few minutes later, we arrive at the brownish-gray trees. Britney and I scurry under them, hiding beneath their long, thick branches. They're wide enough to shelter us from the battering snowfall and allow us to catch our breath from the walk.

I nudge at Champion's hindquarters. "Go potty," I command, and he runs a few feet away, finding a place he likes. I sigh, watching as he squats and defecates in the snow before trotting off happily in the opposite direction. If only it was that easy for me.

"If you gotta go number two, use a rock and dig a hole," Hunter orders. "And make sure it's deep enough so raccoons and coyotes can't get into it."

"Ew. Gross." Britney's face turns green. "I don't go number two."

Hunter gives her a knowing grin. "Sure you don't, princess."

"Jerk." She gives him a shove. "Get out of here."

"Six to eight inches deep. Don't forget," he says, laughing, and blows us a kiss as he walks behind another cluster of trees and disappears from view.

As soon as he's out of earshot, Britney turns to me, her face deathly serious. "Whatever sounds come out, we never speak of this again, got it?"

"Deal." I chuckle, nodding my agreement. That's fine with me.

We turn away from each other so we're back-to-back. My belly spasms again so painfully I wince and throw my backpack to the ground before squatting in preparation and pulling my pants down. Cold air nips at my naked lady parts, but I grit my teeth and go. When it's over, I use the napkins from the car and the hand sanitizer from the front pouch of my backpack to clean up.

"Holy hell!" Britney makes an exasperated noise next to me. "I peed on my shoes."

I peek over and she's sitting butt-first in the snow. Her gross, fur-lined boots are in her hands, and she scrubs frantically at the sides.

"Are you crazy? What're you doing?" I can't believe she's stupid enough to sit in the snow in only her socks. "Put your damn shoes on! You're going to freeze your ass off like that."

She wails. "But these are my favorite boots!"

I watch as she puts her shoes back on and then grab her by the elbow, yanking her up off the cold wet ground. "Here. Use this," I say, offering her some of my napkins and a few drops of my hand sanitizer. "That'll teach you not to wear ugly baby bunny carcasses on your feet." I scowl, eyeing her offensive shoes with repulsion.

"They're designer!"

She tries to snatch the entire bottle of hand sanitizer from me, but I'm too quick for her. I throw it into my backpack for safekeeping and zip the bag closed before she can get near.

"Nice try." I laugh. "This is the only soap we have. No way I'm wasting it on those abominations."

She sticks her tongue out. "The Lord said, 'You shall open your hand to him and lend him sufficient for his need, whatever it may be.'"

"I don't think Deuteronomy applies to shoes," I say sarcastically.

One overly plucked brow raises in surprise. "You know that verse?"

I resist a groan. "We were in the same Sunday school class, Miller."

The funny thing is, I actually believe she'd let me use the soap no matter what I needed it for. She didn't hesitate to give her fancy jacket to Lily yesterday. Not to mention how she let Stuart bleed all over her cashmere sweater earlier. Still, I don't feel bad for conserving our medical supplies. Even if Britney would give me the soap, I'd never ask to use it on something as dumb as a pair of revolting fur boots, and I don't think God would either.

Britney is still grumbling, calling me a soap dictator, when I spot the animal tracks in the snow next to us. My mouth goes dry, a creepy sensation working its way up my spine. No way those are Champion's paw prints. For one thing, there are too many of them.

I take a knee to further inspect and trail a gloved finger around the large, four-toed tracks. The presence of claw marks and the rectangular shape mean it's Canidae, but what canids would run around this deep in the mountains in winter? I still don't believe there's a pack of stray dogs in such a desolate place, and the prints are far too big for coyote or fox—unless it's a mutant variety I've never heard of. That leaves only one other plausible explanation.

Wolves.

Even if possible, it's highly unlikely. Wild gray wolves are protected in California. There are less than a dozen in the state and not many more in the entire Pacific Northwest. Yet even the slightest chance we could run into wolves here fills me with unease. Wolves rarely attack humans, but a domestic dog like Champion? He'd be the perfect meal.

"Naw. Ain't no wolves around here," Hunter says after we catch up to him and I explain what I saw in the snow. "It's probably coyotes. Or bears. Plenty of black bears, though they generally avoid folks."

"Holy crap. Did you say *bears?*" Britney asks, her mouth dropping. "I can't believe I'm saying this, but I like her dumb wolf theory better than yours."

"An Ursidae paw and a Canidae paw are nothing alike," I explain, annoyed at his dismissive tone. I don't care if he is an Eagle Scout—whatever that is; there's no way he knows more about animals than I do. "Come on," I say, grabbing his arm. "I'll show you. Maybe it's no wolf, but it's definitely not a damn bear."

We approach the spot where I saw the animal prints, but in the time it took us to find Hunter, fresh snow has already covered up the tracks. There's nothing for us to see.

"Not only is there no wolf, it looks like there's no bear either. Unless it's an invisible bear," he says, his brown eyes teasing. "You know the saying, right? Black, fight back. Brown, stay down. White, goodnight. Invisible—well, I ain't sure they got a rhyme for what to do if you find an invisible bear."

I cross my arms over my chest. "I know what I saw."

"Relax, sweetheart. There's nothing here but us."

Champion paces uneasily next to me, sniffing at the ground where the prints were visible only a few minutes earlier. His ears flatten back and he looks toward the dark woods behind us, as if searching for something within its midst.

I don't care what Hunter says. The dog knows it and I know it too.

We're not alone.

CHAPTER 7

5:45 p.m.

We return to the car, our teeth rattling. Snow sticks to us like a frozen suit of white armor, and Champion gives a big shake, casting it off in every direction. Britney shrieks as some of it gets on her outfit. Hunter and I exchange looks, trying not to laugh at the murderous expression on her face. Hoping to calm her down, I clean the dog's paws and shoo him inside and away from her wrath before helping her wipe off the back of her jacket and pants.

Once we're all back inside the car, I get Champion settled on the floor in the middle row and check on my brother before climbing over the seats to visit with Lily. Gavin moves aside to give me room, and I scoot in next to her, placing a hand around her wrist to check her vitals. My heart thrums in my chest. I hope for this time to be different—that Lily will wake up and gaze at me with that part-annoyed, part-amused grin of hers like, *I'm fine, what's all the fuss about?* That she'll laugh at us for worrying and go back to reading one of her thick textbooks.

Instead, her eyelids flutter and she lets out a long, strangled moan. She's no better—still stuck in the same half-alive,
half-dead state.

"I can't take this much longer." Britney turns around, her
eyes locked on Lily lying in the back row. "And from the sound
of her, neither can she."

"She's getting worse," Stuart says, his voice tight.

"Actually, the moaning is a good sign," I correct, trying
to keep everyone's spirits up as Gavin helps me back into
the middle row. I prop Stuart's injured leg up on my thighs,
getting him comfortable. "It shows upper brain-stem function
on the Glasgow Coma Scale."

"You're weird." Britney eyes me strangely. "You know that,
right?"

"We're all weird. Some of us are just better at hiding it,"
Gavin says.

Britney pouts like Gavin's taken my side over hers, but I
can't tell if he genuinely means this or is just trying to make
up for earlier.

Not that I need him to defend me. It's not as if Britney is
the first person to call me weird. I *am* weird.

Since I was old enough to walk, I've been obsessed with
animals. I was rescuing injured birds and squirrels in our
neighborhood even before we found Champion, and I started
volunteering at the clinic. Instead of sunning myself at the
Seaside Country Club pool like Britney and the other girls
do, I spent the last two summers playing with strays at the
shelter. And next year I'm going to Central California State
where I'm going to graduate magna cum laude, get into a
top-tier veterinary school, and eventually cure puppy cancer.

"She's going to be okay, right, Sam?" Stuart continues to
watch Lily nervously.

"We should pray for her," Britney says.

Gavin fidgets around in the back seat. "I don't believe in that stuff."

"Why not? Couldn't hurt," Hunter says.

Britney looks at her cell phone, scanning through it. Curious, I lean into the front row to see what she's wasting precious limited battery power on and am surprised to see she's looking at a *Bible* prayer app. I didn't even know there was such a thing. It appears to be downloaded and working fine, even without cell service.

"Found one!" she says a moment later, clapping her hands. She clasps on to the small cross around her neck and begins reading. "Lord Jesus Christ, be near Lily in her time of weakness and pain . . ."

Stuart and Hunter put their hands together in prayer pose and close their eyes as Britney keeps reading. I don't know about the whole God and religion thing, but I won't be the one to mess things up for Lily, so I do the same.

"Our Lord and Savior, sustain her by your Grace and heal her according to your will," she continues. "Oh, and please get us the hell out of here ASAP. Amen."

"Amen," the rest of us say in unison.

Gavin clears his throat. "It's been a long day. I say we head to bed and wait for morning. Things will be better then."

"I'm too wound up to sleep," Stuart says.

"We need a distraction. A game or something," Hunter offers.

I frown at him. "I'm not playing a game. Not with Lil lying there like that."

"It ain't gonna help your friend if we fall apart," Hunter says matter-of-factly. "Morale is the most important survival skill we got. Gotta keep our spirits up."

"What about a story, Stu?" Gavin asks.

"You mean like a bedtime story?" Britney snickers. "What are we—five years old?"

"Actually, stories are a great way to take your mind off bad shit," Hunter says. "Humans been telling 'em since the beginning of time."

She looks unconvinced. "Sounds dumb."

"I don't do that anymore, anyway." Stuart looks at the floor, his cheeks turning red.

"I think it would help, man," Gavin says. He catches my eye, and then I'm back in Stuart's bedroom three years ago, remembering our first homecoming dance freshman year.

Stuart had just gotten out of the hospital the day before and was making a full recovery from his back surgery. The doctors ordered him to bed all weekend. Even though it was homecoming and my first high school dance, I stayed in with him. Never mind this was my first grown-up dance, or that by some miracle I'd found a dress I loved. It was black and velvet and made me feel beautiful. But if Stuart had to stay home, so would I.

"What's wrong with you?" Stuart had asked, eyeballing me from the headboard where he sat propped up by pillows while we played his favorite video game, *Werewolf*.

"Nothing."

I repositioned myself, crossing my legs, trying to avoid eye contact with the creepy movie posters behind his bed. The worst one featured psycho killer Michael Myers from the old *Halloween* movies. He wore a menacing white mask and brandished a butcher knife and always gave me the heebie-jeebies.

"Bullcrap," Stuart said, hitting pause. "You suck but never this bad."

"I don't know what you're talking about. I happen to be great at this game."

"You don't have to pretend," he said. "I know you wanted to go to the dance."

"I'm fine." Just because I couldn't stop wondering what it was like at school tonight didn't mean something was wrong. I bet there was even a live DJ playing music and everything. I sighed, grabbing his controller and unpausing the game. "Better get your claws up," I said right as a monster threw a fireball, obliterating my werewolf player.

Damn. I did suck tonight.

Stuart tried to grab my controller, but I snatched it back, laughing, until a knock on the door made me let go.

"Stuart? Samantha? There's someone here to see you," my mother said, peeking her head around the door, an enormous grin on her face. Standing behind her was the last person I expected to see. In strode Gavin wearing a sash emblazoned with the words *Homecoming Court*—spelled out in sequins, no less—and the shiniest black shoes I'd ever seen.

"Gav!" Stuart was so excited to see his friend he actually clapped his hands.

"What are you doing here?" I asked, not bothering to be polite.

"Samantha!" My mother looked horrified. My entire family adored Gavin. It was so gross. He was around all the time, even though we were now freshmen in high school, and Stuart was still in middle school.

I shrugged. "What?"

She gave me a long, disappointed glance before turning to my brother. "Stu, honey, it's time for your meds."

"I'll do it," I volunteered, grabbing the amber prescription bottles off his desk. "Take two," I ordered, handing him the pills and a bottle of water from his nightstand. He snatched them from my hand, swallowing them both in one big gulp.

"Good boy," my mother said sweetly, and then left us alone again.

Stuart slumped back down into his mountain of pillows. "I can't believe you skipped homecoming," he said to Gavin.

"Yeah, you're gonna disappoint all your groupies," I added.

"This looks way more fun," Gavin said, walking over to the bed and plopping down so close to me our legs touched. Great. Now I'd have to spend the entire night smelling that amazing cologne he wore. "Krissy was driving me nuts in the limo."

I snorted. "Your date's name is Missy, you dumbass! Krissy is her twin."

"Huh." He flashed me a wicked grin. "Maybe that's why she got so mad?"

I swatted his arm.

"Hey, I got you something," he said, his eyes sparking as he pulled out from behind his back a stunning black-and-white orchid corsage. I gasped. It would've matched my dress perfectly.

"It's beautiful!" I exclaimed. "But what . . . how . . . I mean, why?"

He smirked. "I don't think I've ever seen you at a loss for words. That alone was worth the twenty bucks." He leaned in closer, eyeing the collar of my pajama top. "Let me help you pin it on."

"Thanks. Put it wherever."

He bit back a laugh, and I realized what I'd said. I hadn't meant it *that* way. Put it wherever? *Ugh.* I hope he didn't think I was flirting with him. Even if he was on homecoming court and had pierce-your-heart blue eyes, I didn't think of Gavin like that.

Okay . . . so that was a tiny lie.

I was only human. It was impossible to see that face and not think of him that way sometimes, but I always snapped out of it. Gavin was my little brother's best friend and also super annoying. Definitely not boyfriend material.

"On second thought, I'll do it myself," I said, snatching the corsage from him and pinning it on my pajamas.

"Don't worry—I got one for you too, Stu." He pulled another corsage from inside his jacket pocket. This one had enormous flowers and gold glitter. "Pink is your color, right?" he asked, laughing as he pegged Stuart in the chest with the hideous corsage.

"Thanks, you turd." Stuart grinned back, returning the favor by hurling the controller at Gavin's head. Unfortunately, Gavin caught it before it made contact.

We resumed playing video games. Even though he'd barely been able to get out of bed that morning, Stuart was a god on the screen. He beat Gavin and me every single round until Gavin finally dropped his controller, massaging at his left shoulder. "I need a break," he said.

"What's wrong?" I asked.

"I took a spill at the stunt park earlier. No big deal."

"I told you that park is dangerous," I said.

"I wish I could go to the park," Stuart said dreamily.

"I'll take you anytime you want," Gavin offered.

I stared at him, flabbergasted. "Wow. You really are an idiot. He just got out of the hospital. He can't go to the damn park."

"I think I can survive one bike ride," Stuart said with an annoyed groan.

"Over my dead body."

Gavin burst out laughing. "No one has to die. You're always so dramatic."

Heat rose in my cheeks. "Is this why you're here—hanging out with a seventh grader instead of Hunter Jackson and your other football dummies? You think Stu is some kind of charity case? That it's your job to expose him to the skate parks of the world?"

Stuart scowled. "Stop it, Sam."

"He doesn't need your pity," I continued, ignoring my brother. "He's my brother so I'm stuck with him, but he doesn't have to be your problem too."

"Well, maybe unlike you, I don't think of Stu as a *problem*," Gavin snapped.

It took me a moment before I realized my mistake.

Oh, crap.

"Stu, you know that's not what I meant . . ." He lurched away from me, rubbing at his nose, his eyes watering. "I'm sorry," I said, grabbing the controllers and shaking them over my head. "Let's just go back to playing *Werewolf*, okay?"

He crossed his arms over his chest and looked away.

"How about a movie?" Gavin asked him, sounding contrite. "I think that slasher you wanted to see just came out?"

Stuart continued staring sullenly at the wall.

"A story then? We love your stories," Gavin said. "Right, Sam?"

"Absolutely." I nodded along. At least that was one thing Gavin and I agreed on. Perhaps the only thing we would ever agree on.

Stuart's angry expression dissolved as he began weaving a tale about a dance in an enchanted land that lasted 1,001 days and sounded way better than the dance we were actually missing.

"I need a drink," Britney says, bringing me out of the memory and back to the present. "All this waiting around is stressful."

"Make that two, bartender," my brother says, and launches into a coughing fit.

"No more drinking," I tell them.

"Why not?" Britney asks. "It wouldn't hurt you to have a beer either. You were way more fun drunk."

"No beer." I notice she isn't wearing her gloves anymore. This wouldn't be so bad except she isn't wearing her hat either—the god-awful matching one with the furry pom-pom on top. I don't understand how she isn't freezing. The girl has less than an ounce of body fat on her, if that. "And put your gloves back on. We need to stay warm."

"Now that you mention it, I could go for a nice fur blanket right about now," she says, her eyes landing on Champion fast asleep at my feet. A wicked grin spreads across her face.

"Hell, yeah," Hunter says, blowing into his hands. "That's how real men do it. Livin' off the land."

"Dude, what are you talking about?" Gavin asks. "Last time I checked, real men weren't scalping dogs to make blankets."

"I meant other animals," Hunter corrects. "Bears. Wolves. Rabbits. We learned all about it in Eagle Scouts. Cavemen used whatever they could get their hands on to keep themselves warm."

Britney's eyes glitter. "Nothing keeps you warm like a nice expensive fur."

"You two are sick," I say, my stomach turning. "Don't you know where fur comes from?"

"Uh, yeah. From *animals with fur*," Britney says, and laughs.

"It isn't funny. Do you have any idea how barbaric and cruel the fur industry is?" My throat burns thinking about all the bloody undercover animal rights' videos I've seen online. "They put little baby animals in tiny cages in awful, inhumane conditions. They never get to move outside or play. Sometimes they're even abused. And then, when they're big enough, they skin them alive or electrocute them because they get the best pieces of fur that way."

Her tan face whitens. "You're lying."

"It's true," Stuart says, looking squeamish himself. "She made me watch the videos with her. I yacked after. Couldn't eat meat for a month."

"I don't believe you," Britney says, but her voice falters.

In the back row, Lily lets out another strangled groan. I turn around, my heart clenching. She looks so fragile lying there like a broken little doll. Lily has to get better. She just has to. I can't lose her. Besides my brother, she's the only real friend I've got.

I'll never forget the first day I met Lily Zhang. It was lunchtime, and I was sitting in the school library, reading and eating alone like I often did freshman year. I was at my favorite part of *The Black Stallion* where Alec is rescued from the island he's stranded on. They try to make Alec leave his horse because they don't want to take Black on their boat, but even though it's his only chance at survival, Alec won't leave Black behind. I always get choked up at that part.

There I was trying to hide my ugly crying, when this nosy little Asian girl in braids stomped over and slammed her books down on my table. She demanded to know what I thought of the book and if I loved it as much as she did. I couldn't believe it. The place was empty. Why did she pick me to annoy?

I tried to ignore her in the hopes she'd go away, but she wouldn't stop blabbering about how she'd been watching me in the library for weeks and each time she saw me I was reading another one of her favorite books. She said it made us kindred souls and meant we should be friends.

It was weird at first, but I kind of admired her bluntness. It also didn't hurt when she shared her father's award-winning chicken fried rice with me. Even cold and left over from the dinner seating the night before at her family restaurant, it was still one of the best things I'd ever eaten.

We spent the rest of the lunch period bonding over *The Black Stallion* and why Alec and Black's friendship was the greatest in all of literature. After that, we discussed all the other books we loved.

When she and my brother first got together this past summer, Stuart came up with all these nauseating pet names for her, but there was one I did like—Ada Wong. Ada is this badass character in the *Resident Evil* video games that slays zombies with both grace and confidence. The name suits Lily. She's tough. It's what I admire most about her. She lets nothing get in her way. If the undead can't take Ada out, it doesn't seem possible that a stupid concussion can take Lily.

Before long, another storm rolls in for the evening. Snow pounds on the roof as powerful winds rock the SUV back and forth. Gavin and I exchange a somber glance in the dark. I can tell we're thinking the same thing. If this new blizzard had hit only a few hours earlier and trapped us in the wilderness, we'd be dead.

"Why haven't they found us yet?" Britney asks, making a sniffling sound up front in the driver's seat. "Where are our parents? Or the police? Or . . . like . . . the army?"

A shiver of apprehension snakes up my spine. It's been almost twenty-four hours. Six kids don't go missing that long without someone's parents freaking out. Why hasn't anyone come for us?

"Ain't nobody gonna find us in this." Hunter points to one of the uncovered windows where everything outside is coated in white. Any colors like the blue of the sky or the green of the grass have disappeared. I can't make out a single object—not a single tree, branch, mountain, or cloud. "Shit," he says a moment later, and lets loose a string of curses. "We're almost outta gas."

"You've got to be kidding," Britney says.

Hunter eyes the dashboard, worry flickering across his face. "I'm gonna turn the engine off for a while to conserve."

"Jesus—are you serious?" Stuart asks. "I'm freezing."

"It's gonna be a whole lot worse if we run out of gas, trust me," Hunter says, his hand on the key.

At seven p.m., Hunter turns the engine off.

By eight p.m., my teeth are chattering so badly I taste copper and know I've reopened the cut in my mouth.

By nine p.m., I'm having trouble feeling my fingers and toes and am sure I won't make it through the night.

By ten p.m., I'm half-frozen to death when Hunter finally turns the heater back on. Crying out with relief, I thrust my gloved hands and face under the vents to get as close as possible to the hot air spilling out. Warmth rushes through me, feeling so good I can't speak for a moment. I'm like a drug addict shooting up heroin—not that I know what that's like, but I imagine it's pretty much the same.

If it wasn't clear before, it is now. We have to be rescued, and soon. Someone has to get to us before the gas is gone for good.

CHAPTER 8

Day 3 • December 22 • 7:30 a.m.

My stomach gurgles as I wake the next morning. I can't tell if it's from hunger pains or the general foulness circulating the car. There's a yeasty, stale scent percolating that reminds me of cat pee when I'm on cage cleaning duty at the shelter. It's the smell of something gone rancid.

After making sure no one is looking, I lift my arms and take a few discreet sniffs underneath. Thankfully, the stench doesn't appear to be coming from me.

Champion stirs at my feet. He arches his back and opens one coffee-colored eye in my direction, his mouth moving into another one of his happy smiles. Grinning back, I lean down to give him a little good morning kiss on the snout and get close enough to tell the bad smell isn't coming from him either. But then what is it?

I attempt to sit up, my muscles aching as I scan the SUV. *Bingo!*

I spot the culprit right away. Next to Hunter in the passenger seat are two open beer cans, one turned upside down in the cup holder. Yellow stains soil the carpet and the side of Hunter's jeans. His booming snore shakes the car while he continues to sleep, oblivious to the mess he's made. I muffle a laugh, unsurprised that he's the offender.

Besides Champion and me, the rest of the car continues to slumber. Britney appears to be about as comfortable as one can be sleeping in a cramped car. She's almost fully horizontal, sprawled out in the driver's seat and taking up most of Hunter's seat as well, her legs lying on top of him.

Next to me, Stuart sleeps nestled against the side of the door. His pale skin is sallow and his breathing shallow, but overall he looks better than expected. I'm relieved to see his ankle remains propped up on my knees in the same position I left it in last night in order to promote healing.

There's a low, grunting sound behind me and I swivel toward the back seat, assuming Gavin is waking up. For a second, I'm sure I'm still dreaming. I blink and rub my eyes, but she's still there, staring back at me.

"*You're awake!*" I exclaim in stunned surprise.

Lily yawns and rolls to one side. "It appears I am."

My first instinct is to leap into the back row and throw my arms around her, but I know better than to jump on someone with head trauma. Instead, I restrain myself and amble over the seats, squeezing in between her and Gavin. I'm able to fit only because his otherwise long, strapping body is curled into the fetal position and crammed uncomfortably against the window. A part of me registers this selfless act of his, allowing Lily as much space as possible, but I'm far too excited about my friend being conscious to think much more about it.

"Holy shit!" I seize her arm, crushing it to my chest.

"Hey!" Her eyes widen with surprise. "What're you doing?"

Tearing off my gloves, I put two fingers on her wrist and count the pulse beats. *Incredible!* Right under sixty beats per minute! Although still on the weak side, her heart rate almost passes for normal.

I brush back her long dark hair and place a palm to her forehead to take her temperature. No heat. No fever. Her skin is chilly to the touch.

"YOU'RE ALIVE!" I hug her to me, clapping her on the back.

The others wake then, and the car turns to complete chaos. Everyone yells, jumping over seats and falling all over each other to get closer to Lily. They all want to touch her and prove what we're seeing is real and not some figment of our imagination.

"Oh God, Lil!" Stuart's eyes are red and watery as he cries shamelessly. "I was so worried."

"Uh, what's wrong with you guys?" Lily asks, looking at us like we've all gone mad. She reaches back to finger Britney's jacket, which is still tucked behind her head. "And why does it feel like I'm sleeping on a dead rabbit?"

Britney smiles. "That's mine. Isn't it great?"

I peer closer at Lily, assessing her. "Do you know where you are?" I ask, starting off with some simple questions to test her cognitive function.

"Seriously?" she asks. "Are you for real?"

I nod.

"Duh. Of course I know where we are—Gavin's car." She lifts a confused brow and looks around. "But wait—where's the cabin? Why aren't we there yet?"

"What's the last thing you remember?" I ask.

"Stuart hit a tree. We got stuck. And then . . ." She scratches at her temple. "I don't remember." She tries to sit up and winces. "*Cào!* It feels like I got hit by a truck."

"Careful," I say, grabbing her elbow to steady her. "Your body needs time to adjust."

"Adjust from what?" She stiffens in my grasp. "Why are you guys acting so weird? You're freaking me out."

Hunter's laugh is deafening. "You were almost buzzard bait, girl!"

"It's like a real-life miracle," Britney says, nodding along. "Jesus totally answered our prayers and saved your life."

"Saved my life?" Lily repeats, her face paling as she looks to me. "What are they talking about?"

"Will you two shut up?" I scowl at Britney and Hunter before turning back to Lily. "Before I tell you, promise me you'll stay calm." I use my most soothing voice, the one I save for hysterical pet owners at the animal shelter. It's important to keep her vitals stable.

"Just tell me!" she snaps.

"Okay, okay." I back away, raising my hands in the air. "You've been in a coma for over twenty-four hours."

She blinks. "*A full day?*"

I nod.

"This is a joke, right? You're messing with me?"

"Afraid not," I say. "You hit your head during the accident."

"Are you sure?" she asks, raising a hand to the back of her head. "I mean, yeah, there's a bump there. And I feel kind of nauseous." She yawns again. "But a coma?"

"We're sure," Britney says. "Just look at you. No offense, but you're way too pasty." She bends down in the driver's seat and pulls out a big fluffy makeup brush and glittery compact from the purse at her feet. "Here, let me put some blush on you. It'll help."

"I'm Chinese, *bèn dàn*," Lily says with a grumble. "I don't need a makeover. What I need is to know what's going on."

"Suit yourself," Britney says, applying the blush to her own cheeks instead while I catch Lily up on everything that's happened during the last twenty-four hours.

I tell her about her injury. Our hike. Stuart's crushed ankle, which she asks to see for herself to confirm he's okay. He brushes her worry off with laughter, smiling as Gavin and Hunter help me move him to the last row. Now that Lily is awake and doing better, the back of the SUV is the best place for Stuart. This way people won't have to keep jumping over him to get out of the car.

Gavin returns to his old seat in the middle row, and Britney climbs over the center console to join him. Meanwhile, I eye the spot next to my brother where Lily still sits, not sure what to do. I want to be as close as possible so I can check on him, but I worry Lily will feel the same way. He is her boyfriend, after all.

It turns out I have nothing to worry about. Lily volunteers to take the driver's seat, textbooks in tow, murmuring about her pounding head and how I'm much more capable to watch over Stuart because of my vet clinic experience.

"So what do we do now?" I ask, getting Stuart comfortable in the back row while Champion curls into a ball at my feet. Now that Lily's conscious, I feel better than I've felt in days. We've already done the impossible, surviving two frigid nights in the Sierra Nevada mountains. I'm certain the worst of our ordeal is over.

"We work on more survival stuff, obviously," Hunter says in the passenger seat next to Lily. "There's still a shit ton to do."

"But why?" Stuart asks. "We'll be out of here soon, right?"

"Yeah, can't we just relax? I broke a nail yesterday," Britney says, frowning at her now imperfect French manicure. She isn't wearing her gloves again even though I warned her to stay warm. She's so irresponsible, it's annoying.

"Y'all wanna make it out of here in one piece or what?" Hunter slams a hand on the dashboard. "'Cause if so, we got work to do. Stash. Signals. The Rule of Threes."

"The what?" Gavin asks, sounding as confused as I feel.

"The Rule of Threes," Hunter repeats, irritated. "It's the number one survival rule."

We all stare at him as if he's speaking another language.

His mouth drops. "Y'all really never heard of it?"

We shake our heads.

It's funny—and not funny *ha ha* but funny in a twisted and terrible way—how ill-prepared we are for this. Our ancestors lived for hundreds of years in the wilderness and other desolate places like this, but drop off a bunch of pampered kids from Southern California in the mountains and we're clueless what to do. We understand complex math equations we'll never use and how to conjugate verbs in French, but no one ever taught us basic survival skills.

"A'ight, listen up." Hunter hooks his thumbs into his belt loops, pushing his shoulders back. "The Rule of Threes is this guideline my grandpappy taught me to prioritize things. You can live three minutes without air, three hours without warmth, three days without water, and three weeks without food. Get it?"

Lily sits up so fast she almost nails a knee into the steering wheel. "What does that mean?" she asks, sounding worried. "Air isn't a problem, but what about the warmth? What if we run out of gas? And food and water? Do we have enough for all of us?"

"Bingo!" Hunter shouts, pointing a finger in her direction. "That's what I'm worried about. Especially since you burn calories faster in the cold."

"That's right." Britney nods along. "The cheer team did Arctic Freeze right before homecoming."

"Huh?" I stare at her blankly.

"You know, the new cryotherapy place in the mall," she explains. "It was subzero in there. I dropped, like, a thousand calories in three minutes."

Hunter looks at her like she's nuts. "You *voluntarily* went into a tube of frozen nitrogen gas?"

"Uh, did you see my dress?" Her blue eyes widen. "It was pink spandex. Spandex shows everything."

"We're getting off track," Lily says, shifting in her seat. "What about water? We have that twenty-four-pack Sam brought, but is that enough for all of us?"

Hunter tilts his head to the side as if assessing. "Hard to tell," he says. "We gotta drink more than normal to stay hydrated in the cold."

"How much more?" Lily asks.

"Maybe three liters?"

"*Each?*" Lily's eyes go wide. "But that's six water bottles a person!"

"Damn. That's a lot of water," Stuart says. "Where're we gonna find all that?"

"Where do you think?" Hunter grins and tilts his head toward the window.

"Ew, gross," Britney says. "You want us to eat snow? Like from the ground?"

"Not exactly." He laughs. "You'd get dehydrated if you ate snow. We drop it into our water bottles and let our body heat melt it."

Britney wrinkles her cute button nose. "But animals pee in that snow."

"Adapt or die, princess," he says.

She snickers. "More wisdom from Grandpappy?"

"Naw. That's a line from *Pit Bulls and Parolees*," he says with a slow grin.

My mouth drops. "No way! You watch that show, too?"

"You sound surprised."

"It's just . . . it doesn't seem like your kind of thing."

"My kind of thing?" he repeats, his unruly brows narrowing a tad. "What's that supposed to mean?"

I shrug. "Nothing. You know what I mean. You're a jock. That's not exactly a jock show."

"Don't take this the wrong way, sweetheart, but you sound a wee bit judgmental."

"I am *not* judgmental," I say, somewhat defensive by the path this conversation is taking.

Gavin waggles one obnoxious finger at me. "Actually, this is the very definition of judgmental. It's when you form lots of opinions about people you don't know, like Hunt, with no support whatsoever and—"

"I know what judgmental means!" I bark.

"Like saying because I play football means I don't like puppies?" Hunter gives me a look.

"Or what about Krissy and Missy from homecoming?" Gavin adds. "You said they were bimbos, but you never even spoke to them."

"Krissy and Missy *are* bimbos," Britney says and busts up into laughter. Even though I'm annoyed, I can't help but join in. I laugh so hard with Britney that my belly hurts.

"Knock it off. This is serious. We need to focus!" Lily says, frowning at me. "What about the food? Are we going to run out of that too?"

"Depends how long we're stuck," Hunter says. "People can go about three weeks without food, but that depends on all sorts of things. How cold it is. How much energy you use. How much—"

"So what's the real number? Is it days? Weeks?" Lily asks, her eyes darting back and forth. "I need a number!"

Britney yawns and closes her eyes like she's ready to go back to sleep. "Relax, spaz. We'll be out of here by dinnertime."

"We'll be fine, Lil. Humans and animals don't need that much food," I say in what I hope is a comforting tone. I feel bad for laughing when she's obviously freaking out. "Dogs can even go for months without eating. Emperor penguins too. And reptiles—get this—reptiles are cold-blooded, so they can go forever without food. I once read about this crocodile that didn't eat for three years. Cool, right?"

The car goes silent. Everyone is watching me like I've grown two heads.

"What is it?" Heat itches along my cheeks. "What'd I say?"

Gavin turns around in the middle row smiling, his dimples flashing. "Nothing at all. Please tell us more about those crocodiles, would you?"

I grit my teeth. "Oh, shut up!"

We decide to take inventory of our food and water. Gavin and Hunter grab my dad's ice chest and Champion's food from the cargo area and bring it inside the passenger cabin. This way we won't have to keep going outside into the cold every time we're hungry or thirsty. The cooler barely fits on the floor of the middle row, wedged between the seat and the front center console. Champion smells his kibble through the plastic baggie and begins drooling and whining at my feet, staring forlornly toward the front of the car.

Hunter flips the lid off the cooler and sizes up what's left. Minus the food we've already eaten, he counts four chocolate bars, two bags of all-natural pita chips, four string cheeses, about half the party-size bag of peanuts, and most of the sour gummies. To be safe, we all agree the smartest thing is to ration the food, splitting it up and dividing it into small portions instead of burning through whatever we have. It's not a feast, but it's more than enough to last us another day or two. We don't plan to be stuck out here much longer than that.

CHAPTER 9

9:00 a.m.

Before we have time to grab the rationed breakfast we all just agreed to, Champion gathers his hind legs under himself and leaps over the back of the middle row. Gavin lunges forward to grab the dog, but he isn't fast enough to stop Champion from snagging a string cheese from the top of the cooler. Champion's teeth weld into the plastic, and he rockets back into the last row again, tearing into the cheese. He devours its contents before anyone can stop him, and then hides in between my legs.

Sneaky little bastard.

Not that I blame him, even though it leaves us with only three string cheeses now.

"*Bái chī!*" Lily screams at the dog like the world is going to fall apart because he stole a snack. I can't help but giggle at her overreaction. "Stop laughing! It isn't funny!"

She looks so pissed, I try to contain myself.

"Chill out. The poor guy is hungry," I say, swallowing back my laughter and running a hand along the top of Champion's head.

"But we just agreed to ration. We have to be smart, especially when the dog has his own damn food." Her eyes narrow. "Haven't you guys seen that movie *Alive*?"

"The one about the soccer players?" Hunter asks.

"It's rugby," Lily corrects. "The team's plane crashes into the Andes Mountains. They agree to ration their food—like us—but then they think they're about to be rescued, so they eat it all. But they aren't and Ethan Hawke and his friends have to eat frozen flesh to survive, and I'm not going to eat you guys, okay? Because that's disgusting."

Stuart's lips twitch. "It was one string cheese, Lil."

Her nostrils flare with indignation. "That's not the point!" she bellows, but just as I'm sure she's really going to lose it, a tiny smile cracks through. "Just know if it comes down to it, I won't eat people, but I'm not above eating dog," she says. "Understand?"

I pull Champion closer to me and stick out my tongue at her.

"Don't we got anything else besides all this healthy crap?" Hunter rummages through the cooler, pulling out the remaining three organic string cheeses. He holds them up over his head, frowning his disapproval. "Maybe some beef sticks? Or meat sandwiches?"

"Sam here is a vegetarian." Gavin grins down at me over the back of his seat, feeding Champion a handful of kibble out of the dog's plastic food bag.

Hunter goes still. "Gross. Why?"

"Because meat is murder," I say, feeling queasy. Just thinking about factory farming makes me sick.

"Uh no. Murder is murder," he says, shaking his head. "Meat is delicious."

"I think it's cool you don't eat meat, Sammy," Britney says to me with a little smile. "Fish is so much healthier."

I don't bother correcting her. If Britney Miller is sticking up for me instead of making fun of me, I won't tell her that fish is also meat.

"You chicks are joking, right?" Hunter asks. "Ain't you ever tasted baby back ribs? Or a juicy steak? And don't even get me started on bacon cheeseburgers!" He makes a slow, sucking sound and licks at his fingers. "Mmmm."

I try not to gag. I haven't eaten meat since I was eight years old and saw my first cattle farm. That was the year my parents bought our lake house, and we made the short drive from Seaside to Lake Arrowspear.

The windows were down, wind tangling in my hair. Dad and I were playing that game where you call out license plates from other states and get points for all the different states you can find. I'd just spotted Nevada, my second "N" state, when I saw the factory farm. Or I guess you could say I smelled it first. The nauseating odor of feces and dirt overwhelmed my senses even before I saw the rows of cows crammed into tiny, frightening sheds. Something about it felt wrong to me even at such a young age.

Later, I learned those were the lucky ones. That was before they took the cows to slaughterhouses and someone bled them to death on a kill floor drenched in blood.

"Sorry, Hunter. This is all we've got," I say. "If you want meat, you're out of luck."

He lets out a sigh and breaks one of the string cheeses into quarters. "Guess it'll have to do then," he says, and drops a piece of cheese into his mouth, chewing it like it's torture, before breaking off more pieces and passing them around. We let Lily and Stuart split an entire chocolate bar themselves since they've both had injuries and need to keep their strength up.

"No, thanks," Britney says, handing back her cheese to

Hunter, refusing it. "I'll have sushi at the lodge when we get there."

"Good call. Dairy makes you break out," Lily says a little too eagerly as she takes large bites of her chocolate.

I give her a deliberate look. I'm pretty sure this has more to do with her own concern with conserving food than it does with Britney's already perfect complexion.

While the rest of us eat our rations, Britney pulls a brush out of her bag and goes to work on her golden locks. She starts with the ends first, smoothing them out, and then works her way to the crown until the strands shine and sparkle.

I study her carefully, wondering about the school rumors again and if there may be actual truth to them. Anorexia wreaks havoc on a person's body. If you're not eating enough, your brain assumes you're in famine and lowers your body temperature to dangerous levels. It's one of the reasons anorexia can be so deadly.

We haven't been stuck that long and Britney won't keel over and die from not eating for a day or two, but I can't stay silent. A real medical professional—which I one day hope to be—protects the health and well-being of others and would never hurt anyone on purpose. Britney not eating is dangerous, especially if this has been going on for longer than this weekend.

"You should have something," I say to her. "You've barely eaten anything since Friday."

"It's a piece of string cheese," she says. "We're not exactly talking about a balanced diet."

"We need all the calories we can get." I take in a big gulp and rush on before I lose my nerve. "And, you know, I'd be lying if I said I hadn't heard the gossip at school about your, um, eating issues. I know we're not friends or anything, but if you ever need someone to talk to, I'd listen. Obviously, it's complicated, and I can't tell you what to do with your body, but—"

"Screw you!" Her eyes flare. "I don't have an eating disorder, you psycho."

A cramp forms deep in my belly. This was a bad idea. Why couldn't I keep my big mouth shut?

"I'm not trying to pry. I know this is none of my business, but I want to help—"

"You're right, this is *none* of your business," she hisses. "Besides, staying fit for big games is totally normal, and plenty of girls don't eat cheese. Haven't you ever heard of a dairy-free diet?"

I shrink into my seat. "I'm sorry. This isn't coming out right. What I'm saying is—"

"*Sam*! Back off," Stuart warns.

"I just want to make sure she's okay."

"For the last time, there's nothing wrong with me, you nosy bitch!" Britney shouts, but then she smiles the next instant, taking me by complete surprise. "But in an annoying way, I suppose it's kind of nice that you're concerned," she adds. "How about this? I'll eat the damn cheese if you promise to shut up and never bring it up again. Deal?"

"Deal." I nod.

It's not an epic victory, but it's something.

Returning to my own meager piece of cheese, I wolf down my quarter within seconds. My poor stomach cries out in protest when nothing else follows. I rub at my belly, trying to calm it, and eye the rest of the food in the cooler with a sharp, intense longing. Rationing is the smart thing to do, but damn, I'm *hungry*.

Out of the corner of my eye, I watch Britney pick at her cheese, tearing little piece after little piece, like she has no interest in the food at all. It's painful to observe. My hand itches at my side, eager to yank the cheese from her and shove it down my mouth instead. At least I'd appreciate it.

After what seems like an eternity, she finishes her cheese and grabs her purse off the floor. The rest of us brought backpacks on this trip, but not Britney. Oh no. Britney brought along a hideous pink oversize bag that looks like it was made from the skin of some unfortunate endangered reptile. I once saw a video on YouTube about how they chop up alligators and crocodiles alive to get their skins for bags like Britney's. I couldn't sleep for a week after that.

"Want some?" she asks, pulling out a pack of sugar-free bubble gum from the front pouch of the purse. She passes it to me. "You still look hungry. Gum is great for suppressing your appetite."

"Oh my God—yes!" I cry, my mouth watering as I grab the gum from her.

Lily reaches a hand back into the middle row. "I want a piece!" she cries, followed by a chorus of "me too."

An instant later, all Britney's gum is gone.

I chew my piece as slowly as possible, savoring the sweetness as it explodes inside my mouth like the best thing I've ever had in my entire life. And I don't even like gum that much.

"Now that breakfast is over, who wants to help build a signal fire?" Hunter asks.

"A fire in the forest? Isn't that kind of dangerous?" Britney asks. "Do you know what you're doing?"

"Can a dog hunt?" Hunter blows a big pink bubble right in her face and bursts it with a loud popping sound, laughing.

"I'm in," Gavin says.

I raise a hand, grateful for something useful to do. "Same."

"Pass," Lily says, her eyelids drooping shut. "I need a nap."

Stuart eyes her with concern. "You okay?"

"Just tired. And still a little nauseous."

"I'll stay with you," Britney offers. My brother and Lily give her a surprised look. "What? You two invalids clearly need adult supervision."

I'm confused at first. Why would Britney pass up the chance to spend time with Gavin in order to watch over Lily and my brother? For a moment, I consider all the reasons she might volunteer to do this—like she's worried about getting her hair wet from the snow or she's afraid of fire. The first one seems plausible, I suppose. The second idea is a little ridiculous, even to me.

Then all of a sudden it hits me. She's trying to be helpful.

Before I have too much time to dwell on this new idea of a considerate Britney, Hunter rushes outside into the snow and bellows for Gavin and me to join him. I prop up Stuart's ankle on my backpack and some sweaters and then grab Champion by his collar, tugging him along. The dog grunts and falls back down to the floor, burying his nose in between my shins and making me laugh. I'm not looking forward to the cold either, but if I'm going, so is he. He needs the exercise.

"You're not getting out of this," I tell him, leaning down to rain gentle kisses on his cheeks. The dog returns my affection with his own sloppy version, his wet tongue scraping against my neck.

"He really missed you," Gavin says softly.

I glance up to see him peering over the back of the middle seat, studying me. Those bright blue eyes glisten, his lips turning up at the edges.

"Yeah, I missed him too," I say, a sharp pull in my chest. I used to see Champion almost daily until Gavin left for Boston last year. It's been months since I've spent this much time with the dog. "You're still the most handsome boy in the whole world, aren't you?" I scratch Champion under his scruffy chin.

"He gets it from his daddy," Gavin says.

I snort, laughter escaping through my nose. "You did not just say that."

"Sorry. Couldn't resist." Those killer dimples flash my way. "Here, let me help you," he says and folds down the middle seat to grab Champion.

His arm brushes against my leg. It's only for an instant but long enough to make something flutter inside of me—which is seriously weird. There's no reason to get all goofy because a good-looking guy is touching me.

Okay, so yeah, Gavin is hotter than any guy is entitled to be, but that's always been the case. It doesn't make him any less irritating.

And so what if he smells like the most amazing combination of something woodsy and masculine with a hint of the ocean? I don't care at all if—

"Sams? Hello?" He stares at me. "You ready to go?"

"I . . . yeah," I stutter. Geez. Could I be any more of an idiot? "Just get Champ out, would you?"

He lifts the dog up and over the seat and drops him into the snow. The second his paws touch the ground, Champion takes off running for the edge of the woods. I'm still blushing as I follow after them, but I don't have time to ponder why I'm acting like such a freak around Gavin because *holy crap, it's cold as balls!*

I shiver, chills sweeping through my body. My hands shake as I cover my face with my scarf, concealing everything except for my nose and eyes. I thought I'd get used to the freezing temperature outside, but each time I exit the SUV it's the same god-awful experience all over again.

Some commotion at the front of the car draws my attention. Hunter is straightening a red flannel shirt hanging out of the top of the passenger window. It must be one of the signals he mentioned setting up the other day, but I didn't notice it before with all the drama. He double-checks the positioning to make sure it's secure and then rolls the window back up again to keep it locked in place. The shirt flaps against the side of the door; the bright red fabric standing out amongst all the whiteness is sure to get anyone's attention if they pass by. I'm impressed. It's so simple yet effective.

"Y'all ready to get this fire goin'?" he asks us, and then cocks a brow at Gavin. "Where's your spare at? Under the cargo space?"

"Why?" Gavin asks. "Aren't we using wood?"

"Naw, man. Everybody knows rubber burns better in the snow."

Gavin lets out a curse. "Shit. I don't have one."

"What do you mean you ain't got one?" Hunter asks, his voice low and flat. "Everybody's got a spare."

"Well, *I don't*," Gavin repeats, annoyed. "I got a flat last week, and they forgot to put the spare back after they replaced it."

Hunter drops next to the front tires, examining them. "Alrighty then. Pick one."

"No way. You're not touching my brand-new tires. My dad will kill me!" A dark, almost panicked expression flickers across Gavin's face. "He's already pissed about last week."

Hunter's head tilts to the side. "Desperate times . . . yada yada yada."

"We've only been stuck a day and a half," I say, surprising myself by coming to Gavin's defense. He may drive me crazy, but that doesn't mean I enjoy seeing him squirm. Gavin has always had a weird, strained relationship with his father. One I've never quite been able to figure out. "Find another way, okay?"

Hunter sighs dramatically like we're ruining everything but then directs us toward the forest on the side of the road and orders us to gather low branches from the pine trees. There are tons of options to choose from, but most are coated with snow, and Hunter only wants dry wood for the fire. Whatever Hunter deems usable, which isn't much, we place in stacks by their size—big branches in one section, small branches in another.

After we've got the wood secured, Hunter finds a place on the road to build. He shows us how to tap down on the ground to make sure the snow is solid, and we place the wood on top, piece by piece as he directs, until the pile is at least two-feet high. Hunter adds small twigs and sticks and even some pages from one of Lily's textbooks to act as kindling and catch flames. Finally, he takes lint from his pockets to use as tinder and lights it with his lighter before dropping it onto the pile.

Just as the fire starts to take, Champion returns from the woods, smelling like musty dog sweat, tongue lolling. Gavin grabs an extra piece of unused wet wood from the discard pile and throws it to the dog, who jumps almost five feet in the air to catch it in his mouth.

"Good boy," Gavin says, grinning his approval. "Now lie down," he commands, and Champion drops onto all fours a safe distance from the fire. His eyes shut into tiny, tired slits while he gnaws at the stick like it's a bone.

Within minutes, baby flames rise and grow so big they jump up, licking at our faces. We watch mesmerized as the flames dance in front of us, inching higher and higher. I clap my hands, laughter bubbling in my chest. It's like magic.

"You're a genius, Hunter!" I tell him.

He blushes. "I'm no 4.0 GPA like you, but I do okay."

"This is more than okay! I could kiss you right now!"

"No objection here." He smiles at me—wide and without restraint. Our eyes meet. Now it's my turn to blush.

"I wouldn't get too excited just yet." Gavin steps in between us. "Looks like another storm's headed our way."

I look up to see the clouds above have turned a menacing gray color, swollen with the weight of new snow as they race over the eastern horizon. The advancing darkness harkens something sinister is ahead. All around us, the wind blows and dances down the mountainside in little white waves and whirlpools, rattling through the trees, tearing at my hair and coat.

An instant later, small dainty flakes start to fall, suffocating our fledgling fire. We watch for a sad minute as the acrid scent of smoke fills our noses and all our hard work dies a slow, strangled death.

After the fire is extinguished, Hunter races back to the car to make last-minute preparations. Gavin sidles up next to me, staring after Hunter's hulky, retreating figure. "He likes you, you know," he whispers in my ear.

"I like him too," I admit, surprising myself. Champion nuzzles into my side as we walk to the car, and I pet at him absentmindedly. "For a jock, Hunter's not half bad. I think we might even be friends when we get back to school."

"No, I mean he *like* likes you," Gavin clarifies.

I stop in my tracks. "No way. You're nuts."

"I'm dead serious."

"We're talking about Hunter Jackson, right? Starter on the football team? The most popular guy in school?" I ask, and then add, "After you left, of course."

He grins. "Yep, that's the one."

"Hunter could get any girl he likes. Why me?"

The idea is ludicrous and not because I'm one of those insecure girls who thinks she's hideous when everyone else knows she's pretty. Sure, I was an awkward kid growing up, but I'm aware most people consider me attractive now. Even my mother calls me a natural beauty. Albeit, one that would be even better if only I'd wear some makeup and do my hair every once in a while—her words, not mine. But even if I am cute, that doesn't mean I'm Hunter's type. I'm not anywhere near cool enough for a guy like that.

"Hunter's always had a thing for you, if you want to know the truth." Gavin's teeth flash as we continue walking toward the SUV.

"Really?" I find this shocking. I hardly know Hunter. "Why?"

"Who knows?" He shrugs. "Dude beats to his own drum. It's what I like about him," he says. "To be honest, he's probably more interested in hooking up than dating, but he's definitely interested."

I cringe. "You're disgusting."

"So, are you?" he asks, almost hesitantly.

"Am I what?"

He makes an odd noise in the back of his throat, the sound bouncing off the snow beneath our feet, over to the mountaintops and back again. "You know ... interested?"

This feels like some sort of test. Why is Gavin so interested in my love life all of a sudden?

"I'm sure Hunter's just being nice." I nudge him in the ribs. "Unlike some people I know."

"You want me to be nicer, Sams? Say the word." That lazy, patronizing grin of his returns. "Though you'd have to stop arguing with me long enough to make that possible, and I doubt you'd be up for the challenge."

I resist the urge to roll my eyes. "Maybe you should stick with Britney. We both know *she's* up for the challenge."

"Jealous?"

I fake a smile to cover up the weird feeling that's right under the surface, circling between us. "You wish," I say, trying to sound nonchalant, but I'm pretty sure my tough words fool no one.

He swaggers off toward the SUV, laughing to himself like he knows just how jealous I am and wants to make sure I know it too.

CHAPTER 10

11:30 a.m.

Before a new storm can reach full strength and trap us inside the SUV again, Hunter makes us set up the snow-water-bottle concoctions he suggested earlier. Everyone except for Stuart and Lily, who need to rest, grab discarded plastic water bottles from wherever we can find them—in between car seats, on the floor, in the cargo area—and then head outside.

I try to get Champion to come with me, but he jumps into the empty spot next to Stuart and curls in closer to my brother, his fluffy tail resting near Stuart's feet. The dog closes his eyes and stretches out his long front paws. He looks wiped after all his running, branch-gnawing, and fire-circling antics.

The rest of us walk a few feet away from the SUV and then hover above the ground so we don't get our pants wet while we shovel handfuls of snow inside our bottles until they're about two-thirds full. We leave the rest empty, as Hunter instructs us. My teeth chatter fiercely as he darts around, pouring water in each of our bottles to help melt the snow while yelling words of encouragement.

I'm almost finished with three of my four bottles when the weather really starts to deteriorate.

"Are we done yet?" Britney yells over the howling wind.

"Are all your bottles full?" Hunter shouts back.

"No."

He smirks. "Then nope."

"But my hair is getting all messed up," she huffs, though as far as I can tell the wind only makes her look better, like one of those Victoria's Secret models with their sexy beach hair blowing under a fan.

Feeling self-conscious, I pat at the back of my own head with my free hand. My thick tresses are like a matted rat's nest underneath my ski beanie. From the corner of my eye, I catch my reflection in the car window. Just as I suspected, my long auburn strands are a disaster. I sigh and tuck the gnarled pieces into a ponytail and secure it at the nape of my neck. Never before have I so desperately needed shampoo and conditioner.

"You're killing it, guys!" Hunter calls out with enthusiasm. "Keep going!"

"Easy for you to say. Your hair never looked good in the first place," Britney grumbles next to me at the front of the SUV, smashing snow into her bottles. "I can't feel my ears anymore. My hands are numb too. And my—"

There's a satisfying *thwack* sound as someone nails her in the back of the head midsentence. She sputters and her eyes nearly pop out of her sockets. It's so funny, I can't help snickering into my gloves, looking around for whoever had the balls to hit Miss Priss with a snowball.

One by one, I eliminate suspects. It isn't Lily or my brother, who are already fast asleep in the SUV. It can't be Gavin either. Not that he's above flirting by snowball, but he's crouched down by the back bumper of the SUV, with no way to reach Britney from that angle. That only leaves one other person . . .

My eyes land on Hunter.

I'm pretty sure I've found the perpetrator, and not just because of the direction the snowball came from. Hunter's only a few feet away from the front car tires, a stone's toss from us. He's got access and motive, but what convinces me I'm right is the gigantic smile on his face and the wicked twinkle in those warm brown eyes.

"I'm gonna kill you, Hunt!" Two bright pink spots appear on Britney's sun-kissed face as she jumps up, lunging for Hunter.

Guess I'm not the only one who figured it out.

Hunter laughs and yells, "Snowball fight!" and we all drop to the ground, fisting palms of snow into our gloves for ammo. Gavin sprints to the front of the car, heading straight for the three of us. At first, I assume he's coming for Britney, but then he catches my eye and his grin widens.

My feet shuffle for a moment, confused which direction to go. The woods will give me more cover, but then I'll be in the woods, alone, and I think I'd rather get hit by a snowball. The inside of the car is also an option, but I don't think I'll make it in time.

Before I can pick a proper hiding spot, Gavin is upon me. I take off for the road with a burst of speed, but he hooks one muscular arm around my waist so I can't get away. Then he shoves a fat snowball right down the front of my sweatshirt.

"That's for being such a pain in the ass," he says, and runs away before I can retaliate with a snowball of my own. Ice stings as it slides down my stomach.

"You're dead, Farrell!" I shout, sprinting after him.

Damn. He's faster than I remember. No wonder our football team went to the state championship last year. I'm pretty quick myself but have no hope of catching up to him.

With no other avenue of attack, I clench my teeth and a rush of energy gets me close enough to shoot my shot. My aim is right on target, and I land my revenge right between those pretty blue eyes of his.

"Gotcha!" I cheer, jumping up and down to celebrate my victory.

"You're playing a dangerous game, Laken," he says, frowning as he wipes sludge off his face.

I smirk. "You started it."

He stalks toward me. "Give up now and I promise to go easy on you."

Fat chance.

From years of experience, I know there's only one way to play this. Gavin hates to lose. He's tough and strong and the only way people ever beat him sparring in our karate class was if they took him by surprise.

I put my hands up in the air, trying my best to look afraid.

"Okay, I surrender," I say.

He shoots me one of his devastating grins. "I knew you'd see reason," he says and inches forward until we're close enough to share a breath.

That's when I strike. Quick as a cobra, I sweep his legs like Sensei Larrence taught us when we were little. Gavin drops to the ground like a stone, his mouth open into a startled "O" shape. I stand over him, triumphant. It's been too long. Gavin has forgotten I never ever surrender.

I'm gloating and laughing so hard I don't see him reach for my legs. He gives my ankles an easy yank, and the next instant I'm sprawled on top of him.

"You jerk!" I shriek, crying out more from surprise than actual pain. "I can't believe you just did that!" I give him a murderous glare, but I know this is my own fault. He's not the only one forgetting things. I've forgotten Gavin never makes anything easy for me.

"You deserved it," he says, and erupts into laughter. Genuine laughter, open and joyous and kind of adorable—not that I'd ever admit it. Despite the chill around us, his body warms beneath mine. His fingers tighten around my waist as his mouth parts slightly. We're so close our noses almost touch.

Too close.

Much too close.

My pulse races. I tell myself it's all the running back and forth. It has nothing at all to do with that look he's giving me.

"What?" I ask, heat prickling at the back of my neck. "Do I have dirt on my face or something?"

He reaches out and grabs my ponytail, running his fingers through the windblown strands. "Your hair is longer now," he says, his breath tickling my ear. "I like it."

His touch sends little shivers dancing through my body. It occurs to me that if he's trying to distract me to set up for another attack, he's doing a damn good job. The air is too tight, too thin, too strained, between our joined bodies. I can't breathe, much less think of my next move.

"Everyone back inside the car!" Hunter bellows from off in the distance.

I look up, startled, and realize I've been so preoccupied with Gavin and the closeness of our bodies, I've somehow missed the storm worsening. The wind is so loud now it sounds like we're trapped inside a great big tunnel. It's going to start dumping any second.

"We should head back inside," Gavin says, rolling me to one side as Britney approaches.

"There you are!" she exclaims, clapping her hands together. "Time to go, handsome." She flutters her long lashes and stretches out her hand to him. He takes it, hopping up next to her, and they jog back to the car together.

"*Move it, people!*" Hunter yells louder.

Gavin looks back over his shoulder as if I'm now an after-thought. "C'mon, Sam! Let's go!"

I don't budge. I keep staring, my eyes fixated on Britney's tiny hand clasped inside his big one. They really do look perfect together. His tall, muscled body and dark coloring is striking next to her petite, golden figure. They're like real-life Ken and Barbie dolls.

"*Sam!*" he yells again. "*NOW!*"

I force myself to stop gawking at their interlocked gloves. "Right behind you," I mutter, and run after them to catch up.

Hunter throws open the SUV doors, ushering everyone inside as the heavens open and unleash on us. Gavin and Britney get into the middle row together, still holding hands. I step past them, shaking away whatever weird feelings I'm having, and slide the sleeping dog back to the floor to make room for myself in the back row next to Stuart.

From the safety of the car, we watch the tops of the trees sway back and forth. The car shakes and groans with each new powerful gust. Hail hammers at the roof, sounding like hundreds of golf balls raining down on us. I close my eyes, trying to shut out the scary sounds and stay calm, telling myself it's not like this is a tornado or hurricane. We're sheltered and protected inside the car. Still, the trapped feeling isn't exactly enjoyable.

The storm intensifies, the world outside turning white while my mood grows dark. Today is as bad as yesterday. Maybe worse. No chance anyone will make it through this mess to rescue us. It looks like we'll be stuck in the SUV for another miserable night.

Next to me, Stuart wakes and stares out the windows somberly. "I'm so sorry, you guys. This is all my fault."

"You said it," Britney agrees.

"Shut up, Miller!" Even if my brother was the one behind the wheel that caused the accident, I'm not going to let her make him feel bad about it.

"Don't listen to her, man." Hunter flips around in the front passenger seat to give Stuart a kind smile. "It was my whack-ass shortcut."

"Yeah, we all screwed up," Gavin says, nodding along.

Stuart turns to me. "We should've listened to you, Sam," he says, his eyes shining. "I'm sorry."

I blink. Is Stu *apologizing*?

This never happens. I can count the number of apologies from my brother on one hand. Under normal circumstances I'd be thrilled to hear him admit I'm right about something—anything—but just this once I wish I'd been wrong.

He shifts his leg in my lap, readjusting himself, and lets out a low groan.

"You okay?" I ask, little flickers of worry returning.

"All good," he says hastily, like he has a skinned knee and not a bruised and broken leg.

Come to think of it, Stuart has handled this whole thing rather well, all things considered. He's barely complained since the injury happened even though he must be in a ton of pain. I never thought about it before, but all those spinal injections and back surgeries must have toughened him up more than I realized.

Still, just because he's tough doesn't mean he isn't hurting.

"Anybody have something I can give him for the pain?" I ask.

"I got weed," Hunter offers. He props his black cowboy boots up on the dashboard and folds his arms behind his head. "Heck, we could all use a good toke right about now."

"Uh. I don't think so," I say.

Hunter blinks, looking hurt. "What's wrong with pot?"

"My mother would kill me if she found out I got Stu high."

"Why don't you give him a beer and call it a day?" Britney asks.

I stare, amazed. It's actually not a bad idea. I don't know why I didn't come up with it myself.

Alcohol is one of the oldest painkillers known to man. Before anesthesia was invented, doctors used it to numb their patients. Sure, it has its downsides in this cold weather, but at this point a drink will probably help Stuart a lot more than it'll hurt him.

Stuart gulps his beer next to me while we all agree to share more of the remaining peanuts for lunch, saving about a quarter of the party-size bag for later. I inhale my food so fast I hardly taste it. My stomach rumbles as soon as I'm done, and I find myself daydreaming about Christmas Eve dinner and gorging on more food than I can imagine.

My mother can't cook, but every year she orders enough food from Stuart's favorite restaurant to feed a small army. The best thing about Bogart's is that all their ingredients are organic and ethically sourced. And they have the most mouth-watering squash soufflé ever.

I suck at the salt remaining on my fingers as I fantasize about my mother's spread. Warm roasted chestnuts. Buttermilk biscuits with fresh honey. French onion soup with the cheese oozing over the sides. Vegetarian lasagna with layers of buttery noodles and cheese. Creamed corn. Mashed potatoes and butter. Stuffing. Gingerbread cheesecake and eggnog.

Mmmm. It sounds like heaven on a stick.

My eyes slide back to the cooler.

I'm not sure how much longer I can get by eating a few nuts and pieces of cheese knowing there's more food inside, ripe for the taking. It would be so easy. All I'd have to do is wait for the others to take a nap or fall asleep and then I could steal extra. I'm quick enough. I could pull it off with no one finding out. It would be a piece of cake.

Damn. Now I'm wishing I had a piece of cake to eat too.

Champion licks his chops and whines at my feet as he watches everyone else eating their lunch. I feel terrible, but we can't give him any more dog food until dinnertime. The vets back home at the clinic recommend feeding dogs only twice a day anyway, so it's not like I'm being cruel not giving him lunch, but what I'm really worried about is running out of his kibble. Gavin only packed enough for two days since we should've been home by today.

"Here, boy," Gavin says, leaning over the seat to give the last of his peanuts to the dog. Champion gobbles them up and noses at Gavin's hand, asking for more. My stomach twinges again, but this time it's not from hunger. While I've been plotting the best way to steal food from the others, Gavin is sharing his own lunch with the dog.

Could I be any more of a jerk?

"Oh, shit! Score!" Stuart cries out, spotting something under his seat. He grunts, reaching down and grabbing onto a crumpled white-and-yellow paper bag from the rest stop days ago. It must've rolled underneath during the accident and somehow gotten stuck there. The stench of old fast food wafts toward me as he opens the bag, pulling out a few soggy old fries and uneaten pickles from his burger.

Lily makes a gagging sound. "That's disgusting, Stuey! You're not really going to eat that, are you?"

"You bet I am," he says, and pops a fry in his mouth, moaning with pleasure. "Mmmm. Delicious."

"Hey, pass some over here!" Hunter hollers, holding out his hand. Stuart laughs and chucks a few mushy pickles over the middle seat headrest. Hunter gets halfway over the front center console in time to catch them in his mouth. Little bits of pickle fly out and drop onto the floor, but Hunter picks them up off the carpet and eats them anyway.

"So who do y'all think will play us in the movie?" he asks, chewing loudly.

"What movie?" Britney asks.

"The one they're gonna make about a group of fine-looking teens like ourselves getting stranded in the mountains."

Britney straightens in her seat. "You really think they'll make a movie? I've always wanted to be famous."

"Yep, but it won't be us. Not exactly." Hunter pops a few more peanuts into his mouth. I can't stop staring at the food. How does he still have uneaten peanuts? "They'll change things to make it more universal," he continues. "They gotta have a nerd. A jock. A bad boy. A princess. That kinda thing. And a sappy love story so dudes can take their girls." His eyes narrow. "Shit, I'll be lucky to even be in it."

"What do you mean?" she asks.

"Hollywood always whitewashes this shit. It's like all those busted John Wayne cowboy movies." Hunter frowns. "You ain't never seen a Black cowboy on the big screen, have you?"

My brother laughs. "Why would there be? Everyone knows cowboys are white."

Hunter gives Britney a pointed look. "See!"

"Actually, historians estimate that one in four cowboys were Black," Lily explains, turning around to face Stuart. "When the ranchers went to fight during the Civil War, they depended on slaves to maintain the land and cattle. But after the war, the ranchers had to hire them as paid cowhands. Being a cowboy was one of the only jobs open to men of color."

"For real? How do you know all that?" Stuart gazes at his girlfriend, his eyes dilated in astonishment.

"Because I read history books, babe," she says. "There were thousands of Chinese immigrants too. They helped develop the West, building railroads and stuff, but you won't see that in the movies either."

"But why not—if it's all true?" Stuart asks.

"You serious?" Hunter lifts a brow. "The Old West films were racist as hell. That was before the Black Lives Matter movement. Before MLK, even. They couldn't show Black men being all heroic on screen like the white cowboys. Gotta keep the Black man in his place, ya get me?"

"Perception would become reality, right?" I ask.

"Exactly." He nods. "If they made them equal on screen, they'd lose all that power once people left the theaters."

Unlike my brother, I'd heard about the Black cowboys because Lily and I took the same AP history class last year, but I'd never stopped to consider why this wasn't reflected in film or TV. It makes me feel like a privileged, ignorant jerk for never putting two and two together before. Of course, now that Hunter explains it, it makes perfect sense.

"Damn. That's messed up," Stuart says, shaking his head. "I'm sorry, man."

Hunter shrugs. "Ain't your fault. Been dealing with this shit all my life," he says. "People always teasin' me and my family about us being ranchers. They don't understand how hard it was for Grandpappy's family to get our land because no one wanted to sell to Black folk. Or how we had to fight to keep it when those same people tried to take it back." He straightens in his seat, raising his chin. "I'm damn proud of that history, though."

"You should be, Hunt." Gavin reaches across the front center console to grab Hunter's shoulder, squeezing.

The back of my neck grows hot with shame. So this is why Hunter loves to show off his southern cowboy pride. I can't believe I ever thought it was some kind of act. The love he has for his roots and his family as he speaks about them is one hundred percent genuine.

"I'm sorry too, Hunt," Britney says softly, sounding all sincere, until she adds, "Now back to the movie—"

We all groan. Leave it to Britney to miss the entire point of an important conversation.

"What? I said I was sorry," she asks, sounding a bit miffed. "Hunt knows I'm not a racist. We made out in ninth grade playing Spin the Bottle, for crying out loud. I love Black people."

Hunter shakes his head, laughing. "You know that's something every racist says, right? The ole 'I have a Black friend'—or in your case, 'I've kissed my Black friend'—defense."

"Being friends with minorities doesn't excuse white people from doing racist things," Lily says.

"Besides," Hunter adds, grinning slyly at Britney, "*I* kissed *you*. You just kissed me back."

"Oh, please." Britney leans back in her seat and stretches her arms above her head, turning to give him a long, deliberate look. "I rigged the damn game. I *wanted* you to kiss me." Hunter's brows fly up to the top of his disheveled hairline as Britney breaks out into little peals of laughter. "Now back to the movie stuff. I wonder which character they'll make me. The beautiful but misunderstood princess, right?"

"Isn't it obvious?" Lily sniggers in the driver's seat. "You'd be the ditz."

I giggle into my gloves. Holy shit! I can't believe she said that out loud.

"Stop laughing!" Britney barks at us. "That's not funny."

"There's always one of those girls in the movies." Lily shrugs. "The dumb blonde who goes in the garage to investigate a strange noise when she should call the police. You know, the easy girl—"

"I'm not easy!" Britney yells. "*I'm saving myself for Jesus!*"

"Oh, lighten up," Lily says with a tiny grin. "I didn't say *you* were easy. I'm explaining how these tropes work in storytelling.

And . . . well . . . it can only be one of us, right? I'm the brain, obviously, and Sam's the lovable loner. You do the math."

Britney cocks her head, studying Lily. "Okay, I'll consider that an apology—I think. But who says it has to be a girl? Why can't Hunter be the slut?"

Hunter howls with laughter. "You're crazy. The slut's always a chick."

Britney snorts. "That's the dumbest thing I've ever heard."

"Listen, I'm the first to admit I wouldn't make it to the credits either," he says. "The Black guy never survives, but it's always the slut that dies first. It's a simple formula. Girls are the weaker sex. It just ain't believable to have a dude as the first kill."

A little noise escapes my mouth. "That's ridiculous! Females in a species are far better equipped for survival than males."

"Here she goes." A knowing grin pulls at the corner of Gavin's lips. He and my brother trade amused glances.

"Well, it's true." I huff. "For one thing, girls have more body fat, so they have greater reserves. Girls are smaller, so they need fewer calories. And they have a smaller shivering response and higher body temperature for sweating. And thinner extremities and—"

"And listening to y'all yappin' on like this is what kills all the men," Hunter says, turning around to bump fists with Gavin who cheers him on.

"Screw you guys." I respond with a very non-womanly hand gesture. Lily and Britney join me, all of us waving our middle fingers high in the air. We laugh so hard I'm holding my sides until I'm crying. It's such a silly thing, not even that funny, but we're wound so tight it feels good to let loose for a few minutes.

A frightening *BOOM* sound cuts through our laughter, making us jump out of our seats. Champion's ears go flat and he howls as a flash of yellow bursts through the windows, illuminating the dark mountain sky. Another *BOOM* follows, this one even closer and louder.

"Is that . . . *thunder?*" I ask incredulously.

"Thundersnow," Hunter corrects.

"Holy shit. It can thunder in a blizzard?" Stuart asks, staring out the window in amazement.

Hunter shrugs, looking unfazed by the power that shakes the earth with each new bolt of lightning. "So," he asks with a raised brow, looking around the car, "who wants to play a game?"

CHAPTER 11

5:45 p.m.

"**A** game?" I ask Hunter curiously. "What kind of game?" I'm not totally opposed to the idea. It's not like there's a lot else to do to pass time trapped in an SUV in the wilderness, but the look on his face has me worried. I'm not sure Hunter and I enjoy the same sort of "games."

He grins mischievously. "I was thinking a little Strip Poker before bed?"

"Not a chance, Hunt," Britney says.

Lily shakes her head. "*Yīdìng bùxíng.*" Translation: No way.

I wrinkle my nose in total agreement with the other girls. I wouldn't take off my gloves in this cold, much less an article of clothing. Also—stripping in front of my little brother? No, thanks. And also illegal in most states.

"Party poopers," Hunter says, looking all kinds of disappointed. "How about Seven Minutes in Heaven?"

"Now you're talking!" Britney snuggles in closer to Gavin's side, locking her elbow with his. "We'll go first, right, Gavy?"

My stomach lurches. It's weird enough having to watch Stuart and Lily's PDA. I really don't need to see Britney and Gavin make out too.

I can see it now, Gavin and Britney getting paired up and going for it. His fingers stroking the side of her face. Her lips parted against his mouth . . .

Ugh gross.

What we need is a game where we all keep our clothes on, and everyone keeps their stroking fingers and parted lips to themselves.

"What about Never Have I Ever?" I ask.

Hunter's eyes light up. "Love that game! You take a shot of alcohol if you've done whatever the person says, right?" He licks at his lips. "Or we can take off some clothes if you prefer, darlin'?"

And just like that, we're back to stripping. That Hunter—he sure has a one-track mind.

"Our clothes stay on." I grin at him. "We'll use our fingers instead. We can hold them up if we've done whatever's been said."

Hunter rolls his eyes. "Snoozefest."

I laugh and start us off with a softball question about whether anyone has vaped before. Everyone but Lily raises a finger. Even I've tried it once, though I thought it was disgusting.

"My turn," Hunter says, rubbing his hands together and looking around the car with a wicked smile on his face. "Never have I ever had sex?" he asks, and all ten of his fingers go up.

I'm not surprised. It's a given based on Hunter's player status at school. He's dated almost all the popular girls at school at least once. Some even twice.

The finger I don't expect to see is Gavin's. Not that he couldn't get any girl he wanted, but I always thought he was a virgin. At least he was before he moved away to Boston. I wonder when it happened. Was it some girl from boarding school? It wasn't . . . It couldn't be Britney, could it? She said she was still a virgin, and her finger is down, but you never know.

"Wow. You guys are my heroes," Stuart says, gazing at Hunter and Gavin with open admiration.

"Watch it," Lily warns. Ever since we learned in sex ed last year that condoms are only about 85 percent effective, Lily has sworn off sex. She says teen pregnancy would throw a wrench in her plans to snag valedictorian.

"What's the big deal anyway? Even fungus can reproduce," I mutter, pulling my jacket tighter around my body. Why is it so cold in this stupid car?

Lily catches my eye, and we share a sympathetic look. Neither one of us is enjoying this question very much.

"This is fun!" Britney smiles and squeezes Gavin's bicep. "You go next, Gavy."

He hesitates. "Er—I don't know. This isn't really my thing."

I cock a brow his way. "Scared, *Gavy?*"

He presses his lips together and stares at me, his eyes challenging. "How about this—I've never been in love before?" he asks the question like it's a taunt.

The car erupts. Everyone raises their hands and waves them in the air.

"I think we should all go around and say who it is," Britney says, gazing at Gavin like he's just declared his love for her.

"That's not how you play the game!" I snap.

"Mrs. Madison. Fifth grade," Hunter says, his brown eyes twinkling. "Hottest lunch lady ever."

"Mine is Lils, of course," Stuart says, his voice so ooey-gooey I want to gag. He blows a kiss to Lily in the front row and makes loud smacking sounds until she giggles back. It's bad enough that Gavin's life love is better than mine, but watching Stuart is almost too much. How is it possible my little brother is in a full-on relationship and I'm still batting zero?

I bend down and give Champion a big smooch on his black lips. At least the dog loves me.

"Gavy?" Britney asks, nudging him in the chest, grinning. "Your turn."

I shift uncomfortably in my seat. I so do not need to hear him declare whatever feelings he may have for Britney out loud.

"Actually, I—"

"I've never kissed a girl!" Lily blurts, interrupting whatever confession Gavin was about to make, and changing the topic.

"Oh my God—please tell me you have!" Stuart cries out gleefully, and just like that, the boys forget all about who's in love with whom and start talking about hot girls making out with each other. Lily catches my eye across the SUV, giving me a sly wink. I silently mouth "thank you," grateful to have the best friend ever.

"How about cheating? The bad kind that gets you in real trouble?" Britney asks.

Five hands go up—everyone except for Lily.

"I knew it!" Britney smiles, her white teeth gleaming. "What'd you all do? I'm gonna need details."

Hunter flexes his fingers in front of his face, looking bored. "Depends which time we're talking about. Heck, I cheated off you last Friday."

Britney slaps the backside of the front passenger seat. "Hunter Jackson! How could you?"

"Yeah, if you're gonna cheat, why cheat off a cheerleader?" Lily asks, her nose turned up.

"Maybe because this cheerleader has the highest GPA in our senior class," Hunter says.

"Hunter, *shut up!*" Britney hisses, shrinking back into her seat.

"You're lying," Lily says. Her left eye begins to twitch. "There's no way Britney freaking Miller has a higher GPA than I do."

"And why not?" Britney asks, whipping around. "Because I don't geek out about grades? Because I like makeup and go to parties? Or is it because I'm homecoming queen?"

"Yes! All those things!" Lily shouts, her face turning bright red. She has to take in a series of her slow yoga breaths to calm down. "Besides, Principal Jensen told me in confidence there are only two people with GPAs higher than mine and Sam's. Alex Garcia, and he's only half a point, and I'm already doing better than him in AP physics. And there's some other kid. She wouldn't tell me the name, but she said they're not as focused as I am, anyway. Too distracted by social activities and not taking as many AP classes and ..." Lily stops midsentence, looking horrified. "*OH MY GOD. It is you!*"

I try to process this. The idea of Britney as a star student is more than a little disconcerting. Like Lily, I also thought I had a solid grasp of the competition for valedictorian. My best friend. A few kids from my AP classes. It never occurred to me there might be people I'd never heard of with grades as good as mine—or better—or that they'd want to hide such a thing.

"By the way, thanks for the A, sweetheart," Hunter says, clapping Britney on the shoulder. A grin ghosts across his face. "I knew you wouldn't let me down."

"Oh, shut up," she replies, still looking pissed he let her secret out of the bag.

"Mine is so lame. I cheated at *Doom*," Stuart confesses, unable to look the rest of us in the eyes. "I used a special code to get to the last level."

"I knew you were full of shit!" Gavin exclaims, and I remember how they used to compete over who would win that game first.

We go around the car, each of us taking turns confessing our sins. Gavin tells us how he used to cheat in pee wee football. He would grab jerseys, which is against the rules, but he only did it to guys who were jerks on the field. Britney switched around scores at last year's cheerleader tryouts to keep girls she didn't like off the squad. I tell the group how I lied about my age online so I could sign animal rights' petitions. Everyone laughs when I say this, but I don't know why. Lying about your age online is a big deal. Computer fraud is a federal crime. I looked it up.

After we've all gone, we look to Lily.

"What?" she asks, sucking on her lower lip. She hasn't stopped sulking in the driver's seat since she found out Britney has higher grades than she does.

"What'd you do?" Britney prods.

"I don't cheat," Lily huffs and crosses her arms over her chest. "Unless you count skipping to the last page of a book to read the ending first?"

"I don't believe you." Britney smirks. "Everyone's got a secret."

"Not me."

"Come on, Lils. Tell us," Stuart says. "No way yours is as bad as mine."

She sighs. "Well . . . there was this one time—"

"I knew it!" Britney says.

"It was in Beaverman's class last year," Lily continues, ignoring Britney. "He's such a narcissistic egomaniac, you know? Remember how he had a quiz during ACT prep week? I didn't have time to study because I was already pulling all-nighters for exams."

"Such a douche move," Hunter agrees. "No other teachers gave quizzes."

"Wait a second. Are we talking about Coach Beav?" Britney interrupts, choking on her laughter. "You cheated in P-freaking-E?"

"I didn't cheat!" Lily snaps, her voice sharp as any knife. "It was only Visine eye drops in his coffee. It just made him a little sick, and he had to postpone the quiz. No big deal."

A heavy, sickening feeling floods my body. I remember that day.

Coach Beav lurched around the gym like a drunk person, throwing up all over the basketball courts before passing out on the linoleum floor. There was an ambulance and even a fire truck. Girls were crying everywhere. They had to pump his stomach, and the hospital kept him the entire weekend for observation. Someone said he was going to lose an organ, though I'm pretty sure that was kids being melodramatic.

After it was over, the school administration decided it was a severe case of food poisoning even though no one else at school got sick. Never, not in a million years, would I have guessed Lily was behind it.

"That was you?" I whisper.

"Don't start, Sam. He was fine," she says, playing with the knobs to recline the driver's seat and leaning back. "He was back terrorizing us with his stupid quizzes the very next week."

"*Oh my God.* How could you do that?" I can't believe how calm she's being about this. "You put him in the ICU, Lil! You could've killed him!"

"It's not like it was on purpose." Hurt flashes in her eyes. "It was only supposed to make him go to the bathroom."

"I'm with Zhang." Hunter laughs, stretching out and resting his red flame boots on the dashboard. "Coach is an ass. He deserved it."

"It isn't funny. I don't care how big an ass Coach is," Gavin says.

Stuart nods his agreement. "I love you, Lils, but that's messed up."

Her face blanches in the driver's seat. "You don't understand! Beaverman was sick for *one* measly weekend. My entire life was on the line."

"Dramatic much?" Britney asks. "It was one grade."

"Not to my parents!"

Lily has never gotten anything below an A—not because she's ridiculously smart, though she is—but because she studies every single day, even on weekends. While the rest of us are still waiting to hear on colleges, she's already gotten early acceptance to Stanford.

"Whatever you say, sweetie," Britney says, patting at Lily's shoulder. "Remind me never to get in your way."

"It's like my grandpappy always says," Hunter muses to himself. "Never underestimate a desperate fox."

"Huh?" Britney asks.

"It's an old hunting saying," he explains. "Foxes are smart little buggers. They don't stay caught in traps for long. They'll do whatever it takes to survive—even gnaw off their own feet to get free."

"Whatever." Lily clears her throat noisily. "I'm done playing." She turns away from us, grabbing a new textbook from her backpack and flipping on her little reading light.

Game time is over.

CHAPTER 12

7:59 p.m.

We try to pretend we're not trapped for yet another night in a reeking and claustrophobic car, but it's impossible to ignore the biting cold the evening brings.

Stuart and I huddle in close together in the last row of the SUV, Champion nestled into our feet. I cover us with our extra coats until we live in one big wool and nylon cocoon. My gloved fingers shake as I tighten the scarf around my neck and wrap another one over my face, concealing everything except my eyes and mouth. Still, I can't shut out the cold. It cuts through the steel of the car and seeps into my skin. My veins. My muscles. My very organs.

"How is it still snowing?" Britney sighs glumly in the middle seat, cuddling in closer to Gavin. Her head rests on his shoulder.

"We're in the Sierra Nevada mountains," Hunter says, readjusting the front passenger seat to get more comfortable. "The name literally means 'snowy mountains' in Spanish. It's the reason the Donner Party got so screwed."

Stuart's teeth chatter. "I wish we were at a party."

"It wasn't an actual party, my man," Hunter says.

"Did you just sleep your way through all of American history class, Stuey?" Lily asks, laughing at her boyfriend. "How do you not know who the Donners are?"

"If it isn't a video game, he hasn't heard of it," I say, grinning fondly at my brother.

Stuart isn't dumb or anything. He just doesn't apply himself if he's not interested in the topic, which is pretty much everything except for gaming and the TV.

"Very funny." He tries to sit up but doesn't make it far before wincing and pulling at his ankle. "Just so you know, I got As in computer science, game design, and precalc, thank you very much."

"The Donners were American pioneers," Lily explains, resting her head against the driver's-side door and placing her legs up on the dashboard. "They set out for California during the gold rush but got trapped in the mountains. Right around here, actually."

"It's so gnarly," Hunter adds. "They ran out of food and ate dead people."

"Yuck." Britney makes a face. "Do you have any idea how many calories are in a whole person?" she asks, and giggles at her own joke.

I know I'm supposed to be horrified or disgusted, but I find myself laughing instead. I may not like the girl, but I have to admit she's got a wicked sense of humor.

"That's not funny," Lily says with a disapproving tone. "People died."

"Sorry," I say, and Britney and I share a grin. "But it kind of was."

"They didn't just eat the dead, neither." Hunter clicks his tongue, the sound reverberating in the car. "They murdered 'em—bashed their heads in with rocks and shit. Blood and brains going everywhere. You get me?"

"I don't remember that part from class," I say, my skin crawling at the image. I can't imagine how desperate and hungry you'd have to be to resort to murder.

"That's because he's making it up," Gavin says.

"Yeah, that didn't happen," Lily agrees. "The Donners were trying to survive and only ate the dead. Real cannibals are different. They eat people to ensure they're never alone. That's how they keep their victims with them—inside their bellies."

"Uh, you know this how?" Stuart asks, looking a little scared of his girlfriend.

"*Psychology Today*, duh," she says.

"Well, I don't care what your little magazine says," Hunter says. "That's how it happened on Netflix. In the movie I saw, the Donners killed shit loads of people after they got a real liking for the taste of human flesh. And then, at the end, they hosted a body-part buffet!"

Stuart's eyes light up next to me. "Damn, that sounds awesome! I'm adding that one to my watch list."

"It was dope, man! The best part is when they take the blood and the guts and they—" Hunter's stomach gurgles so loudly I can hear it all the way in the back row. "Dang, all this talk about eating is making me hungry."

"You're seriously disturbed, Hunt," Britney says. "How can you be hungry when we're talking about eating people?"

He flips around, grinning. "I'm always hungry."

Seconds later, a loud gnashing noise comes from the front of the car. It's a strange hybrid of chewing and gnawing sounds, like a dog going to work on a piece of furniture or an especially tough bone.

"Who's eating? We agreed no more food!" Lily yells,

jerking her feet off the dashboard and spinning around in her seat. She scans the car for the culprit, until she realizes it's Hunter sitting right next to her in the front passenger seat. "What do you think you're doing? We have to conserve!"

Hunter giggles and extends his hand to her. "Don't get your knickers in a knot. It's tree bark. See?" Tucked inside his black leather glove is a small twig about the length of his radius bone, from wrist to elbow. It's a barren brown piece of wood. Not even a leaf in sight. "I grabbed some when we were filling bottles. Delicious and nutritious," he says, and burps in her face.

"Wow! I thought they only did that stuff in the movies," I say.

"Want some?" he offers sweetly.

It's a testament to how hungry I am that I actually contemplate this for a second, tilting my head to the side, studying the branch. Nothing about it looks or smells particularly appetizing. A part of me understands it's food and I'm famished, but I can't get over the idea of eating a tree.

"I'm okay for now," I say. "But, uh, thank you."

Stuart eyes the bark with interest. "Hell, I'll try it. I'm starving."

"Me too," Gavin says.

Hunter snaps off a piece of the wood and passes it back to each of them before turning to the rest of the car. "Any other takers?"

"Ew. No." Britney shakes her head. "I'll wait for breakfast. Someone's gotta find us by then."

She removes her head from Gavin's shoulder to apply a colored lip balm and moisturizer for the night, rubbing the lotion into her neck and even the backs of her hands. I can smell the powerful scent of lavender and buttercream as she lies down in the middle row. Her head is almost in Gavin's lap, but he doesn't seem to mind. I hope they don't plan on doing anything more than cuddle, because I don't think I'll be able to stomach it if I have to listen to them kiss or . . .

My cheeks heat with embarrassment.

Christ—Gavin was right. I am jealous.

It's not that I begrudge Gavin happiness, and Britney isn't nearly as awful as I thought. She's even kind of . . . nice. Thoughtful and generous too. If this is what Gavin wants, fine. I think I'm just jealous Gavin is dating someone and I'm dating no one.

It's not like I've never had a boyfriend. I just haven't dated anyone seriously since Brandon Johnson my sophomore year. I still don't know what scared him off.

My dad blamed Gavin. Gavin was such a jerk whenever Brandon was at my house, always picking on him, ribbing at him, even though Brandon was the sweetest guy in our class. But it could just as easily have been me. I think Brandon knew my heart wasn't into it.

Sometimes when I was with him, kissing him, I'd imagine those light brown eyes morphing into the bright blue color of topaz. Not that there was any reason to think of Gavin when I was kissing my boyfriend. It's not like Gavin has ever shown any real romantic interest in me.

Gavin only teases and fights with me. He's never flirted. Never put his arms around me like he does now with Britney. He's never dated a girl like me, and I've never wanted to be like the ones he does date. Sparkly and popular. A girl all the boys want.

And yet, just for a moment, I watch Britney cuddle into him and wonder if I wouldn't trade places with her, just this once, if only to see what it's like to be on the receiving end of Gavin's affection.

"So, how long did the Donners survive out here?" Stuart asks in a sleepy voice.

"A few months," Lily says.

"Okay, great." He closes his eyes. "Just wanted to make sure it was longer than three days before they started eating each other."

"Jesus fasted for forty days in the desert and he was fine," Britney says.

Lily turns around in the driver's seat, her face openly mocking. "Oh, were the Easter Bunny and Santa Claus with him too?" she asks. "You know that's all made up, right? It isn't real."

I groan. "Not now, Lil. We're all tired. The last thing we need is an existential debate."

"But she sounds like an idiot," Lily says.

Britney inhales sharply. "I'd be real careful saying anything bad about our Lord and Savior right now. We need all the help we can get."

"I'm just saying if you want to be *saved*," Lily puts air quotes around the word, "you'd better do it yourself."

Hunter raises a fist, smashing it into the ceiling. "Hell, yeah! The power is inside us."

"Shut up, Hunt. Why are you agreeing with her?" Britney's lip curls. Her latest lip shade—a berry red—catches in the moonlight. "Your family is Southern Baptist, you moron."

Hunter frowns at his last bite of tree bark before sticking it in his mouth. "That doesn't mean I gotta confine myself to one religion," he says as he crunches and chews. "I like Christians, but atheists are cool too. So are Jews. And Muslims."

Gavin grins at his friend. "Hunt's been spending a little too much time at the Worship House."

The New Age Worship House is infamous around our town. They're a bunch of cultlike hippie types that preach observing all religions at the same time. I'm willing to bet Hunter's affinity for the Worship House has more to do with the free pizza they give out after services than spiritual enlightenment.

"You sound nuts, Hunt," Britney says. "You have to pick one."

Lily smirks. "If you ask me, he doesn't sound any crazier than people who believe in the Immaculate Conception."

"*Seriously, what's your problem?*" Britney's voice rises, loaded with anger. "Tons of super intelligent people believe in Jesus—like Reverend Martin Luther King. Mother Teresa. Charles Darwin. But maybe you think they're a bunch of idiots too?"

"What I'm trying to say is—"

"And even if we are all idiots," Britney continues on, "Reverend King started an entire civil rights movement. And Mother Teresa—well, she's Mother freaking Teresa! My church ministry built those houses for the Mexican families who lost everything last year, and my mother's Bible study group runs a shelter for battered women." She gives Lily a long, hard look. "What about you? What have you ever done for anybody?"

Lily just stares, looking flabbergasted. I've never seen her speechless.

"You really don't believe in God, Lil?" Stuart asks, sounding surprised and kind of sad.

"Nope."

"Me neither," Gavin says. "If there was a God, there wouldn't be so many shitty things. War. Murder. Disease." He pauses and then clears his throat. "Asshole dads who knock their sons and wives around."

There's a moment of shocked silence as the weight of Gavin's sudden confession registers with the rest of us.

"Oh, shit," Stuart says softly. "I'm sorry, man. I didn't know."

"Why would you?" Gavin shrugs. "You remember my busted shoulder homecoming weekend? I didn't fall off my bike at some stupid park like I told you—that was my father on a bender." His hand shakes as he traces the long scar that runs along his left eyebrow. "This wasn't a skateboard stunt either. I forgot to clean my room when I was eight."

His words send a chill through my body. I can't believe how stupid I've been. How clueless. How could I not have suspected this when it's been in front of me the whole time? All I had to do was connect the dots.

This must be why Gavin never invited us to his house. This is the reason he spent all his free time with Stuart and me instead of his own family. I sometimes wondered about all the bruises and scrapes he acquired, but they always had a neat and tidy little explanation—like a bike fall, or a football fight, or a skateboard. Now that I know the truth, it seems painfully obvious he was hiding something terrible all along.

"That's why you freaked about the tires, isn't it?" Hunter asks, a stunned look on his face. "You're afraid of your dad?"

Gavin only nods.

"Why didn't you tell us?" I ask, feeling ashamed for not realizing this sooner.

"Tell you what? That my dad's a drunk? A mean one too." He snorts. "What would that have changed?"

"We would've helped you," I say. "We could've gone to my parents. Or the school. Someone would've listened."

They have programs in place for this. Counselors. Numbers to call. If I had known what was happening to Gavin at home, I would've figured it out. He didn't have to go through this all alone.

"No one can help me." He says the words so bitterly it hurts my heart. "You want to know the real reason they shipped me off to boarding school?" he asks with a laugh, dark and angry. "It's because I tried to defend myself the last time that bastard hit me. My father said I was a threat—that I was unstable. What a joke."

"I'm so sorry about your dad, Gavy." Britney reaches for his hand. "But that doesn't mean there's no God."

"The bad things only make us stronger," Stuart agrees. "That's what the Bible says."

"Not to mention interfering with free will," Britney adds, matter-of-factly. "God can't keep bad things from happening to every person in the world. It isn't possible. That's why we're not supposed to base our happiness on the physical world. We have to trust that God knows what He's doing."

Lily laughs out loud so hard she starts to hiccup. "That is the dumbest shit I've ever heard." She looks to me, imploringly. "C'mon, Sam, please help me talk some sense into these Kool-Aid drinkers."

Everyone turns to the back row, staring at me as if waiting for me to pick a side in kickball. Like it's that easy to decide the most existential question of our entire existence—what we truly believe in.

When we were little, Stuart and I went to church together every Sunday with our family. We had a regular pew where we sat with our parents' friends and their kids. Stuart and I sang the words to every worship song. His favorite was "Jesus Loves Me" because the chorus repeats the same line over and over. It was the only song he could remember the words to.

Those were the days I kept a Bible by my bed. Every night, my family read passages together. I even had the book highlighted and tabbed at my favorite parts. It made me feel special. Protected. Like nothing bad would ever happen as long as I prayed and followed all the rules in that little book.

But we haven't been to church in years. I stopped believing God was looking out for me after watching all the awful things Stuart went through with his scoliosis.

"Sam?" Lily repeats when I say nothing.

"It's okay not to know," Britney says to me in a surprisingly gentle voice as if she knows why I'm struggling to answer. "If you question things long enough, you'll find Him."

Loud shots ring through the air, startling me. Champion gets to his feet so fast his tail whips me smack in the face, and all thoughts of God and the afterlife fly right out of my head.

"What the hell is that?" I ask, my heart racing.

Hunter laughs. "Relax. It's just avalanche cannons."

"Cannons?" I've never heard of such a thing.

"The snowfall makes things unstable. They gotta break it up for the skiers," he explains.

Lily straightens in her seat. "Is that something we need to worry about now too?" she asks, sounding alarmed.

"Naw. Takes a few more days of snow to get really bad," he says. "Besides, y'all know what to do in an avalanche, don't ya?"

Gavin snorts. "Yeah. Run."

Hunter rolls his eyes at Gavin and proceeds to tell us all these crazy, real-world factoids and statistics about avalanches. How many people die each year in them—over 150 worldwide. That 90 percent of avalanche accidents are caused by the victim or someone in the victim's party. What to do if you get caught in one. Apparently, you're supposed to swim inside the snow if you get trapped. How long you have to live if you get buried underneath. About fifteen minutes if you build air pockets and the rescue team finds you fast enough.

"And that's why all the ski resorts have professionally trained avalanche dogs," he finishes his diatribe. "They don't have long to find you before you're toast."

Another cannon goes off, louder this time.

"It sounds so close." Britney perks up in her seat. "Maybe we're near people after all?"

"Doubt it." Hunter blows into his hands and rubs the warmth against his face and neck. "You can hear sounds out here from miles away. Sure wish we were close, though," he says, flipping around to give me a suggestive little wink. "I'd love a little hot tub action right now."

Gavin groans in front of me. "Leave her alone. She's not interested, Hunt."

"I'm just saying she's smokin' hot," Hunter says.

"Gross." Stuart wrinkles his nose like he's smelled something terrible. "That's my sister."

"Sorry, man. It's the truth." Hunter's voice takes on a light, teasing tone. "I remember freshman year when Sam sat in the back bleachers at our games. We all asked about her," he says, and turns to Gavin with a big grin. "Gav here wouldn't stop yappin'. He went on and on about how cool Sam was, and smart, and, yeah, *hot*—"

"Knock it off. I never said that," Gavin snaps, and looks away. I wish I could see his face because I swear he's blushing.

Hunter laughs out loud. "You sure did! Although that last part I could see for myself." He stares at me from the front passenger seat so long my cheeks grow warm. Hunter isn't turning out to be anything like I expected.

A star athlete like Gavin, Hunter has always been one of the cool guys at school that everyone likes, but now I'm seeing he's way more than just a pretty party boy. It's not only that he treats all of us as equals—even my brother, Lily, and I, who are way behind him in the high school pecking order. He's kinder than I thought. Sweet, even. And smart. Hunter is far more resourceful than I ever imagined a popular jock would be. Sure he's a little rough around the edges, but he's funny and charming in his own oddball way. It's easy to like a guy like Hunter. Maybe even call him my friend.

"Truth is, I've always been curious what it'd be like to take you out," Hunter continues. He rocks in his seat, looking uncharacteristically nervous. "Except I ain't sure how other people might feel about that."

At first, I assume he's talking about his stupid football buddies teasing him because surely he realizes how different we are. I can't see how I'd ever be cool enough to fit into his life. Even after what Gavin said earlier, I'm having trouble believing this flirting is for real. That Hunter Jackson could be interested in someone like me. Then his eyes lock on Gavin's face, and I wonder if this is something else.

Is Hunter worried *Gavin* would be mad at him? That can't be it—can it? Even if my heart's leanings have recently become muddled where Gavin is concerned, there's never been anything romantic between us. Hunter must know that.

Except . . . well . . . there was that *one* time last year right before Christmas.

I still remember how good he looked standing outside my bedroom door, a mysterious half smile on his face. His damp hair was curled at the ends like he'd just showered. The thought of him undressed right down the hall had sent an unwelcome jolt through me as I imagined what that might look like.

"What's up?" I had asked, shaking away the unwanted thoughts. What was wrong with me? I didn't think of Gavin *like that.*

He raised a brow. "Aren't you going to let me in?"

"Uh . . . yeah. Sure." I took a small step back. "But keep it down. You know how my mother is." I wasn't allowed to have boys in my room at night. It was ridiculous since other girls my age were having sex, and I'd only gotten to second base with Brandon last year.

Gavin gave me a mock salute and stepped around me, heading straight for my bed.

"Your parents are back tomorrow, right?" I asked. "Not that we don't love having you lurk around."

"Who knows?" He plucked my favorite stuffed tiger off the hideous lacy pink pillows my mother picked out and jumped on top of them.

"You haven't talked to them yet?" I couldn't imagine going hours without my mother calling to check up on me, much less days.

"Dad's still pissed about the fight."

"Yeah, that was really dumb." I sat down on the bed, keeping a respectable distance.

"Some guy got in Hunt's face at the game. What'd you want me to do? I'm not gonna let anyone hurt my friends," he said, his eyes flashing. "Not gonna happen."

"If you keep it up, you'll get kicked off the team," I warned.

"I'm fine, *Grandma*. I don't want to talk about it."

I cursed under my breath. It was a mistake to bring this up. I just thought . . . well . . . I didn't know what I thought. That the great Gavin Farrell, God's gift to straight women and gay men everywhere, would take my advice for once?

"What do you want? I'm really tired." I yawned, hoping he'd get the hint.

"Here—I got you something," he said, and a box wrapped in holiday paper appeared from behind his back. The edges were messed up, like he couldn't figure out how to fold and tape wrapping paper at the same time.

"Um—why?" I stared at the gift, stunned.

He shoved the box into my lap. "Just open it."

As soon as the silver wrapping paper came off, I recognized the tiny blue box from my mother's favorite jewelry store. Tucked inside was a gorgeous gold heart the size of a quarter. It hung from a delicate rope chain, twisting and glittering in my hand.

"It's no big deal if you don't like it." Gavin studied the ceiling, a flush creeping across his cheeks. "I was going to get you a key chain, but your dad said this was better. You can exchange it, if you want?"

"Don't be stupid. I love it!"

"Really?" Moonlight from the window caught the planes of his handsome face as he smiled, almost shyly.

"Really." I grabbed his hand impulsively, giving it a squeeze.

He stiffened at first but then his smile widened, and he put his hand on top of mine. Heat rushed up my arm at the skin-to-skin contact. Suddenly, I had the strangest desire to touch him more, and not just some friendly gesture. I wanted to feel the muscles of his arm. His skin under my fingertips. His—

"Let me help you put it on," he said, moving closer.

His fingers brushed my skin to lock the necklace in place, but he didn't move away even after it was on. He studied my face, licking his lips nervously, and I had the strangest thought: *He wants to kiss me!*

"So uh . . . there's another reason I came by," he said, breaking the magic of the moment. He stood up and raked a hand through his jet-black hair. "I was thinking we could do something cool for Stu's birthday. What if we sneak him down to Mexico and go parasailing?"

Stuart had just turned fifteen. We'd already celebrated with birthday cake and new video games. Gavin's idea was so outrageous I laughed at first.

"You're kidding, right?"

"He'd love it, don't you think?" he asked, his eyes lighting up with excitement.

I stopped laughing.

"HELL, NO! You're not taking my little brother across the border and hanging him from a freaking balloon."

What was I thinking—imagining there might be something romantic between us? Gavin and I would never work as a couple. There would always be Stuart to fight over.

"Is this why you gave me a necklace?" I asked accusingly.

"You seriously think I gave you that so you'd help me? You're insane." His voice was laced with anger and . . . was that hurt? "You do whatever you want, but Stu and I— we're going."

"How're y'all holdin' up?" Hunter asks, pulling me from the memory. I drop Gavin's necklace, embarrassed. Without realizing it, I'd been holding onto the locket underneath my sweater. What would Gavin think if he knew I still wore it?

"I'm kind of hot." Stuart wipes a hand across his glistening forehead. "Is anyone else warm?"

Gavin cocks a brow. "That's a joke, right?"

"Are you feeling okay?" I ask my brother, another twinge of worry creeping up my spine.

"Eh, I'm just a little light-headed," he says, rearranging his ankle again. I grimace as sharp bone digs into my thigh. Having his leg propped across my lap isn't the most comfortable position with him squirming around all the time, but his ankle needs to be elevated for optimal circulation and healing.

Hunter laughs a deep belly laugh. "It's called a hangover, Stuey."

Please, please, let it be that. I try to wish away my rising apprehension as I reach over and unfold the scarf around his head, checking his temperature. Other than the dampness from the sweat of his skin, he feels okay.

I'm not sure what else to do for him, so I grab some fresh water. If nothing else, staying hydrated certainly won't hurt. He pulls his scarf to the side and drinks from the bottle like he's dying of thirst.

"Maybe you should eat again?" I suggest. The extra calories might help him feel better.

Britney's jaw tightens with disapproval. "No more food, remember? We agreed."

"If he wants food, he's getting food," I say.

"He can have more bark," she offers, like this is a real option.

"You eat the damn bark!"

"Britney's right. We agreed to conserve," Lily says.

I suck in air. I can't believe this. "You're not seriously taking her side, are you?"

"It's fine," Stuart says, letting out a long sigh. "I just want to sleep."

I study his face, debating whether I need to push this more or let it go. Does he look paler? Weaker?

"You'll let me know if it gets worse, right?" I ask, and he places a hand on my shoulder, nodding. Within minutes he's asleep, along with the rest of the car.

While Champion snores softly at my feet, I dig my fingers into his warm fur, hoping for sleep, but I'm too wired to do anything except watch my brother and panic. It's not that I don't want to sleep. Sleep deprivation screws with your motor skills and judgment—things I need to have working in the wilderness. I *need* to sleep. If only I could get my brain to stop analyzing all the things that could go wrong with Stuart.

The threat of infection like the poodle had at the clinic last fall isn't my only worry either. There are so many other dangerous complications from injuries like Stuart's. Though rare, I've read about people getting deep vein blood clots from leg injuries. They break off and travel to the heart or lungs and cause a pulmonary embolism, killing you. There are also fat embolisms where fat tissue from a broken bone can leak into your blood. That kills you too. Even a case of pneumonia can be deadly with no medical help.

A firm hand grabs my shoulder. My eyes dart up to meet Gavin's worried face as he hovers over the back of the middle row. "We need to talk," he whispers. "It's about Stu."

CHAPTER 13

Midnight

"**N**ow?" I whisper back, scowling at Gavin. "You want to talk now? Everyone's asleep."

He cocks his head to the door.

"Are you nuts? I'm not going outside!" Even if it's no longer thundersnowing, it has to be freezing.

"I'll be quick—promise."

I open my mouth to say no again but instead find myself stepping outside the car, following after him. Gavin has this irritatingly powerful effect on me. No one else could get me to leave a safe car to brave the frozen, scary woods at night.

"This way," he says, holding my arm and leading me away from the SUV. He steers me toward a large tree on the other side of the road, a few yards away. It's big enough to provide some shelter from the light snowfall that lands on our jacket hoods and shoulders.

We're in luck. Most of the storm clouds are now gone, replaced by endless clear black sky and a ghostly moon that rises above and bathes us in its eerie light. Never before have

I seen so many stars. They dot the sky like sparkling yards of diamonds. I find myself both hating the wilderness and admiring its splendor.

Gavin clears his throat. "What's wrong with Stu? I can tell you're worried about him."

"You want to talk about Stu . . . *with me?* Since when?"

He sighs. "We need to learn how to work together. For Stu, if nothing else."

"Not a good idea," I say. Even if I wanted to do this, I don't think I can. We'll just wind up fighting about it.

"Come on, Sam." His eyes are warm. "Friends trust each other."

"You think we're *friends?*"

"Aren't we?"

I take a step back, snow crunching underneath my boots. "Let me see," I say, raising a gloved hand, ticking his offenses off one by one. "You never returned any of my calls after you left for Boston. You never e-mailed me back—not once. A whole year gone by, and not even one measly text!" My voice gets angrier as I get more heated. I didn't realize until this very moment how much his ghosting hurt me, and *damn*, it hurt a lot more than I cared to admit. "Not much of a friendship, is it?"

"That's not fair." He kicks at the snow. The toe of his boot gets stuck deep inside the ground, buried under a drift of white powder. "I was busy with school—and football."

"Not too busy for Britney though, huh?"

"That's different."

"Yeah, I bet it is."

A painful ache tugs at my heart. He doesn't need to say it any clearer. What he means is he was too busy for *me*. For a girl he cared about—for Britney—he somehow found the time to stay in touch.

"Forget it," I say, feeling like an idiot. I turn to walk away. I've already said too much. "I'm cold. I'll see you inside."

"Wait." He grabs at my elbow. "Please."

I rip away from him. "I'm done waiting!"

Above us, the tree branches shake and shudder in the wind. He sighs and runs a hand through his inky black hair. "I don't know why I disappeared," he says. "It's not like I didn't want to talk to you, but you were in Seaside and I was in Boston. I figured it was easier this way."

"Oh. Is that all?" I turn on my heel. If he's going to give me bullshit excuses, he's going to get bullshit back.

"What do you want me to say?" he calls from behind me.

"Something better than that, dammit! Do you think I'm some kind of idiot?"

"No. It's not that—"

I stop and spin back around. "Just tell me what I did to make you so mad at me. I deserve to know the truth."

"Leave it alone, Sam." He blinks and brushes stray snow-flakes from his dark lashes. "It's better that way."

I can tell by the look on his face he won't budge. I'm freezing. Exhausted. I just want this whole conversation—this whole night—to be over.

"Fine, if that's what you want." Blood fills my mouth. I've been gnawing on my cheek so hard I bit straight through the fragile, newly healed skin.

"Tell me what's wrong with him. Please, Sam."

I want so badly to ignore his pleas—to run away and never speak to him again. I want to hurt him the same way he hurt me. And yet it's impossible when I know he's only trying to help Stuart, even if he doesn't go about it the right way.

A strong gust of wind ripples through the trees, and I shiver. "It's the cuts in his leg," I say. "I think they're infected."

He swallows hard. "I see."

"He needs medicine—antibiotics."

Confession is a funny thing. I didn't expect to feel better unloading my worries, and yet now that it's out in the open and I'm no longer holding onto this secret all alone, I do. It feels good to share this gnawing fear with someone else, even if it is Gavin.

"You don't have to worry. I won't let anything happen to Stu. I'll get help," he says.

"And how do you plan on doing that?"

"I'll head for the trees again. Our phones should work once we get high enough." He makes a move toward the road beside us as if he's about to leave this very moment.

I scowl. "Oh, drop the hero act, Gavin. Only a nutcase with a death wish would go anywhere tonight."

"The morning then."

"Not if it's storming again."

"I don't give a shit about the storm!" he yells at me.

"This is my problem with you." I push a fist into his broad chest. "You always act first, think later. I want to help Stu as much as you do, but rushing outside half-cocked isn't going to help anyone. You'll only get yourself killed."

A stubborn nod. "I do what I have to."

All the anger I feel for him wells up into one gigantic ball of fury. He's such a crazy, stubborn, insufferable fool.

"*Stop being such an idiot all the time!*" I scream at him.

"Maybe I am an idiot, but I'm not going to sit back and do nothing. Not when Stu needs me," he says, tearing a hand through his scalp so hard a few silky black strands wind up in his gloved fingers. "He's my best friend."

That's when it dawns on me. This isn't Gavin being his usual, pushy jerk self. He's truly terrified for Stuart.

He clears his throat and continues. "You've never understood. It's never been about me being Stu's friend for some stupid ego boost," he explains. "It's not just that I've known him forever or that he's such a good dude, though he is. When I'm with Stu and we're watching scary movies or he's telling his stories, it's like—I don't know—it's like I get to escape my life. Just for a moment, you know? It's as if he gives me some kind of *peace* or something. Is that the word for it?" He bites at his lower lip, his eyes flickering over to me hesitantly. "Am I making any sense here?"

If I weren't so angry with him, I might smile. I understand exactly what he means.

It's easy to get sucked into Stuart's world of make-believe and forget whatever crappy things are going on around you. If you're busy debating whether zombies and werewolves exist, or if Superman or Batman is the better superhero, you don't have to dwell on why Brandon Johnson dumped you with no explanation or why Gavin Farrell stopped talking to you after he moved away. Some people might call it immaturity, maybe because he's younger, but Stuart has an innocence—an optimism about life—that can't help but rub off on you and make you feel better about whatever you're going through.

So yeah, I know why I love being around my little brother. I just never realized anyone else felt the same way.

"Thank you for saying that," I say.

This feels as close to a truce as Gavin and I will ever get.

"I just wanted you to know it's never been me doing Stu any favors." He swallows. "He's the one who does me the favor."

This time I can't help smiling. I always knew Stuart idolized Gavin, but I assumed it was a one-way thing. Now I see Gavin idolizes him right back.

"Gav, please," I say, softening. "Promise me you won't do anything crazy."

"I'm sorry. I can't do that," he says. "First sign of something bad and I'm going, and nobody is going to stop me." He jams his hands into his pockets and turns around, heading to the car.

Back inside the SUV, the overpowering stench of something that smells like skunk fills my nose. I look around in bewilderment wondering how such an animal has gotten loose inside the SUV, but then I see him through a cloud of smoke. In the front passenger seat, Hunter has lit himself an enormous joint. He takes great big puffs from one end and attempts to blow them out quietly.

Lily wakes, coughing and waving away the thick smoke as it drifts from his mouth into her face. "Hey! What do you think you're doing?"

"What's it look like?"

She gives Hunter a murderous look. "Put that out. *Now.*"

"Yeah, man, you're stinking up the whole car!" Gavin says.

"It's called hotboxing," Hunter says.

Gavin scowls. "Hunt—"

"I can't sleep, okay? I need it!" Hunter whines. "It helps me relax." He takes another huge hit from his joint even as he looks apologetic. More smoke fills the car, making my tonsils burn like my throat is on fire.

"At least roll down a window!" I yell at him.

Champion readjusts at my feet, looking annoyed to be woken up by all our shouting. He huffs at my feet, his chest rising and falling with the weight of his breath. I pull my shirt collar up and over my nose, examining the lymph nodes on both sides of my neck. Sure enough, they're swollen and tender to the touch.

That's just great. A sore throat and lymph nodes? I bet I'm getting sick on top of everything else, and this smoke isn't helping.

I start to hack so hard my shoulders shake up and down with each new cough.

"PUT IT OUT!" Lily reaches across the front seat and snatches the joint right out of Hunter's hand. Before he can stop her, she yanks open her driver's-side door and extinguishes it, burying it in the snow.

"What'd you do that for?" Stuart asks, looking crestfallen. "I wanted to try it."

"Me too. I can't sleep," Britney says. "I keep thinking what if no one ever comes for us?"

"They're coming," Gavin says.

"But what if they don't?" Britney's voice rises as she sniffles into her sleeve. "What if we're lost somewhere that they can't find us? What if we sit here, wasting away forever and ever and—"

"Oh, just shut up already!" Lily whips around to glare at Britney. "I'm so sick of your whining! Is that all you ever do?" She rubs angrily at her temples. "*Hùndàn!*" she adds under her breath.

Asshole.

Rarely have I seen my friend so agitated. She's the one who always keeps her cool under pressure—through her mother's daily tantrums, grueling school exams, all of it.

"Take it easy, Lil," I say.

She inhales a few of her deep breaths until her shoulders loosen. "I'm sorry," she says, her hands tightening on the steering wheel. "All this waiting around is making me crazy."

"It's okay. We're all scared," I say.

"You are?" Britney tilts her head in my direction. Surprise lights her eyes. "You sure don't act like it. You didn't even cry when your brother got hurt. You always seem like you've got it all together."

I shift in my seat. "I keep things inside, I guess, but trust me, I'm as scared as you are. About a lot of things."

"I'm scared of spiders," Hunter blurts.

We all laugh at his sudden outburst, the nervous energy spilling over us.

"Don't know what you're laughing at. There's nothing funny about spiders." He shudders. "All those hairy legs and those beady eyes. And spiders can *kill*."

Stuart laughs so hard his body shakes next to me. "Only little girls are scared of spiders."

"Bite me," Hunter says, but he gives my brother a tiny smile.

"Now zombies, that's scary!" Stuart says.

Lily groans. "You really gotta cut out the video games, Stuey."

"You don't get it," he says with a seriousness that takes me by surprise. "It's not the walking corpses, or eating brains, or any of that stuff. It's that these zombies were once someone you knew—someone you loved. And now you have to watch this person who meant the world to you roam the earth forever, half dead. Or even worse, you have to kill them."

"I told you. Zombies don't exist," I whisper, but the reminder is more for myself than for Stuart.

I close my eyes trying to relax, but all I see are the gruesome, half-decomposing zombie faces from *The Walking Dead* episodes Stuart made me watch with him. I never thought about things the way Stuart just explained it. Now it seems not only gross but also kind of sad.

"I'm afraid of tsunamis," Gavin offers.

"Waves?" Hunter shakes his head. "No way that's as scary as spiders!"

"You can kill a spider. Nothing can stop a tsunami." Awe and fear glitter in Gavin's eyes. "That one in Asia killed thousands of people in minutes. I remember watching the news after. Wouldn't go on my board for weeks. I begged Mom to move us somewhere—anywhere—that didn't have a beach. It doesn't matter how strong you are. In front of something like that, you're just . . . powerless." He swallows. "And then you're dead."

"It's snakes for me," Lily says. "I hate those slimy little bastards."

"What about Sigmund?" Stuart asks with a confused look. "You love Sigmund."

Lily has a beautiful pet snowflake moray eel she named after her favorite psychologist and hero.

"Sigmund Freud isn't a snake, you doofus," she says, rolling her eyes.

"Eels are fish. Snakes are reptiles," I explain to my brother.

"And?" He still looks confused.

"They're completely different animal families, Stu." I laugh at him. "You get pissed if someone confuses your PlayStations."

"Only a moron would confuse gaming consoles," he grumbles. "They have different CPUs, graphics processors, and RAM speeds. Even the controllers are different."

Britney looks back at Stuart and then to Lily. "Wow. You two really are a match made in nerd heaven. She has a freak for a pet, and you *are* a freak."

"And what's wrong with eels?" Lily asks, huffing with indignation. "They make great pets. They're independent. *And* pretty. *And* extremely intelligent."

Britney smiles. "I stand by my comment."

"Like I was saying," Lily continues, but not before giving Britney a terrible look. "Snakes are the worst. One time, my sister and I were on our way to the restaurant to help dad when this rattlesnake came out of nowhere. It slithered right in front of us, shaking its freaky tail."

"Holy shit—are you serious?" I ask with a little shiver. We sometimes treat animals who have been bitten by rattlesnakes at the clinic. Vomiting. Paralysis. Not the way you want to go.

"It was so scary." She cringes and looks down at the steering wheel. "I . . . uh . . . I sort of had an accident."

There's a moment of silence before Hunter bursts into laughter, his big shoulders bouncing up and down in the front row. "That ain't nothing to be embarrassed about! Ain't a person in this world that hasn't peed themselves."

"Not me," Britney says, looking horrified. "That's gross."

I scowl at her. "You just couldn't help yourself, could you?"

"Of course, Linds knew exactly what to do. She knew what kind of snake it was and everything," Lily continues, her voice hollow. Lily's older sister, Lindsey, is as Type A as Lily is and even more studious. Lindsey got a full ride to Harvard two years ago and is studying premed. The girl is a lot for Lily to live up to. "She threw a stick at the rattler and it crawled away. She was so calm and brave the whole time, but not me. I couldn't move. I thought I was going to die, and I just . . . *I froze.*"

Out of nowhere, a deep rumbling, sputtering sound comes from the front of the SUV.

"I hope that's not what I think it is," Gavin says, but we all know that it is as the car goes silent and we listen to the last signs of life from the dying engine.

The gas has run out for good.

CHAPTER 14

Day 4 • December 23 • 8:38 a.m.

I wake to the horrible sound of gagging. Across the seat, Stuart sits slumped up against the side of the car, his insides going everywhere. His clothes, the leather seats, the floor—all of it is covered in his vomit. A sweet sickening odor fills the SUV, so thick and pungent it threatens to overwhelm me.

"Oh my God!" Britney bolts up, shrieking. "He's getting puke on everything!"

Hunter laughs in the front passenger seat. "Dude, that's nasty! Someone had too much to drink last night, huh?"

Champion inches toward my brother, sniffing at the ground and inspecting the situation. He looks like he might try to eat the vomit off the carpeted floor.

"Champion—no!" I yell, grabbing hold of his leather collar and hauling him back to my side of the row, away from my brother.

Britney leans over the middle row, looking horrified. "Get him on his back!" she orders, and then seizes Stuart by the shoulders and shakes him from side to side.

"Get off him!" I say, smacking her hands away.

She recoils back into her seat.

"What's your problem? You're supposed to roll someone over when they're puking," she says, and gags, covering her nose. "*Dear Lord.* Make him stop!"

"Rolling makes people choke, you idiot!"

I draw Stuart close and cradle his head against my shoulder, propping him up and keeping him vertical so his airway stays clear. Some of his vomit gets on my gloves and the top of my jeans. It's gross, but I try not to think about it. I'd probably be gagging like Britney, too, if I didn't have so much experience with animals peeing, pooping, and puking on me at the clinic.

"You okay, Stu?" Gavin asks, watching us from the middle row. Concern flashes across his features.

"Just breathe, man!" Hunter shouts encouragingly.

Stuart nods and gives them both a thumbs-up.

"Stuey? Is there anything I can do?" Lily sounds worried, but I notice she makes no actual effort to leave her barf-free spot in the driver's seat for the back of the car where we're in the thick of it.

"I got it," I say, and she looks relieved.

Moments later, Stuart is only dry heaving. He wipes his mouth with the sleeve of his jacket, coughing, as he pulls away from me and slides back to his side of the SUV. "Oh, shit, Sam. Your clothes," he moans, noticing the little present he's left on me. His vomit is everywhere.

"This is so nasty," Britney squeals, pressing a fist to her mouth. "Who's gonna clean all this up?"

"I'll handle it, okay?" I grit my teeth. Is she really this clueless? Can't she see how sick Stuart is? The last thing I'm concerned about right now is my stupid outfit or a dirty car.

I pull my wool scarf off my neck and hand it to my brother to wipe away any remaining speckles of vomit from his face before heading outside to grab new clothes and gloves from the cargo space. The others turn away while I wriggle out of my trashed jeans and put on clean black ones. Stuart changes his sweatshirt.

After we're in clean clothes, I toss our vomit-soaked ones outside, making a discard pile in the snow to be forever forgotten about. While I'm wiping up the soiled bench seats and the floor with extra flannel shirts Gavin hands me, Champion keeps getting in the way. He won't stop trying to jump back into the row and onto my brother. His tongue lolls out eagerly, and I worry he's getting too close to the vomit mess again.

Thankfully, Gavin pushes down the middle seat and climbs into the last row to help. Some of Stuart's throw-up gets on Gavin's hands as he maneuvers closer, but he just wipes it on the side of his jeans, saying nothing, and reaches for Champion. He grabs the dog around the middle and hoists him into the second row.

With Champion out of the way, I turn my attention back to cleaning. Most of the vomit comes off except for a few stubborn spots that have already soaked into the lush gray carpet. The stains won't come out despite my best efforts.

"I've got an idea," Britney says, and digs into her ugly alligator bag. She pulls out some fancy French perfume and passes me the pretty glass bottle. As I open the top, the cloying sweet scent of vanilla and something else sugary overpowers my senses.

I pour a generous amount of her perfume over the most offensive stains, and it seems to work. Mostly. The foul smell is still there, lurking underneath all that sweetness, but Britney's idea is definitely an improvement.

"How're you doing?" I ask Stuart, eyeing the sweat that rolls down his forehead with growing alarm.

He wipes it away with a shaky hand. "Honestly? Not amazing."

Gavin tries to make eye contact with me, but I jerk my eyes away from his searing gaze. If I think about our conversation last night, I'll only start panicking even more.

I press my palm against Stuart's damp forehead and gasp at the heat coming off of him. "You're burning up! Let me see your leg," I demand and lean over to unwrap the first layer of dressing around his ankle. Almost immediately, a horrendous stench fills the car—even worse than the vomit. It's the most terrible aroma of excrement and sewer sludge and rot and dead things all rolled into one.

"What's that *smell?*" Britney chokes.

The last few layers of padding ooze pus and blood, until his mangled flesh comes into view. My body goes cold at the sight, and not cold from the weather, but cold like every single nerve in my body has shut off. His ankle has swollen to twice the size it was yesterday, his toes now a frightening purplish-black color, dripping with juices. The gruesome appearance tells me everything I need to know.

"Well, shit." Stuart stares in horror at his leg. "I'm toast, aren't I?"

Wetness pushes at my eyes as I lower my gaze and clench my jaw. I'm worried if I say something, I'll lose it.

"It's gangrene, ain't it?" Hunter asks from the front row.

I swallow back the lump forming in my throat and nod.

"Damn," he says.

Damn is right.

"Gangrene?" Stuart repeats, looking confused. "How the hell did I get gangrene?"

"The shelf must've cut off your blood supply when it fell," I say, finding my voice again. I look down at my feet, willing myself not to cry. I can't let my brother see how scared I am. "Don't worry. You're going to be fine," I lie, patting at his hand.

"I know what gangrene is, Sam. You don't have to pretend," he says.

"He needs a doctor," Hunter says. "Antibiotics. Oxygen therapy."

"How're we going to find all that out here?" Lily asks.

"Screw this!" Gavin sits up in his seat and reaches for his backpack at his feet. "I'm going for help."

Stuart's eyes widen. "No way, man. I can't let you go back out there."

"There's no *letting*. I'm going," Gavin says.

Hunter nods along. "Me too."

"He's my brother. If anyone is going, it should be me," I argue.

Gavin shakes his head, his mouth tightening. "That's stupid. You need to stay here and help him."

"No one's going anywhere. Look what happened last time." Stuart jerks his chin toward his busted leg, looking distraught. "Tell them, Sam. Tell them they can't go."

My stomach hollows out as I make eye contact with Gavin across the car. His eyes flicker back with defiance, as if daring me to contradict him.

I know I should say something. That's what Stuart wants. The logical part of me recognizes it isn't safe outside, not after what we've seen. Outside all bets are off. It isn't fair to let Gavin and Hunter risk their lives for my brother's. Especially Hunter, who hardly knows Stuart. I'll hate myself if something bad happens to them because they tried to help. All this is true and yet . . .

This is Stuart.

He's my little brother. Despite what I said last night, no matter how conflicted I might feel about it, I'll do whatever it takes to help Stuart. No matter the cost.

"Go," I tell Gavin. I think it surprises us both that for once we've arrived at the same decision where Stuart is concerned, but there it is. A temporary truce.

"Sam! No!" Stuart's mouth drops open.

Britney clutches at Gavin's elbow, holding him. "You can't!"

"I have to," he says, shaking her off.

"But help is coming!" Her lips tremble as she wraps her arms around her body. She looks to the front passenger seat—to Hunter—with an accusing stare. "That's what you said, remember? *You said they were coming.*"

"Look around, princess." Hunter gestures to the uncovered windows. Heavy clouds circle above, snow dancing down the mountainside as lines of soaring trees rock back and forth in the powerful gusts. "Even if they find us in a helicopter, the wind will make it impossible to land."

Britney's eyes flare with desperation. "But you can't leave! I don't feel good either," she says, grasping Gavin's arm again and hunching over, coughing dramatically. "I think I'm coming down with something. You need to stay here and take care of me!"

"You're fine, Britney," I say between clenched teeth. "There's nothing wrong with you."

I can't believe her. We're talking about saving my brother's life, and she's complaining about a silly cold?

"What do you know?" she asks. "You're not a doctor!"

Gavin puts a hand on her knee. "That's enough, Britney."

"Uh, guys?" Stuart asks, sounding petrified. "Something's really wrong with me. I can't feel my—" He slumps over midsentence and vomits again, his hands bracing against the leather seat as his body shakes with convulsions.

I've never seen him scared like this, not even in the hospital after his back surgeries. Not even during his worst treatment days. At the children's ward of Seaside Memorial, they tell kids to rate their pain on a scale of one to ten to know how to treat them. Stuart never put his pain above an eight. The nurses said that's how they knew he was an optimist.

Stuart begins to choke so hard I worry something is obstructing his trachea. I lean in, steadying him first, before using my bare hands to open his mouth and clear vomit from inside. He takes in short, desperate gulps of air as I pull my hands away. My pulse skitters as I stare at my gloved fingers in horror. They're coated with blood.

"We've got to go! *NOW!*" Gavin says, his voice laced with such alarm, I can tell he's seen my hands too.

Gavin hurls his cell phone, water bottles, and his other belongings from the floor into his backpack while Hunter tears through the cooler behind him, grabbing a handful of peanuts and sour gummies to take for the hike. After their bags are packed, the two of them throw open their car doors and sprint to the rear of the SUV.

"Sam! Help me!" Gavin yells from the cargo area, but Stuart is shaking so badly I don't want to leave him alone.

"Lily!"

She blinks her glossy eyes at me. "Huh?"

"I need you to watch Stu."

She nods half-heartedly but makes no attempt to leave the driver's seat. She's like a shell of a person, silent and spacey. It's so unlike her it's almost creepy, but I don't have time to worry about Lily right now.

"Now!" I bark, losing patience. "Get back here!" I point to my seat like I'm talking to a two-year-old.

Once I have Stuart's ankle elevated properly on Lily's thighs, I scramble to join Gavin and Hunter at the back of the SUV. I find them ripping through suitcases, turning the contents upside down and dumping them into the cargo area. Gavin turns to me, breathing heavy. "We need supplies— medicine stuff—just in case. What should we bring?"

The last time we were outside, it was only supposed to be a short hike, but I don't know how long they'll be gone this time or what they might encounter. The best thing to take is a makeshift first aid kit filled with whatever will be most useful in the wilderness. Britney's tweezers. Nail clippers. Shampoo for cleaning. Extra socks for ice packs. I put it all inside their bags.

"I don't know how to thank you enough," I say to them as they throw their stuffed packs over their shoulders and tighten the straps.

"Ain't nothing to thank us for," Hunter says, his brown eyes filling with warmth.

Impulsively, I give him a quick kiss on the cheek, barely feeling his skin through the cold. "Be safe, okay?"

"Don't you worry. Daddy's on the job!"

He pulls me into a bear hug, crushing me against his big chest. I realize I've been so wrong about Hunter. I had him pegged as this stereotypical, dumb jock, but now I see he's so much more than that. He's brave, and caring, and clever. Hunter's one of the good guys.

"You better be ready for that hot tub when I get back," he says, letting go of me.

Swallowing down the lump in my throat, I smile. "You bet."

Gavin steps closer, putting a light hand on my shoulder. "Take care of our boy, Sams."

"You know I will."

I wipe away the flakes that fall from the sky and cling to my eyelashes. They turn immediately to water and disappear, dripping down my gloved fingers. Despite the vicious and gusting wind, snowfall remains minimal so far this morning. Just a light flurry that dusts our clothes and the ground at our feet. I pray it stays that way.

Champion dances at my ankles. He must have somehow slipped outside the car. He barks at us, looking excited, like he can't wait for another mountain trek.

"You stay here, boy." Gavin reaches down to pat his dog. "Where it's safe."

"No, you should take him. He'll help scare predators away," I say, reaching for Champion's leash in the trunk. I hand it to Gavin and Champion yelps louder, more eager. "Besides, he could use the exercise after being cooped up all night."

"This isn't a stroll in the park, Sam. We don't know how long we'll be gone."

"You'll be fine," I insist, bending down and wrapping my arms around Champion's thick neck. I give him a big kiss, hiding my sniffles in his fur. I won't allow myself to cry in front of Gavin and Hunter.

Hunter places a hand on Gavin's arm. "We gotta go, man," he says. "This weather ain't gonna hold forever. We need to make it to the red firs before it starts dumping."

I lean against the back bumper of the SUV and watch as they begin their long journey, heading the same way we went the day before yesterday. All the layers they wear drag them down, making them move slow and clumsy-like as they walk on the thick blanket of fresh snow from last night that covers the road. Though they're big, strong boys, the looming mountains make them they look small and fragile.

Eventually, they disappear from view, vanishing into the frozen wilderness.

CHAPTER 15

11:15 a.m.

Stuart is fast asleep by the time I return to the SUV. Doing my best not to wake him, I motion for Lily to return to the driver's seat so I can slide in next to my brother. He lies there, blissfully out of it, while I reposition his injured leg over my two good ones and tend to his injuries. His lashes flicker but do not open as I unwrap and clean his wounds again with what remains of Britney's expensive shampoo. Not even the final touches of wrapping fresh strips of clothing around his leg wakes him.

His forehead burns my palm when I check his temperature again.

Damn. The infection is progressing even faster than I thought.

I wipe sweat from his face with my sleeve and try to be thankful at least the nausea has passed. Sending Gavin and Hunter out into the wilderness was a risk, but I'm now certain it had to be taken.

While Stuart rests, Britney alternates between crying out loud, clutching at the little cross around her neck, and praying to go home. On the opposite end of the spectrum, Lily says nothing, reading textbooks silently to herself.

Time passes by in an endless symphony of strangled coughs and throat clearing. It moves so slowly, it's as if it isn't moving at all. Seconds, minutes, hours don't exist anymore. Instead, the day is counted from shiver to shiver.

At some point, I make sure everyone eats the rest of the gummies to keep our energy up, but I save the heartier food remaining inside the cooler for when the boys return. We've still got three chocolate bars, two bags of pita chips, two string cheeses, and what's left of the peanuts. Since we have no way of knowing what state they'll come back in, I want to make sure we're prepared with food for them. None of us feel like eating much, anyway. We're too worried.

Instead, we drink water.

Take turns going to the bathroom.

Nap.

By early afternoon, I'm unable to sleep anymore. My throat burns from what I'm sure is an oncoming cold. I would give my left arm for some Chloraseptic right now, but I'm forced to make do with as much water as I can get down. I'd consider eating snow to numb the intense ache if Hunter hadn't already warned us of the dangers of dehydration.

Truth be told, I'm feeling pretty terrible myself, but it seems trivial to complain about a cold—shitty as it may be— with everything else going on. Besides, complaining isn't my style. That's more Britney's speed.

My hamstrings cramp and I readjust, stretching the tiniest bit while taking care not to jar my brother. His leg shifts slightly and a good whiff of puke hits me, churning my stomach. Even with our change of clothes, the scent is still there, as if permanently stuck inside my nostrils.

No matter how I try to distract myself with other thoughts,

I can't stop fixating on Gavin and Hunter. Worries race through my head.

Where are they now?

Have they found help?

Are they okay?

I replay my last conversation with Gavin over and over. Why didn't I say something more meaningful to him before he left besides that measly thank-you? I should have said so much more . . .

I'm reminded of the last time we said goodbye. It was junior year, a few hours before my parents' annual New Year's Eve party. Gavin was grounded after his royal screw-up taking my brother on their half-assed parasailing trip to Mexico for Stuart's birthday. I'll never forget how scared I was driving down with my parents in the middle of the night to some Tijuana hospital. I thought Stuart was going to die. Even my parents were pissed and they adored Gavin.

Still, when he showed up at my doorstep looking upset and needing to talk, I'd caved and snuck him upstairs. I took a seat on the bed while Gavin limped across the carpet, grimacing as he lowered himself into my desk chair.

"What happened to you?" I had asked.

"It's nothing," he said quickly. "Just a skateboarding sprain. Forget about it."

"Okay . . ." I covered my bare legs with my comforter. "So what do you need to talk about?"

"I—I'm moving, Sam," he said, his voice so low I had trouble hearing him at first.

"You're *what?*" I sat up, stunned.

"My parents are sending me to boarding school," he explained. His eyes reverted to my bookcase, studying the shelves like he'd found something fascinating there.

"But we're almost seniors!"

I tried to keep my breathing even. Sure, I was upset with Gavin and planned on ignoring him for a sufficient time period, but that didn't mean I wanted him to go away for good.

And poor Stuart. My brother would be devastated.

"When?" I asked.

"Tomorrow."

I almost fell off the bed. "You can't be serious."

"They want to get me settled in so I can start right away."

"I don't understand. I know everyone's upset about Mexico, but boarding school?" My throat swelled up. "That's not fair. There has to be something we can do. Maybe my parents can talk to them?"

"Nothing's gonna change my dad's mind." He exhaled, sounding dog-tired. "It's okay. Boarding school will be better for me—better for everybody," he said. "At least, that's what my dad says."

Oh my God. Gavin was leaving Seaside!

No more football games? No more lazy Sundays in the movie room?

And what about homecoming? Prom? Graduation? Gavin would miss all those things.

"Listen, Sam," he continued, shadows forming underneath his eyes. "You have to make sure Stu has fun when I'm gone. Maybe don't be a jackass like me and sneak him off to Mexico, but you have to stop coddling him." Sorrow lingered in his gaze, so heavy I worried he might drown from it. "Pinky promise?"

He walked toward my bed, bending down to grab my finger.

"Cut it out." I pushed him away. "Don't make it sound like we'll never see you again."

He shrugged. "Boston is really far."

"But you'll come home to visit. Holidays and summer too," I said. "And we can e-mail and text. Phones work in Boston too, you know."

"Once I leave, it won't be like it is now." He sighed, dragging a hand through his hair. "Out of sight, out of mind."

I flinched, backing away as if he'd hit me. "How can you say that?"

Even if we rarely got along and weren't the best of friends like he was with Stuart, we'd known each other for so long. Was he really going to just forget I existed once he left?

And there was that other thing too. The thing Gavin and I never talked about.

I'd felt it the very first day we met in middle school. It was there every time he sat too close or looked at me for too long. Every time we sparred in karate class and he found little reasons to touch me. Every date he ended early to come to my house and watch movies instead. When he gave me the locket for Christmas the other week, I'd felt it then too. And in the moment after, when I thought he might kiss me.

I felt it right now.

"Just forget it, okay?" he asked, looking at the door like he couldn't wait to leave. "Do whatever you want about your brother. Why would you listen to me, anyway? I just wanted to say goodbye to you in person, and now I have."

He headed for the door and placed one hand on the knob.

"Are you really sure this is for the best? What if—"

"Sam, stop," he snapped. "I don't have the energy to fight with you today. I have to leave, and I don't have any choice— no matter how I feel about it." He didn't even bother to look back as he slammed the door shut so hard the hinges rattled.

I stared after him, stunned. What was that all about? Not even a stupid farewell hug? I didn't know what Gavin and I were to each other, but surely he owed me more than what he'd just given me.

Stupid, inconsiderate asshole!

My hands reached for the locket around my neck. Even though I never took it off—not even to shower or swim—I unclasped it and yanked my bedroom door open, hurling the necklace as hard as I could down the hallway. It wasn't until later—after the anger faded and sorrow took its place—that I went searching for the locket. When I found it the next morning, Gavin was gone for good.

"It wasn't supposed to be like this," Britney says, her sobs bringing me back to reality. She rubs at her red, puffy eyes, no longer made up with mascara or eyeliner. "Car accidents. Comas. Vomit."

Lily pries her wooden gaze from the front windshield to turn and fix a scowl in Britney's direction. "Carrying on like this won't make things better," she says.

"You don't get it." Britney wipes her runny nose with the sleeves of her cashmere sweater. "This weekend was supposed to be special. I've liked Gavin forever, since even before he moved away, and we were finally, like, connecting. I can tell he likes me too. I think . . . I might even be in love with him." She lets loose another earsplitting, anguished sob. "And now it's all ruined."

Wait—*what?*

Did she say LOVE?

A knot forms in my chest as I try to digest this new information. I knew Britney liked Gavin; I just hadn't realized how much. Even I have to admit there's a kind of perfect symmetry to it. The homecoming queen and the football star. Isn't that what every silly teen romance movie is about?

But what about Gavin? Does he feel the same way about her?

He must, I realize with a tiny jolt. I mean, look at her. It's Britney freaking Miller! Even four days without showering, snot running down her face, and bloodshot eyes, she's still gorgeous.

I try it out for size to see how it fits. Britney is in love with Gavin. Gavin is in love with Britney.

Ugh . . . I'm going to be sick.

"I need some air. How about you, Sam?" Lily asks, catching my eye in the rearview mirror.

I recognize that look. She's in caring-best-friend mode and wants to talk. She probably wants to try some psychoanalytical mumbo jumbo from her psych books on me to make sure I'm okay after Britney's bombshell confession. Lily has always suspected there was something more between Gavin and me, no matter how much I deny it.

I don't know. Maybe she's right.

I can't ignore that something has been going on with me. I keep having strange thoughts about Gavin and these weird, unwanted *feelings*. But that doesn't mean I want to talk about it—not even with my best friend.

Besides, this is dumb. Gavin likes someone else, and that someone is so obviously not me. Britney and I couldn't be more different if we tried.

And why am I even thinking about this stupid girly stuff when Stuart is sick and Gavin and Hunter are God knows where? Keeping my brother healthy until the boys return with help needs to be my priority. Not whatever deep-seated, romantic notions I may or may not be harboring for my brother's best friend.

"Sam?" Lily prods.

"I have to stay with Stu."

"Just a few minutes," she says. "He'll be fine."

Britney groans. "If you guys want to talk shit about me, there's no need to freeze outside. Say whatever you want. I couldn't care less."

"That's not it." Lily stammers. "I, uh, gotta pee."

Britney's eyes roll. "Whatever."

I glance down at my brother. His breathing is shallow but steady, his eyes moving back and forth beneath his eyelids so fast I can tell he's in deep sleep. If we go right now and make it quick, he won't even notice. Still, I hate the idea of leaving him.

"I don't know, Lil . . ."

"Please," she begs, placing a hand on the driver's-side car door. "I really have to go."

"Okay, fine," I say, sliding out from underneath Stuart's legs. "But not too far. I need to hear him if he wakes."

We find a clearing beneath a cluster of trees close to the rear bumper of the car. Lily turns to look at me, her eyes heavy with some emotion I can't quite pinpoint. Not quite worry, more like . . . nervousness. The wind kisses a few loose black hairs that have escaped her fastidious bun. She tucks the offending strands behind her ears as she studies the darkening skies above. Another storm is blowing in.

"Sorry to drag you outside," she says. "But I wanted to check on you."

"I'm fine, Lil. I don't want to talk about Britney and Gavin, but I'm okay." I grab her gloved hand and squeeze, feeling a rush of warmth for my friend. Even in the middle of all this insanity, she's worried about me.

She takes a step back, looking surprised.

"Wait—you thought I brought you here to talk about Britney?"

"Didn't you?" Now I'm the one who's confused.

"No, of course not," she blurts. "I mean, yeah, she sucks and I'm glad you're okay, but I'm talking about Gavin and Hunter." She rubs at her upper arms, her fingers twitch inside her thick purple gloves.

"What about them?"

"Oh, come on." Her eyes narrow. "I know how much you care about Gavin, even if you won't admit it. You must be worried about them out there in that," she says, waving toward the jagged, snowcapped mountains in the distance. "We need to come up with a plan."

"A plan?" I repeat. Now she's really lost me. "A plan for what?"

"You know . . . in case they don't come back."

My heart stumbles. "Don't come back? What are you talking about?"

"You have to admit it's a possibility."

"No," I say. "It's not."

I'm willing to concede it's possible Gavin and Hunter might not find help today and have to return, defeated, but there is no scenario in my head where they don't come back at all.

"I've been working this out in my head all afternoon," she says, pushing on as if I haven't spoken. "The longer we sit around, the worse things will get. There's no more heat. Eventually, we'll run out of food too. If Gavin and Hunter don't come back soon, we'll have to get help ourselves."

"You can't be serious," I say. "It's been, what, a few hours? Don't you think you're jumping the gun here?"

"You know I don't believe in leaving things up to chance. We need to strategize," she says. "For starters, we have to conserve more. We're going through food way too fast. We should cut down eating to once a day—even Stuey."

"No way. He needs the calories."

"I'm telling you. I did the math, and we're eating too much." Tiny beads of sweat form above her thin upper lip. She wipes them away with the back of her sleeve, her eyes shifting to the car. "The question is, what do we do about Britney?"

"Uh, what about her?"

She sighs as if I've said something dumb.

"If we have to get help, we both know we can't take her with us. She's too whiny and complains too much. She'll slow us down," she explains calmly. "And we'll have to take the food. We'll need energy to give us the best chance of survival."

"You want to leave Britney . . . *to starve?*" My mouth hangs open.

"No, of course not. We'll leave her what we can spare, but this is the best plan for all of us." She paces back and forth, her feet making tiny tracks in the snow. "This is a zero-sum game. If we all stay, we won't make it, and we can't all go. What else can we do?"

"And Stu?" I tilt my head, examining her. "You want to leave him too?"

I have no idea what's gotten into my friend. Lily is the last person I would peg to panic and overreact in a situation like this. Yet what she's suggesting is extreme. It's only been a few hours since Gavin and Hunter left, and Lily has already gone from zero to one hundred on the hysteria chart, plotting to leave people alone to survive on . . . what? Scraps?

"You know I love Stuey," she says, lowering her voice. "But this isn't about love. We need to sort through this logically or we won't all make it. You and I—we're the brains here. Stuey isn't good at this stuff. And Britney." She groans. "Don't even get me started on that girl. We need a plan now, while we still have plenty of food and water and supplies, and we're still healthy."

I place a hand on her shoulder. "You have to relax, Lil. You're sounding crazy."

She shakes me off. "Don't call me that!"

"I'm sorry," I say, reverting to the practiced, composed tone I've perfected at the clinic for our most panicked pet owners. "I didn't mean it like that. I just think the concussion is messing with your head. Gavin and Hunter are fine. They're getting help. Any minute now, rescue will be here." I reach for her again. "Let's just go back to the car, okay?"

"Just agree!" she yells, her nostrils flaring as she steps away from me. "You don't even like Britney! What does it matter?"

"Because we can't abandon people."

"Why not?"

"Because we just can't! It isn't right."

"*Right?*" she mimics. Her laughter sounds weird and high-pitched. "Don't you get it? There aren't rules out here. There's only living and dying. No one gives out gold stars for being a good person in the wilderness. Darwin wins out here—not Gandhi."

A knot twists in my stomach. I can't believe we're even talking about this.

"What's gotten into you?" I ask.

She takes a deep breath and squares her shoulders. "It hit me today, watching Stuey. He's really sick, Sam, and I don't know if he's going to get better. He could die out here."

"Stu isn't dying!"

"And not just Stuey," she continues, her voice shaking. "*We could all die here.*"

"You need to stop talking like this. You're not making any sense," I say. "Why don't we go back, and you can lie down and—"

"You're not hearing me!" she screams. "I'm telling you it's only going to get worse. You'll see. And then you'll wish you had listened to me!" She shoves past me, running back to the car, leaving me all alone.

CHAPTER 16

3:30 p.m.

For a few moments, I debate whether I should follow Lily and try to talk some sense into her or whether I should give her some space. The last thing I want to do is fight with my best friend, but I don't know if talking more when she's like this will even help. At least now I know why she seemed off earlier. She must have been planning and obsessing over this crap all day.

Was it the coma?

One of the side effects is behavioral changes like irritability and confusion, which she seems to be suffering from. Although I guess it could just as easily be fear. The stress and isolation must be getting to her. It's getting to us all. There's even a medical term for it: cabin fever. It's the claustrophobic reaction you get when you're isolated in confined quarters for an extended period. When it's severe, it can bring on irritability and restlessness. Irrationality. Paranoia.

Stuart made me watch a super gory horror movie about cabin fever last Halloween. Five college students take a vacation in a remote cabin during spring break and encounter locals with some gross infection. The group turns on each other, isolating whoever is sick and then killing them, until eventually they're all dead—either by a friend or by the town police who go on a murder spree. It's not a happy ending.

Tree branches snap in the nearby woods. When I spin around, Champion comes galloping into view. He jumps on me, slamming into my chest so hard he almost knocks me over. Gavin follows seconds after, staggering toward me, shivering violently. He moves like a drunk person, and then collapses to the ground. He's so weak I have to grab him by the waist to help him back up and half drag him to the SUV.

"Did you find people?" Stuart asks, now awake when I open the car door.

"Yeah and where's Hunter?" Britney moves over to make room for Gavin in the middle row. "Is he with the rescue group?"

"Give him a second! Can't you see he's freezing?" I snap at them.

Tears of exhaustion cut trails across Gavin's face as I help him inside the SUV. I kneel next to him and get him comfortable, laying him down horizontally in the seat. His teeth chatter, top row gnashing against bottom. Britney helps me place clothes and anything else warm we can find on top of him, and then Champion jumps onto his chest. The dog lies across him like a blanket, licking away the dirt and crusted snow from Gavin's face and hair.

I cram myself in next to Gavin, leaving Britney no choice but to move to the front passenger seat across from Lily. There isn't enough room in the middle row for all three of us and the dog. With Gavin settled in, I examine him carefully, looking for anything troublesome. Other than being winded and out of breath, I don't see any obvious signs of injury.

"Are you okay?" I ask. "Anything hurt?"

He puts his head in my lap and closes his eyes, saying nothing back.

"I knew you'd do it! I knew you'd find people!" Stuart cheers behind us with barely contained excitement.

Britney preens in the front seat, smoothing down her hair. "How long until Hunt gets here with help?"

Still Gavin says nothing.

I bend down, peering closer to get a good look at him. Dread forms in the pit of my stomach. The others don't notice the look on his face, but I do. I see the tense lines around his eyes. The way his lower lip trembles. Every inch of him screams of some terrible horror. Something awful has happened.

"Gavin?" I nudge him.

His eyes roll around, unfocused. He looks so disoriented I realize his silence isn't mere exhaustion. He's in shock.

"Gav? What happened?" I reach down and grab him by the chin, forcing him to look up at me. We don't have time for shock. If something's wrong with Hunter—if he's hurt somewhere—we need to get to him as soon as possible. He'll have no chance at all once it's dark outside. "*Where is Hunter?*"

"It should've been me," he whispers, his chest heaving.

"What're you talking about?"

"He warned me to stay away from the edge. He said it was dangerous, but we couldn't get our phones to work." Gavin draws in a sharp breath. "*Oh, God . . .* Why did he have to follow me?"

"Who followed you?" Stuart asks. "You're not making any sense."

"There was nothing I could do. He just . . . *slipped*," Gavin says, agony laced in his voice. He buries his head in his hands. "I tried to save him. *I tried!* But when I got there, he was already gone."

A shock runs down my spine, and I hope—I pray—I'm misunderstanding. He can't be saying what I think he's saying.

"Gav, where's Hunter?" I repeat my question.

His entire body quakes.

"WHERE IS HE?"

"He's dead," he whispers. "*Hunter is dead.*"

There's a long, terrible moment of silence, and then Britney lets out a groan.

"That's it! I'm going to kill him," she says.

"What?" I'm not sure I heard her right.

She laughs, high and tinny. "Don't you guys see? This is a joke. Another one of Hunt's dumb, stupid jokes."

"Britney—"

"He obviously put Gavin up to this," she continues, cutting me off. "And it's not even believable either. He must think we're idiots. People don't just fall off of mountains."

"Actually, they do," Lily says in a low, shaky voice. "My dad took us to Yosemite last year. He had us read all these safety books before we went. Falls are the number one cause of wilderness deaths. The park averages twelve to fifteen falling deaths every year," she recites, silent tears trekking their way down her cheeks. "And that's just Yosemite. Way more people die at the bigger parks like Yellowstone. Or the Grand Canyon. Or—"

"Shut up!" Britney plants her hands over her ears. "I don't want to hear your stupid park statistics. You don't know what you're talking about. Hunter is fine, okay? We just need to sit and wait for him."

"He's not fine! *He's dead!*" Lily yells. "What don't you understand?"

This is a dream.

It has to be.

I haven't slept enough, or eaten enough, or something enough, and now I'm having nightmares during the day. No way is this happening. Seventeen-year-old boys don't slip and fall off mountains, no matter what books Lily has read. And definitely not Hunter. Hunter is the most confident, self-assured guy I've ever met.

Someone starts crying big, fat wails. I put a hand up to my cheeks, thinking it must be me, but there's no wetness there. I glance around, confused, and then I see Britney hunched over in the passenger seat, her shoulders curled forward and chest caved in. She's the one crying. Or maybe she's never stopped from earlier.

"Hunter can't be dead," she moans.

And then they're all sobbing, even Gavin, who never cries. Everyone except for me. What's wrong with me? I should be crying too, right?

Why am I not crying?

"We'll never get out of here now. Not without Hunter," Britney says.

Stuart wipes at his tear-streaked face with the back of his gloves. "We have to get out. I'm not dying here too."

"Oh, yes you are! Just look at you. Your leg is a big old mess." Britney jabs a finger, pointing at his ankle. "We all know you have something bad, and it's probably spreading and—"

"Shut up!" I scream at her.

"It's the truth, isn't it?"

"Don't say that. You dumb *biǎo zi!*" Lily curses. Something dark and dangerous flashes in her eyes, like she'd like to kill Britney. I think she might do it, too, if given the chance.

For a split second, I think maybe I'd let her.

It's like we've fallen through a crack in the earth and wound up in some frozen hell. We didn't just lose a friend. We lost our lifeline. Maybe even our sanity. Hunter was the only one of us with real experience in the wilderness. He was the one who knew about hiking in the mountains. About finding water and food. Making a fire. Signal help. Without him, how will we survive?

Oh, God. How will I save Stuart now?

Something breaks and snaps deep inside of me the moment the thought escapes. Disgust sours my mouth, and I realize I'm an awful, horrible person because Hunter is dead and all I can think about is how this affects my brother.

I throw the car door open and run, not stopping until I get to the edge of the woods. Acid and bile rush up my throat as I drop to my knees. What little remains in my belly winds up on the ground below me.

The sound of my retching makes me retch more until the vomit drips down my chin. I wipe it away with my hand, only to realize I've somehow forgotten my gloves inside the car. But so what? What does that matter? What does any of this matter? Even if my hands freeze up and fall off, I'll still be alive. Not Hunter. He'll never be alive again.

He was one of us, and now he's dead.

"Hunter is dead." I say the words out loud, as if trying them on to see how they feel. They feel real.

Finally, my eyes fill. The tears slide down my face and soak into the earth for what seems like ages until the sky turns black and the cold forces me back inside the car.

In a few short hours, everything has changed. The wilderness has transformed from a non-sentient place into something terrifying—a stalking predator that lives and breathes and kills.

And now we're its prey.

CHAPTER 17

Day 5 • December 24, Christmas Eve • 8:55 a.m.

It seems as if morning will never come until, at last, a sliver of light trickles in through the windows. Every bit of me is frozen to the bone, except for my right hand clasped inside of Gavin's left one. Somehow we found each other through the gap in the rows during the night.

I slide my hand out of his grasp to reach for the snow-water bottle in the cup holder next to my seat. Even the simple act of moving my arm brings on a wave of achiness that makes my head throb. I'm certain I now have a low-grade fever to match my cold. At least I hope it's only a cold. It could be anything. The temperature, the lack of food, even the close living quarters—all of it is a breeding ground for serious illnesses.

A loud snapping sound at the front of the SUV catches my attention, and panic grips me as I swivel around just in time to see a giant branch fall from the trees above. It misses the hood by inches, landing with a loud thud next to the front tire.

My heart wallops in my chest as I stare in disbelief. If that branch had fallen just a few inches south, it would've hit the roof and done serious damage. One of us could've gotten hurt, even killed. Thank goodness we're all okay.

I turn an expectant glance toward the front passenger seat and wait for Hunter to make one of his wise cracks. A dick joke with a wood metaphor, perhaps? But then everything collapses inside of me as soon as I see the empty seat and remember.

Oh, God. Hunter is dead.

"Sam? Are you alright?" Gavin whispers.

I realize I'm crying again.

It isn't fair. This whole stupid world isn't fair.

Champion's nose bumps my hand, and he leans his head into my lap, as if trying to comfort me. I rest against him, wiping at my eyes. There's no time for tears, not when this mountain is literally trying to kill us. I have to stay strong.

"Did you see that?" Gavin motions to the downed tree branch, his voice filled with fear. "Shit. That was way too close."

I suppose we're lucky it missed us, but I don't feel lucky. Not after yesterday.

"Hey, get up." I lean across my row and nudge my sleeping brother awake. "You need to eat."

His eyes open into little slits. "Nah. I'm not hungry," he says, readjusting in our row. His feet push into my sore thighs so hard I wince.

"I don't care if you're hungry," I say, moving Champion's furry bottom off my feet and sliding out from under Stuart's legs, careful not to jar his ankle. "You have to keep your strength up."

My dad's cooler is now in the front passenger seat where Hunter used to sit. Gavin must have moved it in the night to make more room for himself and Britney. I slide myself up and over the back of the middle row, crying out as I go flying and accidentally land on top of Gavin. He grabs me around the waist so I don't tumble to the floor.

Next to us, Britney remains asleep, curled up into a ball, oblivious to the commotion. Her head is bent at an awkward angle, resting against the door as she moans audibly. Overnight, her lips have turned a shade so blue it looks like she's eaten an entire container of blueberries. She doesn't wake, not even as I brush up against her legs when I scramble past her to get to the cooler in the front seat.

My breath catches as I pull the top off and gaze inside. *Almost all the food is gone!* What's left—a chocolate bar and two bags of pita chips—is scarcely enough to last us the day. How is this possible? We've been so good about rationing.

Did we make a mathematical mistake planning our meals? Like during Gavin and Hunter's hike yesterday—did we remember to consider all the extra food they took with them that morning? I'm not sure now that I think about it.

Or what about dinner last night? I was so messed up about Hunter that food was the last thing on my mind. For the life of me, I can't recall what we ate after we heard about his death. Did we eat more food because we were all so upset? Anything seems possible. Mistakes are becoming easier to make on such little food and even less sleep.

"Sam? Everything okay?" Lily asks, waking in the driver's seat, untangling her body from its sleeping position wrapped around the steering wheel.

"Uh huh."

"You sure?" Gavin scans my face, worry shading his eyes. "You've been staring at that cooler for five minutes."

It doesn't matter how it happened. We have less food now and once the others realize this, we'll have to make our rations even smaller. I need Stuart to eat before the others find out what's going on. He needs all the calories he can get to fight off this infection. The rest of us—the healthy ones—we'll manage somehow.

"Yeah, I'm fine." I snatch one of the last two bags of pita chips from the top of the cooler and scuttle back to the last row.

As I tear the bag open, the delicious aroma of garlic and thyme hit me in a wave of pure amazingness. It takes every ounce of willpower I have not to pour the entire contents right down my throat.

"Here," I say, ignoring my own cravings and passing the bag to my brother.

"I said I'm not hungry." He pushes my hand away. "My stomach is too messed up."

"C'mon. It'll make you feel better."

He gives me a whisper of a grin. "I don't think pita chips are going to fix what's wrong with me."

"Eat," I demand. "Or I'll force-feed you like we do with the baby birds at the clinic."

"You suck. You know that, right?" He pulls a small chip out of the bag and puts it in his mouth, chewing slowly. His eyes water as he swallows.

"Good boy."

He flips me off, looking like he's about to barf as he finishes the first chip. He takes another chip and then another until he's on a roll, moving through the bag faster than I hoped.

"Don't eat it all, Stuey," Lily warns. "We need to ration, remember?"

I hold up a hand to silence her. "It's okay. Keep going," I encourage him.

Lily gnaws at her lip but doesn't say anything else.

Just as my brother gets to the very end of the bag and I start to relax, he swears, and then his face turns green. Vomit gushes out of his mouth, his loud retching waking Britney. She screams at the top of her lungs the second she sees him throwing up all over the car again, but it's over as fast as it began.

"I told you," he says, his body trembling as he looks at me accusingly. Trails of bile dribble down his soiled chin. He wipes them away with the back of his sweatshirt, looking like he wants to cry.

For a moment, I teeter between wanting to give him time for his stomach to settle down and wanting to get food inside of him before he gets even weaker. I choose the latter, crawling back over the seats to grab the last pita bag from the cooler and bring it back to him.

"Try again. Slower this time," I order, holding the bag out to him. "And more water in between bites."

Britney glares. "No more food. He's only going to puke it up again."

"Shut up!" I snap.

"But that's not fair," she whines. "You have to share with the rest of us."

"I don't *have* to do anything."

I don't care if she's right and I am being unfair giving my brother our last bag of chips when no one else has eaten yet. Stuart *needs* this. None of them are sick like he is. They'll survive a few measly hunger pangs.

"Sam, it's okay," Stuart says. "I don't want—"

"Eat!"

I don't care what he wants. My brother is too clueless sometimes to know what's best for him.

"You aren't God. You don't get to decide which of us gets food," Britney says.

I whirl toward the middle row, hot anger coursing through me. "What don't you get? Stu's sick—really sick—so if you get a few less chips, I don't give a shit!"

"But I'm hungry," she insists.

"That's a first."

"What's that supposed to mean?" Her eyes flash.

"We all know you're anorexic, Britney! Why stop now?"

"Screw you!" Tears spring in her eyes and run down her cheeks. She's so stunned she doesn't even bother to wipe them away.

"Sam! Enough!" Stuart yells, looking at me like he doesn't even know who I am. "What's wrong with you?"

Instantly, the fight goes out of me. I slump into my seat, regretting my words, overwhelmed with the knowledge I've probably said the lowest, shittiest thing possible to Britney. I just want to help Stuart, but even I know I've gone too far.

"We can't fight like this," Gavin murmurs. He puts a hand on Britney's knee, comforting her. "We have to keep it together if we're going to make it through this."

"You're right." I swallow hard and try to catch Britney's eye. "I'm sorry. I shouldn't have said that."

She refuses to look at me.

I can't blame her, but as terrible as I feel about what I've said, I can't let it go. This is Stuart's life on the line.

"I really am sorry," I apologize again. "But Stu . . . he has to eat, okay?"

Gavin nods, softening. "Give him more chips."

"I can't believe this!" Britney jerks around to face him, hurt shining in her eyes. "You're taking her side?"

"I'm not taking anyone's side," he says. "We'll all share the bag, but Stu needs a little more than the rest of us."

"But that isn't fair. He already had his chips." Her red-rimmed eyes scan the car, looking for support.

She won't find it here. Without Gavin, she has no other friends left. I'm certainly not going to change my mind, and Stuart knows better than to keep arguing with me once I'm set on something. And there's no way Lily will—

"She's right," Lily says softly.

"*What?*" My jaw drops.

I don't know what's more shocking. That Gavin has my back for once or that Lily doesn't.

"It's just . . . you keep doing stuff like this," Lily says, fidgeting in the driver's seat. Her short, square nails tap against the steering wheel. "You used all the soap and supplies on Stuey. I know he needed them, but you didn't even ask any of us first. And now the food? Don't you think we should agree how to split these things? It affects all of us."

"But Stu's the only one who's hurt," I say, blindsided by her words.

"Right now, he is," she argues. "But you can't know who might need them next." She looks over at Stuart and gives him an apologetic look. "I'm sorry, babe. But it's not fair. We need to share."

"It's okay, Lils. I understand—"

"Oh, shut up, Stu!" I hiss. My stupid brother never thinks about himself or his health. This is exactly why he needs me. "This has nothing to do with what's fair," I say, whirling back to Lily. "Stu needs this now or he could die. I don't give a crap about future hypotheticals. My brother is what I care about—and you should too!"

"Yes, we're all well aware Stu's your priority. You've made that perfectly clear," she says, her hands fluttering to her face like two little birds. "But that doesn't give you the right to be selfish."

"*Me? I'm* the one being selfish?" I shake with anger. Am I really having this conversation with her? About helping her own boyfriend? "I'm trying to save my brother's life. You're the one plotting to leave Britney here to die."

"Wait—what?" Britney's eyes narrow at Lily. "What is she talking about?"

Lily waves a hand. "Ignore her. It's nothing."

"It's not nothing," I barrel on. "If you two are going to team up, then Britney should know—"

"Shut the hell up!" Lily screams. The wild look in her eyes makes me recoil. I can't help but think back to our conversation in the woods yesterday. Lily hasn't come to her senses at all, like I'd hoped. If anything, she's gotten worse.

"Stop fighting, you guys," Stuart says, his eyes pleading in my direction. "This isn't helping."

Britney's eyes dart back and forth from Lily to me, as if measuring us. "You know what," she says, leaning over the seat and into my row. "I don't even care what you two idiots are talking about. Just give me the chips." She reaches forward and tries to snatch the bag from my hand.

"Don't touch me!" I slap her so hard my fingers tingle through my gloves.

"Ow!" She yanks her hand back, cradling it against her chest. "That hurt!"

"Take it easy, Sam." Stuart sits up, grimacing. He puts an arm on my shoulder. "You need to relax."

Tears prick my eyes, and I feel myself start to lose control. "But you're sick! You have to eat."

His mouth relaxes and his eyes warm toward me. "Sam, I'm fine. I promise."

"Everyone needs to calm down," Gavin says, his voice rising. "I know we're trying to conserve, but we can't keep going at each other like this. Let's just grab more food from the cooler. It'll be okay."

I gulp. "We can't."

"Why not?"

"Because the food's almost gone," I whisper.

"*What?*" Britney asks, her mouth half-open in a mix of surprise and protest.

"But that isn't possible," Gavin says. "We've been so good."

"I'm telling you—there's almost nothing left!"

"I told you we were eating too much," Lily grumbles from the front seat.

"Great!" I snap. "Who cares if we have no food? As long as you're always right, because that's what's important now. Not us starving to death."

The car is silent as the weight of my words hits them. One by one, I watch as the fear enters each of their faces. How long can we survive once we run out of food? What will we do when that happens?

"We'll be alright. It's not like we're in the middle of Siberia. Someone will find us," Gavin says, but even he doesn't sound like he believes it anymore. Not when we're going on day five of being trapped here with no sign of rescue.

"People get stranded and die in America too," Lily says. "It was in those books Dad gave us. Falling. Drowning. Exposure. Snake and spider bites. Even animal attacks."

After a long moment, Gavin says, "I want Stu to have my share of the food."

"No way." Stuart shakes his head. "I can't ask you to do that, man."

"I'll be fine with a few less calories today. And if we don't get out of here soon . . . well . . . we'll deal with that later."

"But—"

"I'm not giving you my kidney," Gavin says with a tiny smile. "It's just chips."

"I'll give Stu my share too," I say, turning the bag over to study the nutrition facts on the back. "It says there are about ten chips in each bag, so that means everyone gets two chips. How about Stu gets six, and you guys split what's left?" I ask Lily and Britney. "Fair?"

Lily nods, though she won't look me in the eye.

"Whatever," Britney says.

After Stuart finishes eating for the second time, I pass

the rest of the bag to the others to finish. Even though I'm starving and it's only morning, I make a promise to myself to hold out on eating, at least until tonight, if it'll help my brother and shut Lily and Britney up.

Ignoring my rumbling belly, I give Champion the last handful of dog food that remains in his bag. I'm almost tempted to sneak a few kibbles for myself, but it smells too disgusting. I'm not that desperate—yet. Plus, Champion would never forgive me for eating his only meal for the day.

The dog continues licking my fingers long after his food is gone, hoping for more. "You and me both, boy," I whisper to him, sighing, feeling his pain.

At least the rank smell coming from the carpet helps. Nothing like fresh vomit to curb the appetite.

"Can someone grab me extra clothes from the back?" I ask the others. "I'll clean the car."

"Here, use these," Britney says, and pulls off her knee-high socks.

She balls them up and chucks them at me. It's hard to tell if she's aiming for my face. I'm not sure I would blame her if she was. Fortunately, I catch them before they make contact.

"You need those. I'll find something else," I say. Bare feet aren't an option in this weather. Not if you want to live.

"Use them. I'm not even cold anymore," she says, propping her naked feet up on the center console between the driver and front passenger seats.

I gasp, taking in a sharp breath. The skin around Britney's ankles is mottled an alarming shade of purplish-gray and covered with fluid-filled blisters. Her toes are even worse. The tips are black as if they've gone rotten and are ready to fall off any minute. Her appendages don't even look human anymore.

"*Jiàn guǐ!*" Lily cries, gawking at the appalling sight. "*What happened to your feet?*"

CHAPTER 18

10:00 a.m.

Britney pales. Shock and disgust register in her blue eyes as she looks down at her ghastly toes and then back at me. "What is it?" she asks. "What's wrong with me?"

I do my best to wipe my face clean of emotions so as not to freak out her or the others, but inside, I'm trying not to panic. "Looks like frostbite," I say, proud that my voice isn't shaking.

"What does that mean?"

"It's when your skin freezes and—"

"*I know what frostbite is!*" she bellows. "What do I do?"

I look away. "I don't know."

Until today, I've only seen frostbite in books—never up close like this. The only thing I know for sure is that it's bad. Really bad. Besides, even if I did know what I was doing, we don't have the right supplies out here to treat frostbite. So far from anyone, with no medicine or medical tools, what could I do to help?

"What do you mean you don't know?" she asks. "You always act like you know everything!"

"It's not like I've seen frostbite before!" I shout back at her. "We live on the damn beach!"

I massage my temples. The pounding in my head grows worse as I try to recall something helpful from the books I've read. There must be something I can do to help her. Something that will—

"Oh!" I snap my fingers as bits and pieces come back to me. "You're supposed to warm up the affected body parts." I know I saw that somewhere.

She immediately moves a gloved hand to her toes, massaging vigorously. Gavin leans over and joins in to help her.

"No! Not like that!" I say.

"But you just said—"

"Rubbing makes it worse."

I climb over the seat and squeeze between her and Gavin so the three of us are shoulder to shoulder. "First, put these back on," I order, handing her back her socks and then wrapping her feet with the sweater tucked behind her head that she was using as a pillow. "Here, like this," I show her, kneading her toes softly but firmly.

Racking my brain, I try to remember more from the medical books that might be helpful. "We need to remove rings, watches," I recite from memory. "Anything that's tight and constricting on the affected appendages."

"I don't have jewelry on my feet!" Britney looks like she's about to cry.

"Oh, right—sorry," I say. "You need to stay hydrated. Drink lots of water."

"What else?" Gavin prods.

I'm out of ideas. No matter how much I concentrate, this is all that comes to mind. I can't help but think if only Hunter were still here, he'd know what to do.

"That's it. That's all I can remember."

"*That's it?*" Britney repeats, glaring at me. "A foot rub and some water?"

"I'm sorry."

"I told you all I was sick!" she says. "Now look at me! I'm gonna die out here."

Guilt washes over me.

Even if everyone else passed off her complaints as melodramatic, I should've paid more attention. I knew she wasn't properly dressed. Drinking too much beer. Sitting in the snow in only her socks. Not to mention the havoc a long-term eating disorder can cause in situations like this. She probably had a weakened immune system from before the trip even started.

I should've listened to her. Watched her closer. Forced her to dress warmer.

This is all my fault.

I close my eyes and take in a deep breath, holding it in for a count of ten.

No, I can't let my head go there. Negativity and blame won't help anyone, not Britney and not my brother. Maybe I haven't been perfect and I don't know it all—maybe Hunter would know more—but there are plenty of things I do know that can help us.

"From this point on, everyone stays covered up. Hats. Gloves. Scarves. Jackets. All the time. Got it?" I give Britney a severe look. "And no more crap about messing up your hair."

She swallows. "Okay."

"And no one goes out into the cold except to go to the bathroom."

"Got it." She nods, looking so scared it makes me feel terrible. Even if she annoys me sometimes, I don't actually want anything bad to happen to her.

"You're going to be okay." I pat at her knee, trying to sound comforting. "But from now on we've got to do everything we can to make sure things don't get worse."

She looks down at her feet and cringes. "There's something worse than *this?*"

"Hypothermia, for starters. But you don't have hypothermia."

"How do you know?" she asks.

"Because you don't have any symptoms." I tick them off on my fingers. "Numbness. Glassy stare. Apathy. Weakness. Impaired judgment. Loss of consciousness."

"But what if we start to get those symptoms?" Lily asks from the driver's seat. "How bad is hypothermia?"

I want to calm them down, but how am I supposed to answer that honestly and not freak everyone out even more? Hypothermia is a huge risk in cold temperatures. Without immediate medical care it can quickly turn deadly. We're alone in the mountains in the middle of winter with a broken car heater and barely any food. At this point, any one of us could get hypothermia.

I glance away. I can't lie to them. "It's bad."

"Things are getting worse. Just like I said," Lily breathes, her voice thick with fear. "It won't be long before the cold starts to do bad things to us all."

Gavin bolts upright, his hands shaking by his sides.

"That's it! I've had it!" he shouts. "I know it's dangerous after what happened to Hunt—" Pain flashes across his face. He has to cough to clear his throat to continue. "But we can't sit around waiting for everyone to get sicker. We have to get help."

"I'll go with you." Stuart nods along. "I'm not dying in this car. At least outside we've got a chance."

"Oh, wake up, would you!" Britney says. "You're not going anywhere with your screwed-up ankle."

"I'm not staying back here again," Stuart says.

"Be reasonable, Stu. There's no way you can go with Gavin. You'd just slow him down," I say. "I don't like the idea of splitting up either, but maybe it's the only way."

Lily makes a nasty sound in the driver's seat. "Oh, wow. This is rich!" Her dark eyes spark with anger as she stares at me. "Yesterday, you said I was crazy, but now you agree with my plan? Now that Gavin says it?"

I flinch at the vitriol in her voice.

"Don't be ridiculous. That has nothing to do with it," I say.

And yet . . . something in my mind *is* shifting concerning Gavin.

I've never agreed with his methods before where my brother is concerned. I always thought him brash. Ill-conceived. Reckless. And maybe he still is all those things, but I'm beginning to realize he has Stuart's best interests at heart too. Maybe he always has.

Even if this isn't the plan I would choose, I don't doubt anymore that Gavin's goal is the same as mine. We'll both do whatever it takes to save Stuart. This is so clear to me now that I don't know how I never noticed it. Gavin and I should never have wasted so much time fighting over what was best for my brother. Not when we've been on the same team all along.

"Well, I don't blame any of you for wanting to go," Britney says, smiling sadly. "If things were reversed, I'd leave and I wouldn't feel bad about it either. No one with half a brain would stay in this car one second longer. Not when there's no more heat or food. You go and let us gimps rot here in peace."

Gavin stiffens. "Now hold on. I didn't say that. I'm not leaving anybody here to rot."

"But those are the facts, aren't they?" Lily asks, wrapping her arms around her body. She begins to rock back and forth in her seat. "Maybe you'll find help and maybe you won't, but at least there's the possibility of rescue. But whoever stays here

... well ... it won't be pretty in a few more days." Her eyes lock on Gavin's face. "I'm going with you."

"I'm telling you guys, I can go too." Stuart tries to stand up only to collapse back down, clutching his ankle and screaming in pain. Tears run down his face. "I can go," he repeats. "You can't all leave me behind."

"I'm so sorry, Stuey," Lily says. "I don't want to leave you either, but there's no other option. Maybe what happened to you and Hunter were freak accidents, but after Britney? It's not safe here anymore." She looks away, swallowing hard. "I keep thinking about my concussion and almost dying, and I can't help feeling ... I don't know ... it's not my time yet."

Stuart's face convulses. "So that's it? You're all going without me?"

"I'm not leaving you." I grab his hand.

Gavin's voice is thunderous. "*The hell you aren't!*"

"Come on, Gav. You know I won't go without Stu."

"Don't be an idiot. You can't stay here," Lily says.

"She's right." Gavin nods along. "What if we can't find help in time?"

"That's a chance I'll have to take," I say, and try to smile. "Besides, aren't you the one always telling me to take more risks?"

"This isn't funny." His breathing goes uneven. "You can't give up, Sam. No matter how bad things are, you can't just quit."

"I'm not quitting."

I lift my eyes to his, willing him to understand. Staying is the only choice I have, like leaving is his only choice. It's who we are. It's how we protect the people we love. This is the way we save Stuart, and we can't argue about it anymore.

"There has to be a way out of this," Gavin says, his voice laced with desperation. "What if ... I don't know ... Why don't we take one of the snowboards? I can rig it up and put Stu and Britney on it and drag them behind us."

Britney snorts. "You wouldn't make it ten feet like that."

"I don't care!" Gavin bangs a fist against the car door. "We have to try something!"

"*Tiān ǎ!*" Lily cries, and picks up one of her history books, heaving it across the SUV. It lands with a loud *thump* in the empty front passenger seat across from her. "How did everything get so messed up?"

Mesmerized, I stare at the book. The spine looks wounded and broken. Pages flutter about. I wonder how many others there are like us inside those battered pages. How many people throughout history have been caught up in similar situations? Impossible situations.

A few days ago, we were a bunch of teenagers heading on a weekend ski trip. Now we're choosing which of us will live and die.

"You better take food if you're going," Britney says, almost calmly as if she has resigned herself to defeat. She leans into the front row and reaches inside the cooler, pulling out our only remaining chocolate bar and handing it to Lily.

"No, uh, that's okay. You keep it," Lily says. Her hands shake as she picks up her backpack off the center console and turns back at me. "Sam . . . I, um, I need to tell you something."

"Take the chocolate, would you?" Britney asks, shoving the candy bar in Lily's face. "You'll need the extra energy."

"I said I don't want it!" Lily pushes her away. "Sam, there's something you should know—"

"Don't bother." I cut her off. "Nothing you can say is going to make me change my mind and leave Stu."

"No, it's not that," she continues. "I mean, you should come, but that's not it." She sighs loudly. "You're going to be pissed when I tell you this—even more pissed than you are right now—but I need you to understand I did this for all of us. I didn't want to go behind your back, but you wouldn't listen to me." She licks her lips nervously. "You left me with no choice."

Britney grabs hold of Lily's backpack while Lily is preoccupied and yanks it closer. "This is ridiculous," she mumbles and tugs at the zipper. "If you won't take the food, I'll do it for you."

Lily whips back around to Britney. "I said I'm fine!"

"And I said to take the damn food!"

"Leave me alone!" Lily reaches one hand out to collect her backpack and uses the other to shove Britney away. Britney goes flailing, the back of her head banging against the top of the middle row seat. She curses, looking like she wants to kill Lily.

During all the chaos, Lily's bag turns upside down, the insides spilling all over the SUV's carpeted floor and going everywhere. Its contents include four water bottles, two string cheeses, one chocolate bar, and all the missing peanuts.

CHAPTER 19

10:50 a.m.

I gape at all the food sprawled across the SUV's floor. There must be an explanation, because what we see—every stinking snack that went missing—isn't possible. Lily has been acting strange and not at all like herself, but there's no way she's been stealing our food. Lily would never do that. She's my best friend. She's a good person.

Isn't she?

"You *bitch!*" Britney's face twists into something frightening as she stares Lily down. "You've been stealing our food?"

"Now, wait a minute—" Stuart starts.

"Wait for what? That's ours!" Britney cuts him off, stabbing a broken fingernail at our provisions now sprawled across the SUV floor.

"I'm sure there's a good reason." Stuart looks to Lily, a hopeful expression on his face.

"Good reason?" Britney repeats with disbelief. "Are you blind? Or just stupid?"

"Lil? What's going on?" I ask as Champion leaps over the back row. I lunge for him, holding him back by the collar with a death grip so he can't grab any of the food.

Lily's eyes are empty as they flick down to the ground, her face disappearing behind a curtain of long black hair. I tell myself that if she says something—anything—I'll give her the benefit of the doubt, but she says nothing.

"Lil?" I prod.

She exhales in the driver's seat, the noise getting stuck in her throat. "I'm sorry," she says, turning to me. "I tried to tell you."

I lean forward into the front row, waiting for more, but nothing else comes.

"You're sorry?" I ask, horror recoiling in my gut. "That's it?"

"I didn't have any choice. You wouldn't listen to me."

"Are you serious? Are you really putting this on me?" I ask, staggered. "Are you *insane?*"

"Don't you do that! Don't make me out to be the bad guy here!" she hisses, her eyes narrowing. "You're always so controlling—always telling everyone how to act and what to do. Stuey and I both think so. We talk about it all the time."

"Lils!" Stuart's face blanches, and he turns to me. "That isn't . . . That's not true," he says, but I can tell by the expression on his face that it is.

My blood goes as cold as the air outside.

"You think I'm controlling?" I ask him.

"It wasn't like that."

"Oh, grow a spine, Stuey!" Lily frowns, throwing her hands up. "I'm sorry, Sam. It's not like I wanted to do this, but I warned you we had to conserve. I *begged* you for a plan," she says, her voice low and full of emotion. "This is your fault."

"How can you say that? None of this is Sammy's fault," Britney says, shocking me by coming to my defense. "She's the one who told us not to go down the road, remember? If we'd listened to her, none of this would've happened, and Hunt would still be here. She's the one that risked her life to get help for *you*. And she's been helping me with my feet and Stu with his leg—she helps all of us."

I grasp onto the back of the seat for support as waves of shock roll through me. What's going on here? Am I trapped in some kind of alternate universe where Lily betrays me and Britney, of all people, is advocating for me?

Lily takes a deep yoga breath and pinches at the bridge of her nose until the redness in her face subsides. "C'mon. You must see why I did this," she says. "I had to look out for everybody."

Britney's eyes flash. "Seems to me like you were only looking out for yourself."

"That's not true," Lily insists. "Sam was looking after Stuey, and Gavin was looking after Sam, but who was looking after the rest of us? No one, that's who. Someone had to step up and make sure Sam didn't waste all our supplies and food on St—" She stops, looking away guiltily.

"Finish the sentence," Stuart says, hurt flickering in his eyes. "You think I'm a waste, Lils?"

"That's not what I meant," Lily says, her voice cracking. "Please try to understand."

"Understand what?" Something darker than just the sickness touches my brother's face. "You were going to take all the food and leave us here alone? *With nothing?*"

"Of course not! How could you even think that?" Her face flushes. "If no one was going to listen to me, I had to be the one to save us. I did it to make sure we didn't run out of food. I was going to share with everyone. I swear. You have to believe me!" she pleads, tears gathering in the corner of her eyes. "I thought if that ever happened, you'd all be so happy we had more food you couldn't be mad at me for doing it."

"I don't care the reason. Friends don't lie to each other," I say.

"You're right," she agrees. "I know I shouldn't have kept it a secret, especially after Stu got sicker. I was about to tell you everything, but then *she* got involved." She looks at Britney, her eyes shooting daggers at the other girl.

"Oh, hell no," Britney says. "Don't you dare try to pin this on me."

"I can't believe you would do this," I say to Lily. Molten hot rage pours out of me. I thought Lily was my friend. I *trusted* her. But she put us at risk—Stuart most of all.

Our argument this morning over the stupid pita chips seems a hundred times worse now that I know it was all Lily's fault. Even after seeing how sick Stuart and Britney were becoming, she didn't tell us about the extra food. Instead, Lily let us fight over scraps.

"I'm not going to say I regret saving the food, but I made a mistake going behind your back. I know that." Silent tears track down Lily's cheeks. "I'm still your best friend, Sam. This doesn't change that."

Lily, to her credit, looks like she might puke. I taste bile and feel the urge to vomit as well.

All the sleepovers, the heart-to-hearts, the promises we made to be friends forever—even after college and grad school and marriage and kids. Did they mean nothing to her? In only four days in the wilderness, has fear stripped away all her goodness and turned her into this selfish, conniving person I don't even recognize?

Or what if . . .

I shake my head, trying to erase my next thought because it's even more frightening.

What if Lily is right? What if it is *me*?

I am controlling at times, even I know that. And she did come to me earlier with her plan. Back in the woods she confided in me and told me what she was afraid of, but I'd dismissed her ideas and called her crazy. I was so certain I was right and that my own wants and needs—to protect Stuart at all costs—were more important than hers. I never even considered what Lily wanted or needed. If Lily was a bad friend because she dismissed my feelings in favor of her own agenda, wasn't I just as bad?

Hunter had called her a fox, doing whatever it takes to survive. That's true enough. But doesn't that make me a fox too? Isn't that exactly what I've been doing to save Stuart?

"Just go," Britney says to Lily, her voice filled with disgust. She shoulders me to get closer to Lily and shoves the smaller girl toward the driver's-side door. "Get the hell out of here already."

"Sam?" Lily continues staring back at me with a desperate look in her eyes. "Talk to me."

I'm sure if she thought I'd listen, she'd tell me she read in one of her textbooks that I need to get my anger out. That it's unhealthy to keep it all bottled in like this. That if we could only talk about it, and analyze it, we could work through it together—or some other psychobabble shit like that.

But that isn't going to happen. I can't speak to Lily right now. I don't even know where to start. Part of me is furious and righteous and wants to yell at her like Britney is, throwing blame so I can take all the helplessness I feel about our situation out on someone else. Yet the other part—the tiny, guilty, self-aware part—wonders if I should apologize as well.

"You need to go with them, Sam," Stuart says. "I can't let you stay here. I don't want to be selfish about this."

I peer closer at him. Sweat no longer dampens his face but soaks his scalp and forehead. It even gets in his eyes, making him squint. Or maybe that's tears.

"Don't be stupid. I'm not leaving you," I say, grabbing his clammy hand and squeezing.

This is what's important right now—Stu's life. He's what matters. I need to focus on my brother and forget all about Lily and our issues.

"Sam, no!" Lily cries. "I know you're upset with me, but you have to be logical. You can't stay here. You'll die in this car!"

"I don't care."

"She's right, Sam." Stuart's lower lip trembles.

"Stu, listen—"

"No—*you listen!*" he yells. "Don't you get it? If this is for me, I don't want it!" His entire body shakes with frustration. "I need you to let me do this. My whole life you've tried to protect me, but I don't need your protection anymore. Just this once, let me protect you. I need to know that you've got a chance to be okay," he begs. "*Please!*"

I stare into his earnest, wide green eyes—eyes that are mirrors of my own. Seafoam green, my father calls it. The color of the ocean right before dusk when sharks and other predators come to feed and the sea is at her most powerful but also her most vulnerable. I know he's trying to be strong and doing what he thinks is best for me, but he doesn't get it. None of them do.

There's no way I'll ever abandon my baby brother. Even if I can't save Stuart, even if the only thing I can do is take care of him until the end, I won't let him die alone.

"I'm not leaving," I repeat, my voice steely and hard. "Don't ask me again."

None of us speak after that.

Lily gets busy shoving her belongings inside her backpack. Her snow-water bottles and whatever warm clothes she can gather go in the bag, but she leaves her beloved textbooks on the floor. It's life or death now, and there isn't enough room to take everything.

While she packs, I help Gavin split up the remaining food inside the cooler and on the floor. It's a lot easier now that Lily has returned the missing rations. We decide that half of it will go to those who are leaving, and the other half will remain for those staying behind.

After Gavin's and Lily's backpacks are packed with food and water, Gavin and I head for the cargo area of the SUV. The two of us go through any remaining supplies and gear, dividing up any warm clothes still left to be used as blankets or bandage dressing. Toiletries are also inventoried and go into packs for first-aid needs.

A car door slams up front, and a moment later Lily appears at the back of the SUV. "Almost ready?" she asks Gavin. She places one gloved hand on the rear bumper and takes in a big gulp of air.

"If we're doing this together, no more secrets. Okay, Zhang?" Gavin asks her in a controlled, measured tone.

She looks down at her snow boots and nods. "Got it."

"If we're out there and you don't agree with something I do, you tell me straight. Understand?"

She nods, tightening the straps on her bulky purple backpack, before turning to me. "Hey, Sam. Can I get a minute?" she asks, giving me a long, meaningful look.

Before I can tell her no, Gavin leaves the two of us alone to say his goodbyes to Britney and Stuart. I stare after him as he steps back inside the SUV. I'm sure he's trying to be respectful and give Lily and me some space, but I wish he'd stayed. For the first time ever, I'm not sure what to say to my best friend.

She clears her throat. "You don't have to be a martyr. Maybe you'll feel guilty if you come with us, I know I do, but you'll still be alive. That's what counts."

"You still don't get it." I slam the rear door shut so hard the sound echoes to the trees and back to us again. "If I abandon Stu, then I might as well die here with him. I'd never forgive myself."

"But I can't lose you both." She sniffles, reaching for my arm. "I hate that you're so mad at me. Tell me how to make this better."

"Just go, Lil. Save yourself. That's what you really care about, right?"

"That's not fair," she says, hurt flashing across her face. "You know that isn't true." She stands there staring at me despondently, as if waiting for something else, some kind of clemency.

I sigh, kicking my boots into the snow drift. It's not easy to rush through my feelings and get past all the hurt and anger I have about what she's done. I won't deny I've played a role in this, too, and maybe I could move past it all and forgive her, if only we had more time.

And yet, time is the one thing we don't have right now.

We're stuck in the most hellish situation anyone can imagine with no idea if any of us will make it out of here alive or see each other again. I don't want her to leave with so much bad blood between us, but that doesn't mean I know how to make it better.

"We're supposed to be best friends, but this isn't how friends are supposed to act, is it?" I ask her sadly.

"I guess not."

"The worst part is, I don't even know whose fault this is," I say. "You did a really shitty thing, but I get why you did it. I can see I wasn't perfect either." I swallow back the lump pushing against my throat. "Maybe . . . maybe we don't deserve each other's friendship."

"Don't say that." She wipes at her runny nose. "Okay, so yeah, this hasn't been our best week ever, but we've had a lot of good times too. You can't just forget all of that, can you?"

Even if we both make it out of this alive, I'm not sure things with us will ever be the same again, but maybe she's right. A few bad acts doesn't have to mean our entire friendship was bad. It doesn't have to mean things can never be good again.

I catch her eye. "Good luck out there, Lil. I'm glad Gavin has you with him," I say, realizing with a shock that I mean it.

"We'll find help and bring them back here," she says.

I nod, tears pricking my eyes.

"Even if I don't . . . make it." She gulps, her throat bobbing up and down. "Gavin will never give up. I think he'd move heaven and earth to save you."

"I know," I say, only wishing I'd seen earlier how much Gavin cares for Stuart. It would have saved us a lot of misunderstandings and fights. "He really loves Stu, doesn't he?"

Her eyes widen with incredulity. "Jesus, Sam! I'm not talking about Gavin and Stu," she says, looking at me like she wants to shake me. "Gavin is in love with you. Can't you see that? And you're in love with him."

I hear footsteps and glance up to find Gavin standing a few yards away from us with Champion's leash gripped in one hand. The dog's tail wags back and forth as soon as he spots me. He pulls at his leash, tugging Gavin toward the back of the SUV.

Lily bends in close to me, lowering her voice so only I can hear. "Tell him how you feel before it's too late," she whispers and wraps an arm around me, giving me a quick hug goodbye before walking away, leaving Gavin and I alone.

Her words jumble around in my head as I stare up into those gorgeous eyes of his. Could she be right? Am I in love with Gavin? *Is he in love with me?*

The fight in middle school. The missed dances. The hospital visits. All those weekends playing video games and watching movies at our house. Was it all only for Stuart?

Or was it for me too?

"I hate this," he says, his face pale, his mouth in a tight line as he studies me.

I take in a deep breath. It's now or never.

"Gav, I need to—"

"Please don't," he says, holding up a hand. "I hate that you aren't coming, but I think I understand why you need to stay." His face is so sad, like he's shouldering the weight of the world. "It's just . . . this can't be the end, can it?"

It's almost more than I can bear. I fall to my knees, burying my face in Champion's warm fur. He licks at my ears, my cheeks, even my chin, so excited for his walk. He has no idea what's happening and what's at stake. How I envy him. What I wouldn't give to believe this was just another fun adventure for us all.

My heart clenches as I take in one last long breath, inhaling his doggy scent, memorizing it. I don't care that his breath is slightly stale and his fur is dirty and musty. The idea of never seeing Champion again devastates me.

"I'll come back for you," Gavin says, kneeling next to me. "I promise." He clutches desperately at my gloved hand, and I warm where we touch, something sparking deep inside me. I know this isn't the right time for a love confession, but maybe there is no right time. Maybe the only time we ever get is right now.

If this is our last chance, I have to tell him how I feel. Except . . . *how do I feel?*

This confused twisty pretzel feeling tightens in my chest, the same one I always get whenever I think about Gavin like this. As much as I want to hate him, even after last year and Mexico, I just can't. He's reckless and infuriating and we never agree on anything, but he's also brave and selfless and has the biggest heart of anyone I've ever met. I can't help but admire and respect him. But how does he feel about me?

I gaze at him, silently willing him to give me any sign he feels the way I do, but he only stares back, those beautiful eyes as unreadable as always. *Why isn't he saying anything?*

"Gav?" I ask.

"Yes?"

A shiver of apprehension ripples through me. If I wait any longer, this moment will pass us by like all the other moments between us. Except this time we may never get another moment. I can't wait for him to speak first. I'm just going to have to do it.

My muscles tighten in anticipation. "Gavin, I—"

"Hey, what's that?" he interrupts, his eyes locking on my neck, widening with surprise. He reaches toward me and lifts the delicate gold chain from underneath my bulky sweatshirt and away from my throat. His mouth drops open as his locket appears. "You still have this?" he asks, his voice filled with surprise.

"Of course, I still have it." I give him a tiny smile. "You thought I'd throw it in the trash because you acted like an asshole after you left?"

He shrugs. "I would've deserved it."

"I would never do that," I say. "Even if you hated me, I would never throw your necklace away."

"Hate you?" he asks, sounding confused.

"I know I must've done something to piss you off. That's why I never heard from you after you left town, right?" I ask. "There's no point lying about it anymore, or trying to spare my feelings, whatever the reason." I'm rambling now, but I can't stop. "Whatever I did to you, I'm sorry."

"Sam, stop—"

"I just want you to know I'd take it all back if I could," I rush on. "Whatever I did to upset you so much."

"I don't hate you, Sams."

I blink. "You don't?"

"There are a lot of reasons I didn't stay in touch," he returns, a bereft tone in his voice. "Some of it was my dad and all his shit. Some of it was Stu and not wanting to complicate things. Some of it was me wanting a clean break and to get away from everything," he explains. "But most of it was me being a stupid idiot." He fixes me with a long, soft look. I'm blown away by the depth of emotion I see in his eyes. It makes me heady. "If we had time, I'd tell you everything. I'd do whatever it took to make you understand just how sorry I am, but we don't. So all you need to know is, yeah, I don't hate you."

It's quiet except for the whirring of the wind when he cups my face and pulls me in close to him. I don't move, I don't even breathe, as his lips touch mine. His mouth is featherlight, sweet at first, as if testing me and unsure of what my reaction will be.

Then I shudder, sinking into his touch, and his fingers weave into my hair. He pulls me closer, closer, closer, until our bodies melt into each other. His hands caress my cheek and the back of my neck, his kiss growing more demanding and desperate. His mouth is hard, insistent, as every inch of him melds against every inch of me.

There was Brandon and before him a boy or two in middle school, but none of those kisses hold a candle to this. Kissing Gavin sets every nerve, every muscle, every bone of mine on fire, and it's the most delicious fire that's ever been lit. We kiss like our lives depend on it, and maybe they do, because this kiss— it's everything.

We break apart moments later. He flashes me a grin—real and true and bigger than any grin I've ever seen from him. "I should've done that years ago," he says simply and without fanfare.

Then he walks away with Champion at his side and Lily trailing after, leaving me with the sickening feeling I'll never see any of them ever again.

CHAPTER 20

1:15 p.m.

You see all these survival stories on TV filled with exciting scenes from moment to moment, but what they don't show you is that for most of the moments there's a whole lot of nothing going on. Nothing except crying and pain.

I find little things to do to keep busy so I don't turn into a puddle of despair, like cleaning and re-bandaging Stuart's wounds. Warming Britney's feet. Checking and replenishing our snow-water supply. Making sure Hunter's window coverings are still holding in place. I even braid and unbraid my greasy, knotted hair.

The hours pass by and it's time to eat again.

After Lily returned what she took and we split up the remains with Gavin and Lily, we're left with one chocolate bar, one string cheese, and a few dozen peanuts. I make Stuart and Britney each eat four squares of chocolate plus six peanuts followed by a full bottle of snow-water. That leaves us with only four pieces of chocolate, the single string cheese, and a handful of peanuts, but it's worth risking what's left of our supply to give them the extra calories they need right now. My own meal, however, consists of just two squares of chocolate.

This time I've learned my lesson. Instead of scarfing my meager portion down right away, I take each piece of chocolate in my mouth one at a time, nibbling slowly to savor each bite of silky richness as it melts on my tongue. When I get to the last piece, I lick the chocolate off my fingers to draw out the meal as long as possible.

My belly gurgles as I chase the food down with water, drinking until I've finished the entire bottle and am bloated and heavy with liquid. The water helps to quell the still-gnawing hunger, which is good because we can afford to be generous with it. The one thing we aren't running out of any time soon is snow to melt.

"Anyone know when the Donners started eating each other?" Stuart asks, yawning next to me. His body trembles with effort as he repositions his head so it's now resting against his arms crossed behind his head.

"Ugh, seriously?" The barely digested chocolate rolls around inside my stomach. "We just ate!"

"I'm just curious. Given our current situation and all." He tries to laugh, and phlegm slips out the sides of his mouth.

"That isn't funny," I say. Not when he looks the way he does, like someone fighting a battle and coming out on the losing end.

"You're right." His voice turns raw. "It's just . . . if you needed to eat my body to live, I'd want you to do it," he says in a rare moment of somberness. "You too, Miller. Even though you're not very nice to me."

"Gee, thanks. I'm sure you'd taste delicious, aside from the pus and all," she says, peering over the back of the middle row, her mouth twitching.

"And another thing." He swallows, turning back to me. "If I die, you can't let Mom dress me in that awful black suit.

You know, the one from Granddad's funeral? No cheesy music either. Or flowers. Or Mom being Mom."

I turn away and grab another water bottle from under the right window console.

"We are not having this conversation," I say, taking a few big swigs to clear the rancid taste from my mouth.

"Promise me."

So much emotion fills my chest, I may explode. I don't want to talk about death, for Christ's sake. Or funerals. Or eating my brother's dead body. If it ever gets to that point, I won't be able to bear it.

"Sam, you have to promise!" He sits up, wincing with the effort, and seizes my hand.

Even though I don't want this morbid agreement with him, I get it. I can't always understand what's in my brother's mind, we're so different in so many ways, but this I can appreciate. It's the same thing I'd want if our positions were switched. I'd want him to live, no matter what.

"Okay." I nod.

"Double pinky promise," he orders, clutching at my littlest finger and we shake on it.

"That's heartwarming and all, but none of you losers better eat me," Britney says.

"Must you always have something to say?" I ask, and blow my congested nose into one of Stuart's old T-shirts until I'm certain some of my brain comes out my nostrils. My phlegm is thick and yellow—almost green—which means my immune cells are starting to work on something in my body. My cold, or whatever is wrong with me, is getting worse.

"I just don't want there to be any confusion if I croak first." Britney smiles innocently. "I want an open casket so everyone can see how amazing I look."

"But you'll be dead? What does it matter?" Stuart asks.

"It always matters, Stu Poo."

"Awesome conversation. Just fabulous," I say. Are we really sitting around listening to each other's last wishes about our funerals? Is this it? Is this all there's left to do?

"It's all so unfair." Britney grunts, readjusting herself in the middle row as she tries to get more comfortable. She rearranges the sweatshirts I've used to wrap around her frostbitten feet and kneads at her toes like I taught her. "I was gonna be a famous bikini designer. Like, super high-end, cover of *Sports Illustrated* stuff."

"Don't be so dramatic. You still will," I say and then add. "God help us all."

"I love bikinis!" Stuart perks up.

"Of course you do, you little pervert," she says, and the ends of her mouth curve into a small smile. I can't help but think again how strange it is to see her lips this sickly bluish-white hue instead of the glossy pink or berry-red shades I've grown accustomed to.

"I wanted to make video games. Gnarly ones too," Stuart says. "I would've been more famous than even Shigeru Miyamoto."

"Who?" Britney asks.

"You know, *Mario Bros. The Legend of Zelda. Star Fox.* He's my hero," he explains. "But I guess that won't happen now."

My jaw tightens. "Can we stop talking like this? No one's dying."

"What about you? What did you want to do?" Britney asks, ignoring my request.

"I'm *going* to be a veterinarian. Future tense," I say and then heat prickles along my cheeks. "Although it seems like everything I've done this week has turned out wrong."

"I think you'd be a great vet, Sammy," she says.

"Seriously?" I ask, taken aback. "'Cause I thought before you said—"

She waves a hand. "I don't know why I say that stuff sometimes. Truth is, it's pretty amazing how you helped with Zhang's concussion. And Stu's ankle."

"Wow. That's nice of you to—"

"Whatever." She grins and sinks into the middle row again. "Don't make a big deal of it."

I stare at the back of her seat, smiling as I digest her words. It occurs to me that Hunter isn't the only one I may have misjudged.

Britney would not talk sweet to me. Or coddle. Or blow smoke up my ass. She wouldn't do read-alongs of our favorite author's books, or Friday night movie marathons, or pull all-nighters studying for AP exams, or do any of those things I had done with Lily. And yet, there was so much good in Britney once you knew where to look.

She told the truth—brutal as it was. She was smart too. And kind, though it was in unexpected ways. She would watch over a girl and a boy she didn't really like while the boy she loved built a fire with everyone else. She would let an expensive sweater get stained with another person's blood. She'd give her clothes away—literally right off her back. She'd even travel to another country to build houses for people she didn't know simply because she could, and they needed the help.

All this time, I've disliked her solely because I'd made up in my head this image of who I thought she was. I'd believed Britney was the mean girl, but it turns out the mean girl was me.

"You're not so bad yourself, Britney Miller," I say to the back of her head.

"Yeah, I'm a regular Mother Teresa," she says, her peals of laughter quickly turning to high-pitched, whistle-like wheezes. I pass my water over the seats, watching as she takes small, delicate sips from the bottle.

Outside, the storm starts up again.

The wind screams so loudly I worry one of the nearby trees will topple the car any second. The now-familiar cloud of white nothingness surrounds us until I can't see anything out the windows anymore. Hail falls, slamming the car roof like a boxer going to work on his opponent in those fights Gavin would make Stu and my dad watch on Saturday nights.

BANG. BANG. BANG.

I don't want to think about it, but if Gavin and Lily aren't somewhere safe and sheltered by now, chances are that something awful is happening to them.

"How about a story, Stu Poo?" Britney asks suddenly.

"Really?" He looks hesitant as if waiting for the punch line.

"It's probably all the frostbite going straight to my brain, but yeah, a story sounds nice. I need to focus on something happy right now."

"I can handle that." He laughs and takes a quick moment to collect his thoughts. "Okay, our story takes place at the circus," he begins. "Our heroine, Billie, grew up there. They called her The Living Rapunzel because she had long blond hair that went down to the floor. Billie was the top act at the circus even though all she did was stand around and look pretty."

Britney coughs noisily.

"Just trust me," he says and continues. "So as I was saying, Rapunzel Billie was used to being the top dog until one day a new act arrived—The Razzle Dazzle Kids. The Razzle Dazzle Kids were a brother-sister act named Scottie and Stefanie. Before long, they became the most popular act in the circus, and not only because they were siblings, which is pretty awesome, but because they could shoot fire from their fingertips."

Britney huffs. "I think beautiful blond hair is better."

"You would," I say, laughing.

"Naturally, Billie hated Scottie and Stefanie," Stuart goes on. "She tried to sabotage them any chance she got. One time, she stole all the candles so there was no light for their show. When that didn't work, she filled their tent with rats, hoping Scottie would get too scared to perform, but Stefanie found the rats first and made them into her pets."

I grin. "I do like my rodents."

"Still can't believe Mom let you keep Mr. Whiskers," Stuart says, making a face beside me. "He was disgusting."

"You mean adorable," I correct, thinking of my first and only pet.

I still miss Mr. Whiskers. My dad got me the albino rat for my sixth birthday. My mother almost had a heart attack but eventually decided it was better than the dog I'd begged for. At least Mr. Whiskers was confined to a cage and couldn't pee on her designer furniture. Mr. Whiskers passed away freshmen year, and my parents said no more pets. That's another reason I spent so much time volunteering at the shelter, playing with the animals.

"One day, a tornado blew through the circus," Stuart says. "The tornado sucked Billie, Scottie, and Stefanie into its funnel and carried them far, far away, dropping them off only when they reached the top of the highest mountain in town, miles from the circus.

"At first, all they did was fight about how to get home. Scottie and Stefanie wanted to use their fire fingers to escape. Billie thought her blond hair was the answer. But none of it worked, and they each blamed the other for being trapped." He stops his story and looks at Britney. "What's your position on the squad? Flyer, right?"

"That's right!" She puffs up in her seat. "I'm the only one good enough to do a kick double full basket."

"That's what I thought." He grins. "So what Scottie and

Stefanie didn't know was that Billie had a secret. Turns out, Billie was an even bigger freak than they were. Beneath all that glorious blond hair, Billie was hiding wings."

"Wait—like bird wings?" Britney asks.

Stuart nods.

"Gross!"

"Funny, that's what Billie thought too," he says, laughing. "That's why she grew out her hair—to hide them. Except now, stranded on a mountain, Billie wondered if they might be useful. What if she could use her wings to fly them all to safety?

"That's where Scottie and Stefanie's powers came in. After Billie confessed her secret, the siblings used their fire fingers to burn away her hair so her wings could work, and Billie flew the three of them right off the mountain. They passed over hills and lakes until they found a house with a huge chimney. Billie swooped the three of them inside, where they used a phone to call the circus ringleader for rescue.

"To this day, the three of them are still friends. Each night, they perform together in a flying fire show that's the most successful one in all of circus history." He smiles widely. "And, of course, they lived happily ever after."

Britney gives my brother a nod of approval. "Wow. That was actually pretty good. I'm shocked."

"Um, thanks?"

"Billie was cool." She sounds thoughtful. "Even the Razzle Dazzle Kids were okay, I suppose. Almost makes me wish I had a brother."

I wink at Stuart. "I guess it can be alright sometimes."

She tilts her head to the side, studying us. Envy darts across her face.

"I've got two older sisters, but we don't get along," she explains. "Chels is in New York modeling, and Taylor moved to Hollywood to act. They're gonna be the next big thing. At least, that's what my mom says." She looks away, picking lint off her jacket sleeve. "Wanna know what they gave me before they took off? A diet book and a lesson on how to make myself throw up."

I swallow uncomfortably.

"That's really shitty," Stuart says.

"That's just how they are, I guess. Besides, you can't fly in a basket toss if you're fat." She shrugs. "Honestly, they probably did me a favor."

"You know that isn't true, Britney," I say.

"You wouldn't understand. You don't hang with the same crowd I do. It's impossible to keep up." She smiles sadly. "Anyway, you're lucky you two have each other, that's all."

Stuart and I share a grin, and my heart pulls in my chest. I can't help but compare Britney's sisters' "gift" to the gorgeous bouquet Stuart sent me freshman year so I wouldn't be a complete loser on Valentine's Day.

I *am* lucky. Stuart and I may have our differences, but we're always there for each other when it counts.

"You guys aren't as awful as I thought." Britney yawns loudly. "I shouldn't have said all that mean stuff before. Like all the Stu Poo jokes. Truth is, I kinda lied the other night. I totally peed my cheer spankies one time. It wasn't my fault or anything. Coach made me drink way too much Gatorade. I'm just saying gross stuff happens to everybody."

"It wasn't Stu's fault," I say. "What happened was—"

"Shut up, Sam," he hisses at me. "Before I really do die—*of embarrassment*."

"It was after his back surgery," I continue, ignoring him. "The doctors had him on all these different drugs for the pain. That's why he had the accident."

"I get it," she says, sounding tired. "But if you guys ever tell anyone what I told you, you're dead, understand?"

"Deal." I grin. "And I'm sorry too. For all the rude things I said to you."

Her breathing turns shallow, worrying me. I realize somewhere along the way I've started to like and care about Britney Miller.

"Hey, I have an idea," she says. "I may not have wings, but I've got something that'll make us feel better. Sam, would you be a doll and grab my toiletry bag from the back?"

I groan. "You're kidding, right? It's freezing outside."

I may not hate her anymore, but I'm not going back out there for anyone.

She lifts a brow. "I may be dying, like, actually *dying*. Are you really going to deny me my last wish?"

Well . . . it's kind of hard to refuse when she puts it that way.

A few moments later, I drop the giant duffel on the floor next to her in the middle seat. I shiver, rubbing at my aching biceps. The bag must weigh thirty pounds. How can one person have so much makeup?

She yanks the zipper open. Instead of pounds of beauty products like I'm expecting, she pulls out an honest-to-god miniature Christmas tree packed with ornaments and strings of garland and everything. She flicks a switch on the back of it, and lights flash as the branches dance to the sounds of joyous holiday music.

"Merry Christmas Eve!" she shouts, clapping her hands to the beat of "Holly Jolly Christmas."

"Holy shit!" Stuart's mouth hangs open. "That's awesome!"

"Thanks." A radiant smile bursts across her face. "I was going to surprise the girls by decorating our cabin for the holidays."

She digs further into her bag and more trinkets appear. A hideous-looking elf cap that she shoves onto Stuart's head. An ugly red-and-green Christmas scarf she wraps around my neck. Handfuls of colorful ornaments emerge, and she forces me to scramble into the middle row and help her arrange them around the seats. She even has reindeer stuffed animals that she makes me place on the dashboard so we can all see them.

"We can't be home for Christmas Eve tonight, but this is almost as good, don't you agree?" she asks, putting on a ridiculous hot-pink Santa Claus hat.

Tears wet the corners of my eyes. I'd almost forgotten tonight was Christmas Eve.

For the first time in my life, I'm not spending the holiday at home with my family curled around a crackling fire watching Christmas movies. Instead, I'm stuck here in this freezing death trap of a car while my brother fights for his life. Britney's holiday junk and knickknacks, well-meaning as they are, isn't enough—it's not even in the ballpark of enough—to cheer me up.

"Decorations aren't what Christmas is about," I say, looking away so they can't see I'm about to cry.

"Maybe not, but everything doesn't have to be so black and white, Sammy," she says. "Christmas is about Jesus, and Jesus is about joy. Maybe these things are silly and plastic, but they're symbols of His love for us."

She opens the bag one more time and pulls out a tree topper. It's an exquisite-looking star with ornate gold wire points and sparkly ribbons. She holds it high above her head, her eyes lighting up as she glances at it lovingly. It looks handmade and very old.

"I saved the best for last," she says. "This is the star of Bethlehem. It's the light that guides us to Jesus. Obviously, it's not the actual star—it was my grandmother's—but it's a symbol of hope. Maybe it'll bring us good luck, huh?"

"It's really pretty," Stuart says, giving her a sweet smile.

I have a flash of inspiration and lean back over the center console. "May I?" I ask, reaching for the star and placing it front and center on the dashboard between the three reindeer.

She nods her approval at me, her gaze unwavering as she stares at the star.

"Do you feel it? God is all around us tonight." Her teeth chatter as she shivers, but she doesn't turn away, not even as the snow pounds on the roof again and the darkness closes in. "I just know everything's going to be okay."

As she begins to pray out loud, I return to my seat next to Stuart. My mind wanders to thoughts of my parents. Even though tonight is Christmas Eve, they won't be celebrating this year like usual. I see them in my head, wide-awake in that enormous kitchen of ours.

My mother is probably sitting at our white marble round table, the outrageously extravagant one she had my dad import from Italy. I'm sure she is refusing food or drink, while my dad likely sips on his coffee. Extra hot. No sugar. That's the way I like mine too. Though it feels like I've been gone for ages, the milk in his coffee must be the same milk carton I used in my breakfast cereal on Friday.

Has it only been five nights since I was home?

It seems like a lifetime ago.

As I think of my dad, I feel an urgent—almost violent— longing to be with him. Loving and pragmatic. He always remains so stoic and strong, no matter the circumstance. We're a lot alike in that way. I wish I could hug him now and have that strength seep into my bones.

Stuart groans next to me and whimpers out loud as he drifts asleep. I whisper words of comfort in his ear that seem to soothe him but do nothing to quell the suffocating sensation that tightens my own ribs. Drawing him in closer like a shield against all my fear, my love for my brother swells in my chest and drives everything else away. I remind myself it isn't over yet. Stuart's here with me. He's alive.

We just have to make it through the night.

CHAPTER 21

Day 6 • December 25, Christmas • 2:30 a.m.

A sharp scratching noise jolts me awake. Something is grating against the steel metal of the SUV, as if something—or someone—is on the car roof and trying to get inside. Shivers skitter down my spine, but I tell myself this is impossible. There's nothing out here but the three of us and miles and miles of wilderness. We're all alone.

I slink back into my seat and shut my eyes again, trying my best to relax. Except the sound continues.

Louder. Shriller. More desperate.

Hunter's scary story from days ago flashes in my mind, and I picture an ax murderer standing on top of our car. The killer's masked face—a near replica of the Michael Myers poster over Stuart's bed—gets closer, until he's near enough to pry open the car door in front of me. Moonlight glints off the sharp edge of his knife, blood from his last victim dripping onto the snow below us.

My breathing goes rapid and shallow. After wondering for so long what will happen to us, now I know. We're about to be murdered, hacked into a thousand little pieces, to never be seen or heard of again. A voice inside my head screams: *This is it! This is the end!*

I have to shake myself to banish the ghastly thoughts from my head.

Get a grip, Sam, I order, and smile in the dark, thin and self-mocking. The reality we're dealing with is far scarier than whatever stupid horror story my brain can conjure. What I need to do is stop freaking myself out and go outside to investigate the actual source of the strange noises.

And yet, even though I know it's ridiculous, the image of slasher killer Michael Myers ready to butcher me won't leave me. I'll go check things out alright, but I'm not going alone.

The inside of my gloves are damp with sweat as I lean across the seat and grab Stuart's shoulder, turning him over. His sleeping face comes into view, and I immediately change my mind. He looks so peaceful after a night of crying and moaning, I don't have the heart to wake him.

I call out softly to Britney instead, hoping she'll brave the outdoors with me. I give it a few moments, but there's no answer from the lumpy pile of makeshift clothing-blankets in the middle seat, not even as I whisper her name louder and louder.

Great. I guess I'm on my own.

As I sit up, a familiar dull ache runs through my body, but I'm so used to the throbbing pain of cramped muscles from sleeping awkwardly in the SUV that it only half registers. I sneeze a few times and blow my nose before sliding out from underneath my brother's legs and pulling on the seat lever to get into the middle row. Before exiting, I give one last hopeful glance in Britney's direction in case she's now awake, and I freeze. Up close, I can see there isn't anyone under that big mound of clothes. The bench where Britney should be sleeping is empty.

I don't understand.

Britney doesn't seem like the type to go outside alone in the middle of the night. At least, not without telling me first. So then where is she? She didn't just disappear into thin air. If she's not inside the car, that only leaves one other explanation. Strange as it seems, Britney must have gone outside alone—but why?

It seems I now have two missions: find Britney and confirm Michael Myers isn't out there.

Bracing myself for an arctic chill, I step outside and am surprised to find it's nowhere near as bad as it's been the past few nights. It's not even snowing anymore. We must've reached a lull in the storms.

A lightness fills my chest. While I don't want to get my hopes up too much, this has to be good news for Gavin and Lily. I pray they've somehow found shelter or help, but if that isn't the case, tonight seems at least survivable, even if they're making camp somewhere in the wilderness. Maybe we have a chance to get out of this alive, after all.

My ears prick as I hear soft moaning beneath the light whirring of the wind. I cup my hands over my nose and blow air into it, warming myself as I look from left to right. The low, hollow sound differs from the clawing noise I heard earlier inside the car. It almost seems human.

I strain, trying to make out where it's coming from. It sounds like the front of the SUV. Driver's side.

As soon as I walk around, Britney comes into view lying under the body of the car by the front tire. She's slumped up against the rubber wheel, wearing only a pale pink bralette and pants. Her fuzzy white socks and ridiculous fur boots lie next to her, discarded on the ground at her bare feet. The rest of her clothing, her sweater, jacket, gloves, scarf—even her pink Santa hat—all hang from a nearby tree.

My eyes widen with horror as I see for the first time how skinny she is. Her collarbone juts out from her chest and her ribs protrude from a skeletal-thin abdomen. From behind, I can see every single vertebrae of her spine as it pokes through the skin of her back. Her half-naked body is already turning purple, like some rare hypercolor praying mantis.

The only sign she's still alive is the sad keening and occasional shiver that rocks her body as her hands claw against the SUV's tires, as if she's trying to get the trapped car loose. Every one of her once-perfectly manicured nails are broken and cracked, bits of bright red blood dripping down, leaving scarlet trails in the snow.

"Britney?" I whisper, my voice cracking as I inch closer. "Can you hear me?"

Even as I come up behind her, she doesn't look up or give any sign she's aware I'm here. She just keeps digging at the snow and tire.

"Oh, Britney. What have you done?" I ask, dropping next to her and wrapping my arms around her freezing body.

"Home," she says, her voice trembling. "We have to get home."

"Okay." I nod, tears pricking my eyes. "I'll take you home."

I pry her away from the steel and she collapses into my arms. With my hands locked underneath her armpits, I drag her backward and throw the car door open. My breath goes fast and heavy as I use all my energy to haul her back inside the SUV. Stuart wakes right as I've gotten her into the middle row.

"What's going on?" His lips tremble as he takes in Britney's ragged appearance. "Where are her clothes? Who did that to her?"

"She did it to herself."

"*What?* Why the hell would she do that?"

"Because she's hypothermic," I explain. "She doesn't know what she's doing."

A low moaning sound escapes Britney's lips. She won't stop shivering, even as I get in beside her and begin to clothe her. I start with her core, taking the sweaters she was using earlier as blankets and slowly wrapping them around her stomach like a mummy. If I warm her extremities too soon, it will drive the cold blood straight into her heart and could cause shock.

After she's covered up, I check her vitals with a shaking hand. Her skin is like a block of ice as I place two fingers against her vein. Her pulse is faint and sluggish, almost nonexistent.

"You have to help her!" Stuart cries.

I cradle Britney's stiff body in my arms to add my body heat to hers. "Can't you see I'm trying!"

"*Try harder!*"

"I'm doing the best I can!"

Why can't Stuart see this is far beyond my ability? I don't have access to any of the life-saving supplies they'd have at a hospital. No hot chemical packs or moist oxygen. I don't even have anything warm for her to drink.

"Please—home?" she asks, looking up at me with glazed, unfocused eyes. The Britney Miller of glossy blond hair and perfectly made-up face is gone, replaced by this desperate creature.

"It's okay, Britney. You'll be home soon." I rock her in my arms, watching helplessly as her tremors grow worse.

Her eyes close, and her breathing slows so much it's like she isn't even breathing at all. She stills then, falling into a deep slumber. I lay my head on her chest, listening for any kind of heartbeat. It's there, but barely.

Oh, God. Why is this happening?

"Do something, Sam!" Tears stream down Stuart's ashen face, his green eyes swimming with emotion. "Save her!"

It's useless, but I try anyway.

I lay Britney flat on the seat and kneel next to her, doing my best to remember the directions they gave us in CPR training. My hands tremble so badly I have trouble getting them centered over her upper body. Using my full body weight, I push the heel of my hand against her chest and compress a few inches before tilting her head back and pinching her nose shut. Just like they taught me, I cover her mouth with mine and breathe into her for what seems like forever.

"Come on, Britney!" Stuart screams, his voice going hoarse. "Don't do this!"

Even though I do everything by the book, it doesn't matter. All the studying, all the practicing in class, none of it makes any difference. There is no fanfare or hysterics as she drifts away. Just a soft, horrible blue that creeps into her face as rigor mortis sets in, stealing her last breath. Britney was the kind of girl who would've wanted to go out all fireworks and spitfire, but the cold robs her of this too.

My throat constricts and tears escape, dripping onto that repulsive fur jacket of hers. I shake with great heaving sobs until I'm crying so hard I can't breathe. Britney was so beautiful and bitchy and funny and bossy and full of life, and all of that energy can't just disappear into the ether. She can't now be this empty nothing shell in front of us, can she? This can't be the end for her, can it?

Unable to look at Britney any longer, I cover her with extra clothes, burying her body from view. Then I hide her face. I can't bear to see what she's become.

"Wait," Stuart says, grabbing my shoulder. "Grab her star of Bethlehem."

"What? Why?"

"Just do it!"

I blink, taken aback by the intensity in his voice. It seems like such a silly thing for him to be concerned about. Who cares about stupid ornaments right now? But I'm too upset to argue with him, so I lean forward and reach between the center console to snatch the star off the dashboard.

"Here," I say, shoving it at him.

"It's not for me." He shakes his head, sniffling. "It's for her."

"Britney's dead! She doesn't need a god damn star!"

"But she said this leads you to Jesus."

"Look around, Stu! Take a good hard look at where we are! *Hunter and Britney are dead!*" Rage runs through my veins. "There's no Jesus here, okay? It's time you get that through your thick skull!"

A long beat goes by before he speaks again.

"It doesn't matter if you believe," he says. "Even if you think it's all bullshit, Britney didn't. And I don't either."

I watch as Stuart places the beautiful gold star above Britney's heart and then gathers up armfuls of her Christmas ornaments from the seats. Traditional glass ones in beautiful shades of gold. Silver ones with sparkles and crystals wrapped from end to end. Colorful red and green spheres decorated with polka dots and zigzag patterns. Tenderly, he places them over her body, one at a time, covering her. He doesn't stop until she's shielded from head to toe, surrounded in the things she loved.

My fury dulls as understanding dawns on me.

We can't save Britney or bring her back to life, but we can honor her memory the way she would have wanted. This is how we keep her spirit alive. Maybe death gets to take part of us when we die, but it doesn't get to take it all.

CHAPTER 22

7:15 a.m.

I wake to a sight so glorious I forget where I am for a moment. The sun rises in the east and juts out over the top of the peaks, basking the white mountainside in glorious reds and oranges and pinks. It's like the most beautiful watercolor painting I've ever seen. Warmth from the rays beats through the windows and makes my face and hands tingle. The heat does such cheerful things to my brain, it's as if the last few days never happened.

But then Stuart wakes next to me, clutching at his ankle, moaning in agony, and reality comes crashing back down. Even the most magnificent sunrise in the universe can't change the fact that my brother is battling for his life and two of our friends have already lost theirs.

A tear slides down my cheek as a terrible thought rears its ugly head.

What if this is it? What if this is the end for us?

It would be so easy to go down this spiral of despair, but I force myself to brush away the salty wetness with my gloved hand and steel my shoulders. No matter how bad things are,

I won't give in to desolation. If Mother Nature wants my brother, she'll have to pry him from my cold, dead hands first.

Stifling a groan, I force myself up and over the seats to get to the cooler in the front passenger seat. Pins and needles prickle throughout my muscles and joints, and my leg brushes up against something hard buried beneath the pile of Christmas ornaments—some body part. An arm? A leg?

A sick feeling tickles the back of my throat with the realization I'm touching a dead person. No—not just any dead person. *Britney.* The knowledge that we're now sharing this small space with her corpse is almost more than I can take.

I fight against the sudden and intense urge to throw open the door and shove her lifeless body outside, except that seems even worse somehow. Britney isn't a piece of trash to discard and leave by the wayside. We'll just have to wait unless things get worse. If she starts to . . . to smell or something. My stomach roils at the idea, but I shove the rising nausea down. We'll deal with it later if it comes to that.

"Stu? Are you up?" I ask, returning to the back row with our last string cheese tucked inside my glove. Besides the handful of peanuts remaining, this is all we've got left. I nudge his shoulder and his eyes flutter open. "Here, eat this."

"I can't," he says. "Not with Britney's dead body one row in front of us."

"That's exactly why you should eat. Maybe if Britney had eaten more, she'd still be alive."

"Sam!" He gasps. "I can't believe you just said that."

Part of me hates myself for putting this on Britney, but I can't sugarcoat things for him. Britney could've done more to save herself, and so can Stuart. Now isn't the time for tact. We have to survive, even if I have to shove food down his throat.

"*Eat!*" I order, ripping the cheese in half and thrusting it at him.

He tries to whack my hand away and misses, catching only air.

"I said I don't want it."

"I'm not doing this with you. Just eat the damn cheese."

"No!"

"Jesus Christ." I clench my teeth, holding back a scream of frustration. "Why do you always have to be such a baby?"

"Screw you!" he yells, his face turning red and puffy. "Stop telling me what to do!"

For a moment I only stare in shock, reeling from his outburst. I've never seen him this mad at me before. Doesn't he know I'm only trying to help?

I hate that he's upset with me, but then something red-hot flares inside my chest and my entire body burns with my own fury. So what if Stuart is angry? I'm angry too. I'm angry at God for putting us in this hellhole. I'm angry at Gavin and Lily for leaving me all alone and at Hunter and Britney for making me care about them and then dying on me. But most of all, I'm angry at my stupid, selfish, ungrateful little brother.

"How dare you act like this!" I shout at him. "After everything I've done for you!"

"*Me?*" His eyebrows fly up. "This has nothing to do with me."

I laugh. The sound is bitter and hollow in my ears.

"Of course, it does. It's always about *you*," I say. "Mom and Dad are constantly coddling you—treating you special. Everything we do is planned around you and how you feel. *Is Stuart well enough to go? Let's stay at home because Stuart can't do that.*"

"That's not fair." He draws in a pained breath. "You're the only one who still treats me like an invalid, but I'm fine, Sam. I've been fine for a long time, and I don't need your pity. I know you resent me—"

"I don't resent you! You don't know what you're talking about."

"Yes, you do! Just admit it already!"

I look down at the SUV's floor. "Shut up, Stu."

"Admit it!"

I can't tell if it's the exhaustion or the fear or both, but something deep inside me cracks, twisting and splitting wide open.

"Alright, I do! I do resent you!" I scream. "*Sometimes I wish you'd never been born!*"

And there it is. Stranded in the middle of nowhere, with nothing around but wilderness and death, my most treacherous secret slithers out from the darkest corner of my heart. I've never realized until this very moment how I really feel.

Stuart has always been my mother's favorite. Her entire world revolves around him—her sweet delicate son. So many sacrifices were made in the name of Stuart.

From the little things like eating whatever Stuart wanted for dinner because he had to keep his strength up, even if I hated the food, to the big things like my parents missing my middle school graduation because Stuart was in the hospital or having to skip homecoming because Stuart couldn't go. Maybe he never asked any of us to do those things for him, but he let us. He allowed it to happen, even when he must have known how much it hurt me.

"Finally!" He crosses his arms over his chest, looking almost pleased with himself. "Now was that so hard?"

That's it. That's all he says.

"Did you even hear me?" I ask, panting in great, rattling gulps. It's like someone has shredded my insides, my guts hanging on the outside for all the world to see. "Did you hear what I just said?"

"I may be sick, but I'm not deaf."

I see pain and sorrow in his eyes but no condemnation.

"But then how . . . how are you still talking to me?"

"C'mon, Sam. This isn't news to me. I've just been waiting for you to admit it to yourself," he says. "Ever since we were little, you always looked after me. You always put me first. And when my back got worse, it's like you decided it was your job, no—*your mission*—to protect me, but I know what you missed out on because of me. I know what it cost you. And I know, even though you never said it out loud, that sometimes you must've hated me for it."

I shake so hard the tears spill from my eyes and run down my cheeks.

"I'm so sorry, Stu," I whisper.

His arms go around my shoulders. They're as skinny as craft pipe cleaners, and yet I've never felt so warm and comforted by anything in my life. Not even my dad's hugs are this good, and his hugs are the best.

"That's all over now. Do you understand?" he asks as I lean against him, my body quaking with sobs. "You can't save me. No matter how hard you try, you can't protect me. If I die, I die, and it'll suck, but that'll be on me and maybe on God, but not on you. None of this is on you. Got it?"

"I'm so afraid something bad will happen to you," I say, my voice cracking. "I can't lose you."

He grabs me by the shoulder, his hand surprisingly strong. "I'm your brother. That's forever. You're not going to lose me," he says, and his words envelop me like a shield of protection. "You know you can't go on like this, right?"

I shake my head. "I don't know how to stop."

"I can help, if you let me."

The sun shines on his face through the uncovered windows of the car. His eyes are soft, but there is steel in there too. My heart fills as I look at him in wonder. I'm blown away by how clear and confident he looks. He's strong. So much stronger than I realized. I'm not sure how I missed it before, but Stuart's not a little kid anymore. He doesn't need me to protect him. Maybe he never did. All this time, maybe I'm the one who needed him.

In that instant, I realize a truth so simple I can't believe I never saw it before. Fear is nothing but a thief.

I've lost so much time worrying over my brother. So many moments that should've been carefree were instead filled with anxiety. So much energy wasted feeling guilty for everything I could do that Stuart couldn't and then resenting him when I decided not to do those things either so he wouldn't get hurt or be alone. Precious time was lost, and I can never get it back.

"We'll make it through this, Sam. You just have to trust me," he says.

"I do."

Saying it out loud works some kind of magic on me, like an oath. I'm no longer my brother's keeper. We're equals now. We're the last ones left, Stuart and I. If we're going to survive, we have to do it together.

"It's time to go. We can't stay here any longer," he says, squinting at the sun as it continues to rise high in the morning sky.

It's a force of habit as I open my mouth to disagree. I don't want to go anywhere. As long as we stay here, in this car, we're both still alive. The moment we step outside, anything can happen. Except I've just promised things will be different. I guess I have to start somewhere.

"What are you suggesting?" I ask.

"We head back to the gas station. If we found that, there are other things nearby. We didn't go far enough last time, but I know there's something else that way," he says. "I can feel it."

I give him a flat stare. "While I appreciate your *feelings*, that's hardly scientific proof. Why don't we give it one more day to see if anyone finds us here?"

"You know why." He looks down grimly at his leg. "We have to go now, after we've rested and still have enough food and water to hike. While I can still move. While I'm still . . . me."

I exhale a long, slow breath. As much as I want to change—to trust him—it's not easy for someone like me who is used to being in control.

"Stu, you can hardly move," I argue. "You sleep half the day and vomit the other half. I don't see how this can work."

"This is the first day we've seen the sun. It's a sign. We have to listen."

"I don't believe in signs."

"Fine," he says, and holds out his hand. "Give me the damn cheese."

I blink. "What?"

"You want me to eat, right? I'll do whatever you want, but we gotta go."

"One string cheese isn't going to suddenly heal your ankle," I say.

"Why not?" he asks. "People do superhuman shit all the time. Like moms that lift cars to save their kids. Or that James Franco movie—the one where he cuts off his arm to survive. If they can do it, why not me?"

Here he goes again with that superhero bullshit.

"Because this isn't a movie. It's real life," I say.

He smiles. "It's all one big movie, Sam, and ours is getting a happy ending."

"But—"

"Look, if we stay here, we're both dead. You know that as well as I do." He gives me a severe look. "I won't be the reason you die. We're done with that, right?"

Slowly, I nod my agreement. Yes. I think we are.

Stuart eats half the cheese while I pack the other half into my backpack along with our last few peanuts. He isn't strong enough to carry anything, so I fill my pack with supplies and as much water as I can handle. Grunting, I secure the straps around my shoulders and waist. It's heavier than I'd like. Not only must I bear the burden of the bag on our hike, but I'll also have to shoulder the bulk of Stuart's weight.

As soon as we step out of the car, Stuart's breathing turns rough and raw simply from the effort of putting pressure on his smashed ankle. Though he does his best to hide it, I can tell he's already in pain.

In a last-minute flash of inspiration, I leave him propped up against the side of the SUV and run toward the forest, spying what I'm looking for. Hanging from one of the smaller trees is a branch about two inches in diameter that looks as long as Stuart's armpit. I snap it off and hand it to him to use as a walking stick.

We start down the long road ahead, and a lump forms in my throat as I get a premonition of finality. We won't be spending another night in these mountains, of this I'm sure. But whether we'll be dead or alive, I can't say.

Despite the uncertainty, it feels good to be leaving the car behind. To be doing something—anything—and not just waiting around for something to be done to us.

I glance back one last time at the broken and discarded SUV and make a silent promise to Britney. If we have the chance, we'll come back for her. She deserves the proper burial she asked for.

"What do we do if we don't find anything by nightfall?" I ask Stuart.

His arm drapes across my shoulder as he hobbles along next to me. "We'll find something."

"Stuart, be real." I'm trying, I really am, but my new trust only goes so far. "We need to prepare for the worst possible situation."

He scratches his head, looking thoughtful. "Alright, if that happens, we dig holes in the snow and hide in them," he says. "I saw that in a horror movie once. Seemed to work."

"Seriously?"

I can't believe our lives now depend on one of Stuart's ridiculous slasher flicks.

"This will work, Sam," he says with an encouraging smile. "You just have to have a little faith."

CHAPTER 23

I t's painfully slow work juggling my brother, my backpack, and my own body down the road ahead. It's been snowing for so many days that deep drifts cover the concrete, almost up to our knees. With each step we take, we have to lift our legs high enough to make sure we clear our boots. This is not easy under normal circumstances, but with Stuart's screwed up ankle it takes twice as long to move one measly step forward.

My body heaves with exertion and soon I'm huffing and puffing in big, deep breaths of mountain air. The crisp wafts of pine and oak and other delicious scents are almost enough to block out the sickly odor of gangrene and vomit, but I can still sense it somewhere, lurking right below the surface. It seeps out from Stuart's splint and skin, wafting around us like an invisible cloud.

By the time we make it to the old gas station, it feels as if days—not hours—have passed. The place looks the same as the last time we saw it. Still no sign of people, and still spooky as hell. Out of the corner of my eye, I spot the window Gavin broke. Glass shards lie beneath it, right where we left them.

My eyes burn and I wipe the wetness away with the back of my glove. It's hard to believe it was only days ago that we were here. My brother was healthy. Lily was about to wake up from her coma—not lost, wandering around somewhere with Gavin in these god-awful mountains. Hunter and Britney were still alive and waiting for us back at the car. We were all safe with no idea how terrible things would soon become.

Stuart and I continue past the gas station, walking along in silence, neither of us looking at the other. I wonder if my brother is lost in the same depressing thoughts I am, but now is not the time to give up. We keep pushing onward.

After the sun climbs to the dead center of the sky and we've somehow made it another mile or so down the road, Stuart yanks my arm so hard it jars in the socket. "Look!" he cries, steering me over to the edge of the road where pavement falls off into cliffside. "Do you see that?"

I blink, mesmerized by the sight.

A crystal-blue lake lies below us, stretching on for what seems like endless miles. Light reflects off the water, twinkling and glittering all around us. It's so stunning it pierces through my exhaustion, and a sweet pang bursts in my heart—a sense of gratitude—to witness something so spectacular.

"Wow. It's beautiful." This must be what heaven looks like. If heaven exists, that is.

"No, not the lake!" His voice rises with excitement. "*The smoke!* Don't you see it?"

"Huh?" I lift a hand to block out the sun's glare and squint past the surface of the water. Over the tops of the trees surrounding the lake's edge, something dark and gray is swirling. "Oh—that? It looks like more storm clouds to me."

"It's not clouds," he snaps. "There's something here, like I told you. Campers, maybe? Aren't they usually by water?"

"I don't—"

"Hello?" He cups his hands around his mouth and screams at the top of his lungs. "*Is anybody down there?*"

I put a hand on his shoulder. "Stu—"

"We're too high." He shakes me off impatiently. "We gotta get down there."

I step back, my jaw going slack. "You can't be serious. That lake must be hundreds of yards below us."

"You got a better idea?"

"Uh, yeah. Any idea is better than that one."

"Okay, then what do you suggest?" He scowls in my direction. "Should we keep stumbling down this empty road, hoping someone miraculously finds us before we freeze to death?"

My stomach clenches as I lean down and glance over the side, inspecting the terrain. Sun blazes down on the tree-covered slopes lining the way to the lake and reveals brutal ridges and narrow peaks. There's no way to tell if the snowy path below is stable and could hold our weight. Even if it was safe to walk on, enormous boulders lie scattered about, looking like they might come crashing down any second on anyone unlucky enough to be underneath them.

"Stu, be real," I say, straightening again. I make a frustrated noise in the back of my throat. "You're barely standing upright on a flat road—do you really think you can walk downhill? Not to mention, we know nothing about mountain climbing. We've got no tools. People have tools for this kind of stuff. Like axes, I think? And picks? And they wear those special cleated-shoe thingies, I can't remember what they're called. And—"

"You're babbling," he interrupts me.

I throw my hands in the air. "Of course I'm babbling, you idiot! *You want to walk down the side of a damn mountain!*"

"Relax. I've got a good feeling about this."

"What is it with all these feelings of yours?" I ask with a groan. "Did you suddenly become a mystic?"

He gives me a long, measured look. "Sam, there is no other option. This is all we got."

I peek over the edge one more time. The only bright spot, if you can call any of this a bright spot, is we wouldn't have to descend straight downhill. There appear to be gradual inclines and declines rising up and down along the wide mountainside, plus plenty of trees and sprawling rock walls are available to grip onto and offer support during a descent.

Not that I'm seriously contemplating his dumbass idea.

"I don't understand. Why can't we keep walking this way?" I ask.

"Because we'll be dead before we ever get to town!"

"And the lake is better?" I ask, shaking my head in disbelief. "How?"

"*At least we can see the lake!*" He pinches the bridge of his nose. "There are people there—I know it. And quit asking me how. I just do. Sometimes you have to let go and trust in something bigger than yourself."

I sigh hard. It doesn't matter which way we go anymore. Nothing is safe. Either way, we're probably dead. Might as well take a chance for once.

We lean against each other for support and begin descending down the side of the cliff in a deliberate manner, little inch by little inch. Our boot heels dig into the ground, securing our footing as we walk.

"I bet the smoke is from a chimney fire. Like my story!" Stuart says, slipping away from my steady grasp to move faster. He's so excited he trips over his own two feet and almost goes plunging right down the side of the mountain.

"Careful!" I yell, my heart lurching in my chest as I lunge forward and reach for his arm, steadying him.

"Relax." He throws me a big grin. "I got this."

"I doubt that very much," I mumble as he pushes forward again with only his walking stick to guide him.

We should be cautious, but it's good to see him this way. This is the most energized he's been in days. Clumsy as he is, this surge of adrenaline is exactly what we need right now. Much better than watching him puke his guts out or shake uncontrollably in the SUV.

Plus, I'll admit it. I could use the break of not having to shoulder his weight for a bit. My head cold has returned with a vengeance. It feels as if someone has screws at my temples, tightening them over and over.

A sudden burst of pain explodes, and the path in front of me swirls and spins. I trip, flailing, reaching for something—anything—to stop my fall. My hands latch onto an enormous boulder jutting up from the snow, and a piece of rock the size of a basketball breaks off.

It tumbles to the ground, barreling straight for Stuart. He lets out a scream, dodging left as the rock tears downward right past him. It narrowly misses his head before rolling harmlessly off the edge.

For a long moment, we stare at each other, speechless. If that rock had been a few inches closer . . . I don't want to even think about what could've happened.

"You're gonna have to try harder than that to kill me," he says in a shaky voice, and then we're laughing so hard the sound echoes off the mountains and back down to us again. Tears roll down our faces as we howl, holding onto our sides.

This whole damn thing, it's like the most ridiculous situation ever. It doesn't matter how careful we try to be. We don't have control over anything anymore. Every step we take is a potential disaster. One mistake and it's all over. It's so terrible, there's nothing left to do but laugh.

After a while, the surface we travel on weakens and our feet sink into the newly softened snow. It has the consistency of wet, sticky mush. It's like wading through mud. Stuart's walking stick no longer works, so we thrust out our arms making a "T" shape, which helps to maintain our balance. Our movement now requires such concentration we stop talking and take frequent breaks, bracing against the gigantic trees lining the slope.

"I don't feel so good," Stuart says, panting next to me. I glance over in time to see his eyes roll backward and catch him before he hits the snow.

He gasps as I pull him next to me and give him a moment to steady himself, taking time to recharge myself as well. My fingers are thick and bungling as I wrap my arms around a generous trunk and press my forehead against cold bark. I gasp for air as if I've run a thousand marathons. No matter how hard I wheeze, I can't fill my lungs fast enough. Never have I been this exhausted. All I want to do is lie down and sleep for hours.

Forward, I command my shaking legs, putting one foot in front of the other and dragging Stuart along. I keep my grip on his hand, terrified that if I let go, I'll lose him somehow. *We need to keep moving forward.*

Soon every tree we pass becomes a small victory.

I ignore the horrible moaning sounds Stuart begins making as he stumbles beside me, because I know it's what he wants. It's as if we've made some secret sibling pact not to address the misery and pain that hangs thick between us.

Just when I think things can't get any worse, the earth spins before me. It's the kind of dizziness where trees and snow and sky all swirl together until everything looks like one of those expensive abstract paintings of my mother's. It causes me to stumble, and we both crash into the cold, mushy ground.

"We need water." I dig through my backpack and come up with two bottles. "Drink," I command, handing Stuart one. Sweat pours off me in droves as I gulp mine down.

Within seconds, I've drained half my bottle. My body screams for *more, more, more*, but I need to save the other half for later, so I stash it away in the bottom of my bag where I won't be tempted to finish it.

"Stay here," I order Stuart after I'm able to catch my breath again. "I'm going to get a better look around." I get to my feet and wipe snow off the back of my pants, heading for the side of the mountain.

Before I get far, I hear heavy panting behind me and turn to see Stuart is already standing. I have no idea where all his energy is coming from, but I'm grateful for it.

As we approach the edge, my excitement builds. We've walked so far and for so long now, there must be something for us to see. Perhaps the ski village? Or if not the village, I hope for at least a few cabins or some sign of life. Getting as close to the side as I dare, I suck in an anxious breath and look down.

My heart plummets with despair.

In every direction are legions of snow-covered mountains, each as forbidding and daunting as the one we're standing on. Hard angles of ice and rock. No softness. No life. Only an impenetrable fortress of swells and peaks with tapered valleys running between an endless labyrinth. We're no closer to people and civilization than we were hours ago when we first left the SUV.

"Looks like this is where you and I part ways, sis," Stuart says, his head lifting to mine.

"Don't joke."

"C'mon, Sam. You see the same thing I do. There's nothing here. We must be miles and miles from anyone." He smiles his silly, crooked grin, but his eyes are sad. "Sure, I can keep stumbling around a little longer. An hour? Maybe two? But we both know I'll never make it."

"Just keep walking. We'll find your smoke and whoever was making it."

"No." His mouth tightens. "You gotta do this without me."

I strengthen my grip on him. "No way."

"Without me slowing you down, you might have a chance."

"I know you're hurting, believe me I do, but—"

"Don't you dare tell me this hurts you more than it hurts me. Because if you say that, I swear I'll vomit on you again. This time on purpose." He makes a sick, gravelly sound as he takes in another painful breath of air. "Just listen, okay? If I don't make it, I want to say thanks for always being there. For always fighting for me." His eyes fill as he leans forward and wraps his arms around my shoulders. His entire body shakes as he holds on to me. "You're the best big sister a brother could ever have."

"Knock it off!" I push him away, fighting back the tears that threaten to consume me. "You're not saying goodbye. Not like this." If I have to throw him over my shoulder and crawl, I'll do it.

"Sam, please—"

"*I said no!*" I scream, my voice raw. "You're the one who made us leave the car, remember? You said we could do this! Why do all that if you were just going to give up now?"

There's a long beat of silence.

"You know why," he says.

It takes a moment for me to understand, and when I do, it hits me like a ton of bricks. I have to brace myself against the tree next to me so I don't fall over. Yet again, I've underestimated my brother. My dear, sweet, conniving, manipulative brother. This was his plan all along.

"You lied to me," I whisper.

"I couldn't let you die in that car."

He knew I'd never leave without him, even if it was my best chance at survival. And now it's too late to go back to the SUV and hunker down and wait it out together. The only option is for me to keep going. Alone. He knew his plan would cost him his life, but he did it anyway.

He knew.

"I'm so sorry, Sam."

Tears stream down my face. "I don't care. I won't leave you!"

"You have to."

Suddenly, a distant roaring begins high in the mountains. It's the sound of something huge breaking wide open, like the crack of a shattering window magnified a millionfold. At the top of the horizon, an enormous cloud of snow charges down the mountainside. It tears through everything in its path, annihilating massive trees and giant boulders alike.

All the terror I've been holding in since we got stuck—fear of a slow, drawn-out death from hypothermia or illness or starvation—converges into one great big fear of the mountain itself. I see now it needed none of those other things to kill us. If it really wants to, it can do the job within seconds.

The deep cracking sound grows louder as snow rushes toward us. Even though I've never experienced anything like this, something buried deep inside the most primal part of my brain recognizes what I'm seeing right away.

Avalanche.

Stuart turns to me, his eyes white around the edges, and screams one word.

"RUN!"

CHAPTER 24

1:30 p.m.

Our fight from seconds ago is forgotten in the face of the real and immediate danger of an avalanche. Stuart grabs me by the elbow and pulls me toward the thick, piney woods to our right. "The forest!" he yells. "The trees will slow it down!"

And then we're scrambling through snow and rock, trying not to imagine what's racing after us. Our feet pound against the ground going *faster faster faster*, until we're moving so quickly my legs burn and I can barely breathe. Even Stuart, God bless him, is somehow running beside me like a superhero.

Seconds later, we get to the trees.

Low-hanging branches claw at our faces while roots and rocks rise from the snow, threatening to trip us and take us down. My lungs feel like they're about to explode, my muscles screaming for oxygen, but I don't dare stop as trees topple behind us like a row of dominoes.

Below me, the earth starts to shake and undulate like waves of the ocean. My knees crumple and my legs slide out from underneath me. It happens lightning fast—in a matter of nanoseconds. One second Stuart is next to me; the next I'm watching in horror as the avalanche tears him from my grasp, leaving only white air in his place.

"*Stu!*" I claw at the empty space now beside me. Terror—undiluted, pure terror—slams into me, but I'm powerless to do anything but scream as the avalanche thrusts me forward and away from my brother.

A line of trees rushes up to meet me as I hurtle downhill, my teeth stinging as I collide into them, face-first. The pain is so bad it almost knocks me unconscious, but somehow I stay lucid enough to grab hold of the trunk. Wood meets my gloved fingers—solid and sturdy. I wrap myself around the tree, my arms burning as I hold on for all I'm worth. The taste of copper floods my mouth, and I realize I've bitten through my old wound, drawing blood. Or perhaps this is a new wound? It feels as if my jaw is broken.

Blocks of ice slabs roar past me, each one closer than the next, while more snow sweeps in behind me. The force slams me into the tree and brings on another wave of torturous agony. A howl erupts from my throat as pain like nothing I've ever known explodes through me. Still, I manage to keep holding on, my body shaking with the effort.

Off in the distance, I hear faint screaming that I'm certain is my brother. Instead of being horrified, I'm glad for the sound. As long as he's screaming, he's still alive.

We will not die here, I promise Stuart. *I'll make it through this and then I'll come find you.*

With a powerful tug, the avalanche tears my tree from the ground and throws me dozens of feet. My body rolls over and over like I've fallen inside a giant, deathly washing machine. It rips my hat and gloves off and snow goes everywhere—down my back, up my pants, even inside my ears. It's like I'm drowning in it.

Somehow, this last thought of drowning makes me remember Hunter's words in the car about swimming in an avalanche to stay afloat. With a burst of energy, I make myself go straight and long like I'm on my surfboard again and heading for the next big wave. My body executes in alternating movements. One arm moves backward, propelling me forward. The other goes above my torso, preparing to take its place. My legs join in next, flutter kicking downward and upward with pointed toes.

Right away, I fall into a familiar rhythm. Inhale. Stroke. Kick. Exhale. Repeat.

Just like Hunter said, the faster I swim, the closer to the surface I stay. Bone and sinew strain to almost snapping, but I'm no longer sinking—I'm riding the avalanche. It's as if all those years I spent behind our house swimming and bodyboarding were solely to prepare me for this very moment. Like whatever force had compelled me as a kid to love the water had somehow known this day was coming.

Sweat slides down my spine as exhaustion creeps in. I try to coast, knowing I can't afford to expend all my energy too soon. My strokes skip a beat, and the avalanche throttles me downward for a moment.

Shit! Too slow!

Snow roars in my ears and creeps over my head. Something in the debris pulls my legs under, and fear slams into me. I claw upward, trying to get back to the surface, but it's too late. I'm too deep inside. All I can do is take in one last gulp of air as I sink further into the depths below.

Reality disappears and then falls away completely.

Seconds, minutes, hours go by—a lifetime of darkness.

The next thing I know, the world has become the terrifying white of endless snow. A massive weight presses down against my chest, making each new breath a grueling task. Even the smallest movement is next to impossible.

My pulse races as I realize what's happened. The avalanche has trapped me under its depths! *I've been buried alive!*

Adrenaline surges as I tear and push my arms against the snow. I punch and punch again some more, but nothing happens. I don't even move an inch. That's when I know it's all over for me. Snow will soon pack in and suffocate me. I'll never get out; I'll never save Stuart. We're both going to die alone, in the snow, and—

A scream rips from my throat.

I can't breathe. I can't breathe. I can't . . .

STOP!

From somewhere deep within my soul, the voice comes. Strong. Confident. Calming.

Maybe it's coming from inside me, or maybe it's the God that Britney and Stuart believe so strongly in. I have no way of telling for sure. All I know is that the voice won't allow the black panic to overtake me. It knows that if I lose control, it'll only hasten my death. It tells me I cannot become the mountain's next victim.

I am smart. Strong. I'm a survivor. There is a way out of this. I just have to *think*.

What do I know about the mountains? Snow? Avalanches?

I rack my brain, scouring every corner, every memory, no matter how insignificant it might seem, and then . . . I find Hunter's words again. He said the first fifteen minutes after an avalanche were crucial. The important thing was to act fast to ward off asphyxiation long enough for the rescue dogs to find you. Once the avalanche stops moving it seals you inside, giving you only seconds to preserve pockets of air around you before the snow packs in like a rock.

With Hunter's words as my guide, I get to work using my hands to dig an air pocket near my mouth and nose. Like he instructed, I take a deep breath and hold it in so my chest expands to give me more breathing room after the snow settles.

Seconds later, the loose snow makes a wet, screeching sound as it firms itself into something more concrete-like around me. It locks my body in place, but I don't let myself give in to the claustrophobia. Hunter warned this would happen too. The thing is to stay as relaxed as possible. The calmer you are, the slower you breathe and the less oxygen you use. This is when I'm supposed to relax and wait to be saved by the rescue dogs.

Except—*what dogs?*

The full impact of my realization hits me, stealing away any last remaining silly notions of salvation. No animal rescue team is coming to save me. I'm all alone out here. When my air pocket runs out, the snow will push in closer until it fills my mouth and nose and steals all the oxygen, gradually killing me.

There's no hope for me. No hope for Stuart, who will surely die without me. If he isn't dead already. Like all the others . . .

Hunter.

Britney.

Probably Lily and Gavin too.

We're all going to die out here.

The panic takes hold of me again. I claw against the snow, knowing I'm only wasting precious oxygen but unable to stop myself.

After only a few seconds of this, I gasp and pant, so tapped out I can't move. My pulse skips, my blood pressure skyrocketing as the cold on the surface of my skin works its way to my internal organs. Massive cramps overtake my body as the blood leaves my extremities, trying to save my heart instead. Soon there'll be nothing left to save. My body is starting to die.

I let out a savage sound that's part scream, part death cry. After everything we've been through, Stuart and I are going to wind up at the bottom of this damn avalanche.

Despair consumes me, my heart shattering in a way I didn't know was possible.

I'm sorry I couldn't save you, Stu. I telegraph this last thought to my brother.

As the darkness overtakes me, wetness starts in the corners of my eyes. The tears well up and pour out. And then ... the strangest thing happens. Instead of snaking down toward my chin like expected, my tears go in the other direction—they flow toward my forehead.

That's odd.

At first, I don't understand why my brain fixates on such a silly little observation. It shouldn't matter what's happening with my tears. And yet, something in my mind tells me this is *IMPORTANT*. It demands I pay attention.

Think, Sam!

My heartbeat explodes as I solve the riddle. If my tears are flowing in the opposite direction, that means I'm upside-down! That's why nothing happened when I clawed and punched at the snow with my arms. I need to use my feet!

The realization gives me renewed strength. Instead of striking upward, I strike downward. Almost instantly, the smothering, suffocating pressure around me gives way at my lower body. My feet break through the snow, creating little pockets of air, and I realize I'm so much closer to the surface than I imagined.

That's when the barking begins.

The sound is so strange and unexpected, I'm sure I'm hallucinating at first. I recall the animal tracks I saw in the snow days ago, and my foggy brain cries—*WOLF!*

Except that doesn't make any sense. No wolf barks like this. The sound is long and insistent. This is a bark I know.

I gaze up through the small holes I've made in the snow, and warm brown animal eyes peer back at me.

I know those eyes . . .

Someone yells my name. They tell me to stay with them. To fight.

An instant later, strong hands grab me under my arms. I have the vague sense of being torn from the ground so fast, my nose and throat burn. And then air—crisp, wonderful air—before I black out one last time.

CHAPTER 25

One Month After
January 20 · Martin Luther King Jr. Weekend · Friday · 3:00 p.m.
Seaside, California

Around town, some people call it the "Christmas Miracle" that Gavin, Lily, and I survived all those days stranded in the mountains. I try not to think about what the families with children that never returned call it.

Hunter.

Britney.

I wonder about them often—their mothers and fathers. Hunter's grandpappy. Britney's older sisters.

I regret not being able to give my condolences in person at the funerals. The doctors kept me in the hospital for an entire week after my rescue. My left leg was all torn up from the avalanche with over two dozen stitches and bolts holding it all together. I still walk with a slight limp.

Instead, I sent flowers and cards and tried to explain what happened that week in the wilderness. I wanted their families to know how Hunter sacrificed his life for us and how comforting Britney was at the end.

Of course, there was no funeral for my brother. You need a body to have a funeral.

"You sure you're ready?" Gavin asks, glancing over at me as he takes his spot behind the wheel of his new truck. After they recovered it in the mountains, his parents sold the GMC Denali. Though it was salvageable after a replaced tire and bodywork, no one wanted to drive it. No amount of repairs could erase the terrible memories of what happened inside.

"Yeah. Let's do this," I say, getting in next to him and readjusting the passenger seat and air controls, preparing for the long drive ahead.

"It's going to be okay. Whatever happens, we'll handle it—together." His blue eyes smile down at me, and I think my heart may burst.

God, he's beautiful.

Sometimes, like right now, I find it impossible to believe he's really here in front of me and not some ghost or figment of my imagination.

"I'm so glad you're here," I say, my throat tightening with emotion.

"Stu would be proud of you. Taking chances. Breaking the rules."

My eyes burn as I think of my brother. "You two were always a bad influence," I say, blinking the wetness away.

Lying to my parents for the first time wasn't as hard as I always thought it would be. They think I'm headed to Palm Springs for the three-day holiday weekend with some other seniors from school. Everyone has Monday off for Martin Luther King Jr. Day, and my family thought it was a good idea for me to get out of the house and try to do something "normal" for a change. With the exception of school and classes, I sleep more than I should and find it difficult to leave my bed some days.

What my parents don't know is that Gavin snuck out of boarding school late last night using his monthly allowance to purchase a round-trip plane ticket from Boston to Seaside. His folks are in New York for business, so they have no idea he's back either. Our parents would never let us go if they knew what we're really up to.

We're heading back to Mount Sierra. We want to memorialize and remember our friends and my brother. Pay our respects. Face what happened and try our best to move on.

We've loaded Gavin's SUV to the gills with camping gear, hiking supplies, and enough food and water to last us a month—not that we'll need that much. If all goes according to plan, we'll be back by Sunday night. We even splurged for a satellite communicator with GPS this time, just in case.

"You printed out the maps, right?" Gavin asks.

"Yep. Got 'em right here." I point to the backpack at my feet and he puts the car in reverse, pulling out of his driveway. After what happened, I'll never rely solely on car navigation technology or cell phone service again.

As Gavin gets on the highway and accelerates, Champion lets out an eager bark in the row behind us and wags his tail excitedly. I turn around to ruffle the top of his messy head, giving him a big kiss.

Champion has been staying at my house ever since I got out of the hospital. The doctors tried prescribing drugs like Xanax and Valium, but Champion is the only thing that helps with my insomnia and the nightmares. At first, my mother protested having the big dog around so much, but I think she's grown to love him even more than she loves me. He is a hero, after all.

The way Gavin tells it, he and Lily got disoriented after they left the SUV and wound up lost somewhere in the middle of the woods. It was Champion who heard barking. He found dogs in a campground only a few miles from our SUV and led Gavin and Lily straight to them and their owners for help.

Champion is also the one who found me. After the avalanche, he took off running uphill, knowing Gavin would chase after him. I guess he heard me. Maybe sensed me somehow? It's incredible, if you think about it.

Some big Hollywood producers came by last week to meet Champion and see what he's like. Just as Hunter predicted, they want to make a movie about us. When everyone hears our story, they're always amazed it was a dog that saved our lives. We all like to believe humans are superior to every other species, but the truth is we're helpless once you take away all our fancy technology. After our car stopped working and we had no cell service, we were at nature's whim. Only Champion adapted to our harsh new surroundings.

"Do you think we might find something?" I ask Gavin, my intestines rolling like I'm going to throw up as I recall those last few moments with my brother. That's the last time anyone saw Stuart alive, but I refuse to accept he's dead. He's out there somewhere—I feel it in my bones.

Gavin sighs deeply. "We already talked about this—"

"But what if there's a clue . . . or . . . I don't know, *something?*" I'm unable to meet his eyes. I know very well what he thinks about this topic, but I can't ignore how I feel.

If my brother was dead, I'd *know* it.

"Sams, you promised," he says as we turn onto the I-6.

I clear my throat in an effort to rein in my emotions, but a few sniffles escape. "Flowers. Say a few words. Then leave," I recite what we discussed earlier as Champion gets onto all fours behind me and pops his long snout against my shoulder. He nuzzles in as if he can tell exactly how I'm feeling.

Gavin and I agreed to start at Hunter's shortcut, placing flowers and two crosses along the road where we last saw him and Britney alive and saying some words to honor them. Afterward, we'll head to the site of the avalanche and visit with the family that rescued us to give our gratitude in person. Gavin packed a third cross to leave there—for Stuart. He says it'll be good for me to say goodbye.

"We have to be realistic, okay?" he says, firm but not unkindly. He squeezes my shoulder.

"I'm just not ready to give up on him."

My brother is a fighter. It might have taken us going to the edge of hell and back, but I finally understand who he is. How brave and capable. How strong.

After Stuart's back brace didn't work and his scoliosis surgery almost failed, he didn't give up. When the doctors told him he might never stand upright again, he told them to suck it. And that nightmare week in the mountains? He should've died inside that damn SUV, but he didn't. If anyone can survive an avalanche, it's him.

Even if it sounds inconceivable, there are crazier survival stories out there, if you look for them. I should know. I've spent countless sleepless nights researching and reading them all: the Hotel Rigopiano guests in Italy who were rescued fifty-eight hours after an avalanche; the young football players who survived seventeen days trapped underground in Thai caves; the Alaskan woman, Ada Blackjack, who survived two years alone on Wrangel Island; the Uruguayan rugby team Lily told us about who lived for 72 days in the remote Andes mountains; and, of course, the infamous Donner Party who endured almost four months in these very same mountains.

If all of them survived, why not Stuart?

After a few hours on the highway, the sun dips behind the horizon and the Sierra Nevada foothills come into view. Outside the truck's windows, I spot a few of Hunter's lodgepole pines. A sad laugh escapes me as I remember those orange trunks and my bathroom hike with him and Britney. It wasn't that long ago, but the moment seems worlds away, as if it happened in another life.

I have no idea where Hunter and Britney are now. Though I hope for heaven, I'm not sure if that's true or just a fantasy. I close my eyes and try to imagine them there, anyway.

If only I could go back in time and fix everything. Make this all go away.

"I should've tried harder to keep Hunter in the car," I say, the hot sting of guilt rising in my throat. "I could've been tougher on Britney too—made her eat and drink more."

"Don't do that," Gavin says. "We can't change the past."

"But I should've made you turn around. Right at the beginning."

"People take shortcuts all the time. They don't die," he says more forcefully. "You didn't cause this, Sam. It just happened."

I appreciate what he's trying to do, but these are only words. They won't bring our friends back. My chest tightens with the weight of endless regrets. There are so many things I would take back if I could.

"How is she doing?" I ask.

His gaze shifts to mine for a brief second. He knows Lily is still a touchy, complicated subject for me.

"She misses you," he says.

"I miss her too."

Though I haven't spoken to Lily since Mount Sierra, the two of them are still in touch and have grown close over these last few weeks. Gavin says he never would've made it down the mountain without her. Though her obstinate determination may have caused the rift in our friendship while we were stranded in the SUV, that same quality of hers also helped save my life.

"Maybe it's time to give her a call?" he asks, prodding.

"Maybe."

This is a game we play. He tells me to call. I'm noncommittal.

It still hurts my heart to think about Lily. When she first betrayed me back in the mountains, I was devastated. I wasn't sure I'd ever get past it, but over time things have changed.

I've changed.

Life is so short and precious. I don't want to waste any of mine holding on to anger. I'm not upset with Lily anymore. We'll talk again one day; I'm just not ready yet.

Even though I forgive her and take blame for my own mistakes, I'm not sure if I can ever truly forget or stop wondering what might have happened if only Stuart had more food back when he needed it. It's not that I believe what happened to Stuart is Lily's fault. She's no more to blame than the rest of us. We all played a part in what happened in the mountains.

Still . . . it's hard.

"Anyway, thanks for doing this with me." I swallow thickly. "No way I could do it alone."

"You don't need to thank me. I *want* to be here with you." His hand reaches for mine, tucking my fingers inside his. He kisses my knuckles, soft and tenderly. "I love you, Sams. Always have, ever since that very first day."

Despite myself, I laugh. "You fell in love because I got in a fistfight?"

"Smartass," he says, chuckling back. "No. I fell in love because seeing you standing up to those bullies was the most amazing thing I'd ever seen. You wouldn't let anyone hurt Stu. No one ever did anything like that for me." His voice lowers to almost a whisper. "God, Sam. I don't know what I would've done if I'd lost you too." He gulps hard, his Adam's apple bobbing up and down. "Now that I've got you back, I'm never letting go."

We turn off the highway, setting out for Hunter's old shortcut, and my thoughts take over again. There are so many pieces to this puzzle I still can't quite figure out.

What if we'd left Seaside earlier that day?

What if we'd all stayed inside the car?

What if we had found help sooner?

But of all the questions I still have, it's the avalanche that really gets me.

At the time, it seemed like the absolute worst thing in the world that could happen. That was before the rescue team told me they weren't sure they would've found me without the avalanche pushing me so far down the mountain. Without the avalanche, would I still be alive?

Somehow, I don't think so.

I don't know if that's God or fate or something else, but there's a reason I'm still here today.

As we get closer to the highway exit and are ready to turn off, I can't help hoping that whatever spared me also spared my brother. Even if it seems impossible that Stuart could be out there and alive, I choose to believe. It's like Stuart said that last day on the mountain. Sometimes you just need to let go and have a little faith.

ACKNOWLEDGMENTS

Thank you to everyone who has supported me on this path to living my lifelong dream of creating stories and putting them out into the world. Publishing is filled with many challenges and *Ski Weekend* is a story that almost didn't get told. The book you now hold in your hands had to fight for its survival, just like the characters within it. What kept me going was the solid belief that this day would come, thanks in large part to the love, support, and help of so many. I could not have done this without you. To quote my favorite fictional attorney, Elle Woods, "We did it!"

Thank you, Amy Tipton, my amazing editor and also my coach, quasi-agent, and friend. I love being a Feral Girl! Thank you also to Stephanie Elliot and Trae Hawkins, who lent an editorial hand. This book would not be the same without you.

Thank you to Brooke Warner, Shannon Green, and everyone at SparkPress for making this book come to life. Thanks to Julie Metz for helping design such a wonderful cover. Thanks as well to my publicists on the BookSparks team—Crystal Patriarche, Taylor Brightwell, and Hanna Lindsley—for your hard work in getting my book into so many hands.

Thanks to those in the writing community who have provided me with their expertise and support throughout the years, especially those first early readers of *Ski Weekend*. Thank you, Evelyn Skye, Lauren Kate, Jeff Zentner, Eileen Cooke, Paul Grecko, and Laurie Elizabeth Flynn. Thank you to my LEVEL UP WRITERS family, Mary Weber and Sorboni Banerjee, and all the friends we've made along the way during our chats. Thank you to my SWP/SP cohort publishing sisters. Cheers to our books! Thank you to the SCBWI and Pitch Wars community, who gave me extra pushes when I needed them, and thanks to all the other writer friends who have had a kind word of support when I needed it most—you know who you are and I am forever grateful.

Thank you to all the booksellers, librarians, and media who have championed *Ski Weekend*. I cannot thank you enough for your early and eager support. It has meant the world to me.

Thank you to the online communities that have embraced all things "Rektok Ross" on Instagram/Bookstagram, Book-Tube, BookTok, and Clubhouse, and in my Facebook Book Nook group. People like to knock social media, and while there are definite downsides, I will always be grateful to the community I have found online and all the incredible book lovers and content creators I call friends. Thank you also to my "Shine(y)" ladies, who encourage me in all things entrepreneurship: Jennifer, Alicia, Amy, Marilee, Sarah, Sharifa, Sheila, Sherie, Anna, and Stephanie.

Thanks to all my friends and colleagues at my former law firm who encouraged me when I said I wanted to start writing again. Practicing law with you was a true pleasure.

Thanks to my street team and friends who have been both my sounding board and my greatest cheerleaders on FaceTime calls, Zooms, and late-night texts—you mean the world to me. Special thanks to those of you who have literally given me HOURS of your time to answer the most ridiculous book-related questions like what color swag you like the best, including but not limited to: Pri, Kate, Ash, Angel, Joannie, Natalie, Nancy, Ryka, Jenn, Lynn, Gena, Ye-hui, Sepi, AC, Kathy, Filly, and Nicole. I owe you one!

To my family. I feel blessed to have had a mother who loved books as much as I do and instilled in me a love of reading from day one. I know you are reading this from Heaven, Mom. Dad, L, and Lance—thank you for always supporting me. Thanks to my "sister wife," Hilary, and the entire DeCesare clan for embracing me into this special modern family we have. Thanks especially to my amazing stepkids—Derek, Dani, and Ro—I am so grateful to have you in my life. And to my wonderful husband, Michael, thank you for all your love and support.

Finally, to my readers, thank you for choosing to spend your time with me and my book. I hope you have fallen in love with these characters as I have. Sam, Stuart, Gavin, Hunter, Lily, Britney, even Champion—they each have pieces of me (and maybe you too, Dear Reader) in them. Remember, life is too short to not live out your dreams. So go out and follow your heart, explore your passion, and have a little faith. (Just don't forget to tell people where you're going, pack an emergency supply kit, and bring a map.)

ABOUT THE AUTHOR

Rektok Ross is the pen name of Liani Kotcher, a trial attorney turned award-winning young adult author and book blogger. An avid reader since childhood, Liani writes exactly the kind of books she loves to escape into herself: exciting thrillers with strong female leads, swoonworthy love interests, and life-changing moments. She graduated from the University of Florida School of Journalism and obtained her juris doctorate at the University of Miami School of Law. Originally from South Florida, she currently splits her time between San Francisco and Los Angeles with her husband, stepkids, and her dogs. You can find her online just about anywhere at @RektokRoss, as well as on her website, www.RektokRoss.com, where she blogs about books and writing.

Author photo © Agency Moanalani Jeffrey

SELECTED TITLES FROM SPARKPRESS

SparkPress is an independent boutique publisher delivering high-quality, entertaining, and engaging content that enhances readers' lives, with a special focus on female-driven work. www.gosparkpress.com

But Not Forever: A Novel, Jan Von Schleh. $16.95, 978-1-943006-58-8. When identical fifteen-year-old girls are mysteriously switched in time, they discover the love that's been missing in their lives. Torn, both want to go home, but neither wants to give up what they now have.

The Goddess Twins: A Novel, Yodassa Williams. $16.95, 978-1-68463-032-5. Days before their eighteenth birthday, Arden and Aurora's mother goes missing and they discover they belong to a family of Caribbean deities. Can these goddess twins uncover their evil grandfather's plot in time to save their mother, themselves, and the free world?

A Song for the Road: A Novel, Rayne Lacko. $16.95, 978-1-684630-02-8. When his house is destroyed by a tornado, fifteen-year-old Carter Danforth steals his mom's secret cash stash, buys his father's guitar back from a pawnshop, and hitchhikes old Route 66 in search of the man who left him as a child.

The Leaving Year: A Novel, Pam McGaffin. $16.95, 978-1-943006-81-6. As the Summer of Love comes to an end, 15-year-old Ida Petrovich waits for a father who never comes home. While commercial fishing in Alaska, he is lost at sea, but with no body and no wreckage, Ida and her mother are forced to accept a "presumed" death that tests their already strained relationship. While still in shock over the loss of her father, Ida overhears an adult conversation that shatters everything she thought she knew about him. This prompts her to set out on a search for the truth that takes her from her Washington State hometown to Southeast Alaska.

ABOUT SPARKPRESS

SparkPress is an independent, hybrid imprint focused on merging the best of the traditional publishing model with new and innovative strategies. We deliver high-quality, entertaining, and engaging content that enhances readers' lives. We are proud to bring to market a list of *New York Times* best-selling, award-winning, and debut authors who represent a wide array of genres, as well as our established, industry-wide reputation for creative, results-driven success in working with authors. SparkPress, a BookSparks imprint, is a division of SparkPoint Studio LLC.

Learn more at GoSparkPress.com